Lord Apollo & the Colleen

Suzanne G. Rogers

...

Idunn Court Publishing

Lord Apollo & the Colleen, Copyright © 2015 by Suzanne G. Rogers

All Rights Reserved. Except as permitted under the U.S. Copyright Act of 1976, no part of this publication may be reproduced, distributed, or transmitted in any form or by any means, or stored in a database or retrieval system, without prior written permission of the publisher.

This book is a work of fiction. While references may be made to actual places or events, the names, characters, incidents, and locations within are from the author's imagination and are not a resemblance to actual living or dead persons, businesses, or events. Any similarity is coincidental.

Idunn Court Publishing
7 Ramshorn Court
Savannah, GA 31411

Published by Idunn Court Publishing, June 2015

ISBN: 978-1-947463-10-3

This book is licensed to the original purchaser only. Duplication or distribution via any means is illegal and a violation of International Copyright Law, subject to criminal prosecution and upon conviction, fines and/or imprisonment. No part of this book can be reproduced or sold by any person or business without the express permission of the publisher.

Published in the United States of America

Editor: Kathryn Riley Miller

Cover Design: Suzanne G. Rogers

Lord Apollo & the Colleen is dedicated to
Kathryn Riley Miller,
whose ancestors came from the Emerald Isle

May the Road Rise Up To Meet You
(traditional Gaelic blessing)

May the road rise up to meet you.
May the wind be always at your back.
May the sun shine warm upon your face;
the rains fall soft upon your fields
and until we meet again,
may God hold you in the palm of His hand.

Chapter One

Bound for Ireland

Liverpool. 1867

The sun was dipping into the west, but it was difficult for Padraig Shields to tell how much daylight remained because of the thick fog drifting across the River Mersey. With his cap pulled down low over his forehead, he hastened along the pier toward the steamship *Banba*, the hull of which was partially obscured by outgoing cargo. Deckhands were busy loading the crates onto the ship, although occasionally a man would pause for a cigarette. As Paddy approached, he scanned their faces until he spotted an acquaintance.

"Riordan!" He lifted his hand and waved.

The man's lips quirked up in a smile. "What about ye, Paddy? Long way from home."

"So 'tis."

Paddy offered Riordan a cigarette and a box of matches.

As the man lit up, he gave Paddy a sidelong glance. "Ye didn't come down to Albert Dock to offer me a smoke."

"I didn't, to be sure."

"What's the story?"

Paddy jerked his head toward the ship. "She headin' for Belfast?"

"She is."

"Ye have a spot in the hold for a fellow countryman?"

The deckhand laughed. "Why don't ye book passage on a passenger ship?"

"The thing is, I'm after leavin' England in a hurry."

Riordan shook his head. "Och! Ye want me to lose me job?"

Paddy spread his arms out in supplication. "Have a heart! It's me sister's thirteenth birthday the day after the morrow."

"Megan's thirteen already?" The man shook his head. "Here I was, thinkin' she was still a wee wain."

"Och aye. Time flies, don't it? Surely there's somethin' ye could do, especially if there's somethin' in it for ye."

Padraig flashed a pound note, but as the deckhand reached out for it, he pulled his hand back. "Not so fast."

Riordan frowned. "What are ye playin' at?"

"I've not lost me senses. Ye don't get paid until after I'm secure on board."

The large man stared at the money. "Come back at midnight, and I'll sneak ye into the hold."

Paddy grinned. "Cheers. See ye then."

As he retraced his steps, an early spring breeze cut through his coat and turned the tip of his nose to ice. Despite the chill, his spirits were high; he'd be home soon with a full wallet and good news. Although he'd left Ireland penniless, he now had the opportunity to better his circumstances, and those of his sister. If he could convince Megan to come back to England with him, perhaps he could find her a gentleman to marry. She'd been a very pretty ten-year-old when he'd seen her last, and he had no doubt she'd grown into a beauty who'd turn the head of even the most confirmed bachelor.

Paddy turned up the collar of his coat, hunched his shoulders, and hastened toward the nearest quayside tavern. Dinner, a pint or two, and perhaps a game of billiards or darts would help kill time until midnight drew nigh.

••••

Numb and distraught, Theo stumbled down the gangplank of the luxury passenger liner alone. As he stepped onto the pier, he heard a bell echo at his back, warning friends and family of the ship's imminent late-afternoon departure. Since he knew Mariah wouldn't be at the railing to wave good-bye, he didn't bother to turn around. Nothing he'd said just now in her cabin had swayed her from her chosen course of action. His former fiancée was eager to sail to America—away from England, and especially away from him. He couldn't blame her, really. After his father had disinherited him for stealing Mariah away from his younger brother, he had nothing to offer.

He headed toward town, wondering what he would do with himself now. Wandering aimlessly around Liverpool, especially dressed in expensive clothes, was an invitation to disaster. Pickpockets and criminals couldn't possibly know that his costly attire belied his true financial condition—which was quite close to penniless. In fact, he could scarcely believe it himself.

As he walked, a painted woman in a low-cut dress fell into step beside him. She gave him an admiring glance through her eyelashes. "Aren't you a pretty lad? I could almost mistake you for one of them Greek gods. Do you fancy some company?"

"I'm sorry, but I'm not in the mood for company. Is there any place around here where I could get a drink?"

A flash of pique crossed her face. "Nothing fit for a toff like yourself."

"It doesn't have to be fancy, I can assure you."

She pointed. "The Froggy Cups is about a half block that way."

Remembering his manners, Theo touched the brim of his hat. "Thank you, miss."

The tavern wasn't difficult to locate, but the place was full of ruffians and unpolished dock workers. After Theo purchased a glass of ale at the bar, he glanced over the crowded tables for a place to sit. As a gentleman, he was clearly out of his element—and not particularly welcome. A few patrons shot hostile looks in his direction, but nobody tried to start any trouble at least.

Theo spied a booth in the corner, occupied by a young man about his age. He brought his glass over.

"Would you mind awfully if I shared this space with you for a little while? There seems to be no other place to sit."

As the man regarded Theo, his eyebrows rose. "Yer in the wrong part o' town, so ye are." He gestured to the opposite bench. "Yer welcome to sit. Nobody ever called Padraig Shields inhospitable."

"Thank you." Theo slid into the booth. "Irish?"

"That I am."

Theo reached out a hand. "Theo."

"Paddy."

The two men exchanged a handshake.

"Are ye lost, Theo?"

He sipped his drink. "Not exactly."

Paddy chuckled. "Ye look downcast. I'm guessin' ye have lady troubles?"

"I have no lady now." Theo averted his eyes. "I also have no family, no fortune, and no future past this glass of ale."

"That's hard."

"Don't feel sorry for me; I brought it on myself." He smiled. "I'll travel to London and get a job to earn my living."

"I've just come from London. Lots o' work to be had, if ye know where to look."

"I was hoping to work with my hands."

Paddy looked at him askance. "Nobody'll hire ye, Theo. Yer hands are too soft."

Theo's heart dropped. If he meant to avoid anyone from society, what position would he be fit for? "Well, it was just a thought. Perhaps I could work in a shop?"

"Sure ye could, but with a face like yours, ye should take to the stage."

"The stage? Do you really think so?"

"If ye can memorize lines proper, I reckon so. When I was in London last, I saw fellers in matinee melodramas who weren't half as good lookin' as ye."

Theo turned the idea over in his mind. Although it seemed bizarre at first blush, becoming an actor would be the perfect way to start a new life. With an assumed name, stage makeup, and a wig, none of his former friends and family would ever be the wiser.

"That might work." He smiled. "Thank you for the suggestion."

"I've another suggestion, if ye'd care to listen. If ye show up lookin' like a toff, ye'll ne'er get hired."

Theo glanced down at his attire. "I've haven't the funds to purchase anything else. In fact, I may have to beg rides all the way to London."

"Tell ye what; I'll trade ye my hat and jacket for yers, buy yer fancy pocket watch off ye, and throw dinner into the bargain."

"Why would you do that?"

"As it turns out, I'm filled with generosity." Paddy grinned. "My employer gave me a wee sum o' money to go visit my sister. It's been goin' on three years since I've seen her."

"I'm very happy for you." Despite his words, Theo felt a pang of sorrow at the realization he'd never see Graceling Hall or his family again.

"I've been Mr. Osbourne's driver these past three years, see, and he's always been kinder to me than I deserve. Anyway, I'm headed home to Ireland tonight to collect my sister and bring her back with me."

"Why bring her to England?"

"To find her a gentleman husband, o' course! Mr. Osbourne's always takin' up one cause or another, and I told him about Megan. He seems to think if he buys her the right sort o' clothes and shows her off proper to his society friends when she's eighteen, one o' them elegant gentleman will bend his knee."

"Is that what your sister wants?"

"I'll not be askin' Megan's opinion unless I'm desirin' an earful." He laughed. "At any rate, if I was to arrive home lookin' a bit like a gentleman meself, the stubborn lass might be more easily convinced that comin' up in the world is the right thing to do."

Desperate for cash and hungry to boot, Theo was hardly in a position to refuse the man's offer. Although he was particularly reluctant to sell his pocket watch, he'd no longer be using the name inscribed on the back. Since he was estranged from his brother and father as well as disinherited, a clean break from the past was probably the best course of action.

He nodded. "Done."

••••

After a dinner of shepherd's pie, Paddy challenged Theo to a game of billiards. To Paddy's surprise, he didn't manage to best the gentleman as easily as he'd imagined. At half-past eleven, he directed Theo to an address where he could obtain cheap lodgings for the night. They exchanged jackets and hats, Paddy gave him money for the pocket watch, and they shook hands.

"May the road rise to meet ye, as they say. Safe home."

"Thank you, Paddy. I hope our paths cross again."

After Theo left the tavern, Paddy took a moment to admire his new timepiece—marveling at the fact the beautiful object was now his. The engraving on the back—Theodore Nathaniel King—could perhaps be undone by a jeweler...or maybe he'd just have his own name inscribed underneath. He tucked the timepiece into an inner pocket of his new jacket so he wouldn't lose it, and then made his way outside. The elegant jacket was a slightly tight fit through the shoulders, but the expensive garment made Paddy feel like a gentleman nevertheless. The smooth, black silk top hat was also unlike anything he'd ever owned before, and he enjoyed how it felt on his head. Wouldn't Megan be amazed when she saw him! Paddy counted himself fortunate he'd met Theo that night, and to such mutual benefit.

Admittedly, Paddy had had too much to drink, but his slight inebriation would help him pass an uncomfortable night in the hold of the *Banba* more comfortably. If he was clad in his ordinary workingman clothes, he might have indulged in a loud chorus of "Rocky Road to Dublin." Since he wore the clothes of a gentleman, however, he made a conscious decision to affect a gentleman's upright posture and demeanor.

The wind had died down somewhat, but the temperature was still brisk. Paddy strode toward the docks, retracing his steps from hours before. Thick fog had rolled inland from the Mersey, transforming the dark of night into heavenly whiteness. As he walked, footsteps seemed to echo from behind. He paused every so often to look back, but could see nothing but billowing clouds. With a shrug, he turned down the pier that led to his final destination. Halfway to the *Banba*, he heard a whooshing noise. He meant to turn around to see what had caused the noise, but then something hit him on the head. As he fell, his last thoughts were of the damage that must have been done to his hat. Something prodded him in the side, rolling him over and off the side of the dock. Not even the chill of the water could wake him from his barely conscious state.

Padraig Shields would never see his beloved Ireland again.

••••

Sergeant O'Hara shook his head in dismay as he surveyed the bloated body his men had just pulled from the Mersey. Although the dead fellow's features were largely unrecognizable, he appeared to be a young gentleman—if his waterlogged jacket was any indication. As far as O'Hara could tell from its advanced state of decomposition, the body had been in the water for weeks.

"Any wallet?" O'Hara asked.

"If he had one, it's long gone—either stolen in a robbery or at the bottom of the river. He has a crack on his skull, but it's hard to say if it showed up before or after he went in the water. Lots of ships come through here and could have crushed the body up against the dock."

"It's the bloody fog. Can't see anything in the river."

"We did find this in his pocket." The policeman dropped a timepiece into the sergeant's hand.

The hands on the watch face had stopped at a quarter to twelve, probably when water had intruded into its inner workings. "Couldn't have been robbery if this was left behind. Maybe the man's death was an accident…or suicide."

When O'Hara turned the watch over, he discovered an engraved name. He frowned as he contemplated the unpleasant duty that lay before him.

"Looks like I have very sad news for Mr. Theodore King's family."

Suzanne G. Rogers

Chapter Two

Intentions

Graceling Hall, Newcastle. Five years later...

Theo King rode to the chapel on horseback, where several men were working in his family's burial ground. As he arrived, the workers hoisted a heavy granite headstone into a waiting wagon and lifted a small marker into its place on the grass instead.

Theo dismounted just as Lady Clarissa Alderforth emerged from the chapel, followed closely by a berobed vicar and the always elegant Earl of Rowe, Jensen Alderforth. The pretty woman crossed over to Theo and gave him a dimpled smile.

Theo bowed. "Good afternoon, Clarissa. I'm grateful you and Rowe could attend today."

"What else are friends for, if not to support one another?"

"I'm fortunate indeed to have such good friends." He exchanged handshakes with the other two men. "Thank you both for coming."

"Glad to be of service," the vicar said.

"It's my pleasure," Rowe said. "I presume the mystery is solved?"

"Yes. I sent a letter to the Liverpool police department detailing what I could remember about the man buried in my grave, and the chief inspector wrote me back."

Rowe raised an eyebrow. "How much could you recall after so much time has passed?"

"Well, I remembered his name was Paddy and he was returning home to Ireland that night."

The vicar frowned. "An Irishman named Paddy? I can't imagine that narrowed the field much."

"Not ordinarily, but the police wrote back to say the man's sister had arrived in Liverpool quite recently, trying to figure out what had become of her long-lost brother, Padraig Aengus Shields. Apparently, the information in my letter helped the inspector solve his disappearance."

"It's all so dreadfully tragic," Clarissa said. "I wish she'd had better news regarding her brother's fate."

"I do as well. I feel I owe him a great deal."

"Why is that?" Rowe asked.

"The night we met, I was emotionally distraught and without funds or family." Theo produced his timepiece, now repaired and restored. "The money Paddy gave me in exchange for this pocket watch paid my expenses until I got a job in London. Since the watch is legally his property, I forwarded the sum he gave me to his sister at her lodgings in Liverpool, with a note of thanks."

Rowe nodded his approval. "That's more than most men would do, and I expect the money is far more welcome to her than a timepiece engraved with your name."

"I hope so."

The vicar gestured toward the family plot. "Shall we get started?"

Clarissa fell into step beside Theo as they headed down the path. "What a shame Brandon and Larken couldn't be here. I understand they took little Myles to see the house Larken inherited?"

"Yes. Actually, it was my idea they should visit Wynstone Park today. I thought it would be best if

Brandon was elsewhere while we re-dedicated the grave. Since he believed me to be dead all these years, I suspected the graveside service would bring back too many painful memories."

"That's very considerate."

At the gravesite, the vicar gave a short funeral service, and Clarissa laid a wreath of roses on the grave marker.

Theo thanked the vicar and slipped a gold coin into his hand. "I hope we may have the pleasure of your company at our ball a week from Friday?"

"Indeed you may, and I thank you for the invitation. Now, if you'll excuse me, I've an elderly mother to attend to. She's been a trifle ill."

"I'm sorry to hear it. Give her my regards."

After the vicar departed, Theo turned to his friends.

"I know I'm giving you no notice, but are you free for dinner tonight? I've decided to have an Irish wake in Paddy's honor."

"We'd be delighted," Clarissa replied. "Will Brandon and Larken be back in time?"

"Oh yes, they said they'd be home for tea." He paused. "They've only been gone since this morning and the house is already too quiet for my taste."

"I daresay Graceling Hall will feel terribly empty when Brandon and his family move to Wynstone Park permanently," Rowe said.

"Indeed it will. In returning the house and my inheritance to me, my brother wishes to do the decent and honorable thing. In the absence of family, however, I'm afraid the house will feel like a tomb."

"Quite so, but the solution is clear," Rowe said. "You must marry as soon as possible and start a family of your own."

"Jensen!" Clarissa frowned at her brother. "Unsolicited advice is seldom welcome."

Theo laughed. "I agree with Clarissa. Besides which, I can hardly take marital advice from a man who has thus far escaped the institution himself!"

The earl shrugged. "If I had more than two sovereigns to rub together, I'd eagerly join the hunt. Unfortunately, I'm an impoverished earl forced to earn my living and I've nothing to offer but my considerable charms." He winked.

Clarissa rolled her eyes skyward. "Not every woman wishes to marry for money!"

"Perhaps not, but a man with money is infinitely more attractive."

"That's true," Theo admitted. "When Mariah realized I'd been disinherited, her affections cooled remarkably quickly. Even worse, she broke her engagement to my brother for me and I'll bear the guilt of that for the rest of my life."

"She wasn't worthy of you—or Brandon for that matter," Clarissa said. "Besides which, Brandon is far better off married to Larken. He adores her, and he never would have been happy with Mariah."

"Your brother would be the first to say it all worked out for the best," Rowe said. "And don't forget, if it weren't for Larken, you and Brandon wouldn't have been reunited."

"I suppose so." Theo's gaze rested on Clarissa. "What about you? Have you never happened to think of marriage these past five years?"

"I've had other things to occupy my mind."

"Clarissa will never admit it, but she's had many offers. For some reason, however, she's turned her nose up at all of them," Rowe said.

"Oh? Were your suitors anyone of my acquaintance?"

"Never mind that; we all know I'm far too sensible for marriage." Clarissa joined arms with him and her brother. "I'm much more interested in seeing the two of you wed to the most amiable ladies imaginable."

"So each of us is resolved to stay single and yet see the others married off?" Theo shook his head. "This should prove interesting."

••••

Clarissa and Rowe climbed into their gig—one of the last remaining vestiges of their former wealth. As the small open carriage drove away from the church, the earl gave his sister a sidelong glance. "Well played back there."

She peered at him. "To what are you referring?"

"Someone has been leaving flowers on Theo's grave the past five years. The person's identity is a mystery to everyone but myself."

"Please don't embarrass me." She stared straight ahead. "My feelings for Theo are of friendship only."

"Come now, Clarissa. Why don't you give the man some encouragement? Perhaps that's all he needs to set his feet on the right path."

A dull ache burned inside her chest. "I encouraged him once before, and he chose Mariah."

"Anyone can make a mistake."

The ache intensified. "The mistake was entirely mine for believing there could ever be anything between us. I've made my peace with it, and so should you."

"If you'd truly made peace with it, you'd have accepted one of the proposals you'd received since then. How many have there been...five or six at least?"

"I wasn't in love."

"Or rather, you were already in love with someone else."

Her anger flared. "If you continue, I swear I'll strike you with the horse whip!"

"Temper, woman!"

"I'm quite serious, Jensen. If you care anything at all about me, you'll not speak of my encouraging Theo again!"

Although her brother fell silent for a long while, his hands continued to fidget on the reins. Finally, he sighed. "I *do* care about you, Rissa." The nickname from her childhood grated on her nerves, but Rowe was oblivious. "I want you to marry while you're still young."

"Perhaps I *will* marry someday soon, but it won't be to Theo King. Don't you *dare* say anything to him about me or I'll never forgive you."

She hated the tears welling up in her eyes. To mask her distress, she took the reins from her brother and gave them a smart snap. The horse surged forward, and Rowe's hat nearly tumbled off his head.

"There's no need for haste," he managed.

"I beg to differ."

Fortunately, Rowe left Clarissa to her thoughts on the remainder of their drive. She hadn't counted on his keen powers of observation, but she supposed it would be naïve to assume he'd been oblivious about her feelings. Nevertheless, she'd tucked her romantic heartbreak away long ago, and had no wish to revisit it. Although Theo's return had indeed brought her a deep sort of joy, she'd tried to accept the fact he cared for her only as a dear friend.

Her brother was right about one thing, however. She'd mourned the man long enough. Perhaps she'd emerge from her cocoon at the Kings' ball and see what came of it. She had some uncommonly pretty gowns put away from seasons past, and one of them would do nicely. It was time to wake up and get on with her life. In fact, the invitation had indicated she could bring an escort...and she knew exactly whom to ask.

Although Clarissa tried to keep her amusement to herself, Rowe noticed the smile on her lips. "Your head seems to be full of bees. What has you so jolly?"

"I'm looking forward to the ball with great anticipation."

He peered at her. "Are you sure that's all there is to it? I've never seen anyone's mood change so quickly."

"I've just thought of someone to escort me, if he's not otherwise engaged."

Her brother winced. "Not Sir Willard."

Clarissa made a sound of disgust. "I wouldn't stoop *that* low. Papa would roll in his grave if I should ever give that man a second glance."

"Indeed, he would. I've often regretting selling him the manor house, but we received no other offers." His brow furrowed a moment. "You can't mean Graham Quinlan?"

"I most certainly do. And you're not to discuss him with anyone. I'd like my escort to be a surprise."

"Quinlan annoys Theo to no end."

"He's to be *my* escort, not Theo's. Besides, I like him."

"Really? Then why do you turn down his proposals?"

She shrugged. "My feelings forbade it before, but it's a new day. Perhaps I'll feel differently the next time he proposes."

"What a fine situation! I was planning to take you to the ball, and now you've left me in the lurch for Quinlan of all people."

"So ask someone else."

"I'd rather go alone."

"Suit yourself."

As they drew near the cottage, Clarissa noticed a familiar horse tied to the fence outside. "We have a visitor waiting for us, it seems."

Rowe clicked his tongue and muttered, "Speak of the devil. I suppose we'll have to ask Quinlan to stay for tea."

"Why not? It gives me the chance to ask him to the ball."

"That's a bit forward, isn't it?"

"There are ways to make an invitation seem as if it's the man's idea."

He peered at her. "You continue to astonish me."

A handsome man, clad in finely tailored clothes, emerged from the house. When he spotted the gig, his face assumed an expression of pleased surprise.

Clarissa brought the horse to a stop. "Good afternoon, Mr. Quinlan."

"Good afternoon, Lord Rowe and Lady Clarissa! I was about to give up hope of your return. I'm so glad I waited."

"As am I." Clarissa handed the reins to her brother and allowed Quinlan to assist her down from the carriage.

"I'll put the horse away and be in very shortly," Rowe said.

"I'll tell Cook to have tea ready."

Rowe's reply was sardonic. "Wonderful."

Quinlan, seemingly oblivious of the sarcasm, offered Clarissa his arm. "Shall we go in?"

••••

Although Theo settled himself in the drawing room with a good book, he had difficulty concentrating on the story. Clarissa had artfully dodged his question about her suitors, and he kept turning over the possibilities in his mind. He glanced down at the golden retriever puppy curled on the rug at his feet.

"Who do you suppose were Clarissa's suitors, D'Artagnan?"

The puppy opened his eyes at the sound of his name and lifted his head.

"I daresay Graham Quinlan could be included."

A growling bark came from deep within D'Artagnan's throat.

"I agree with your assessment," Theo said. "That ne'er-do-well popinjay broke the hearts of half the girls in the county before he'd reached the age of one and twenty. Although I remember him pursuing her quite ardently at one time, she had far better taste than to encourage him, apparently."

The golden retriever cocked his head.

"Sir Willard Vandenberg probably made her an offer, too. He made a rather impertinent remark about her figure in my presence once, for which I took him to task." Theo frowned. "I know the fellow is well-off, but he's far too old for her, in my opinion. If he were a peer, his age might not be a drawback, but he's only a baronet."

Quinlan and Vandenberg might account for two of her suitors, but who were the others? As he continued to tick other possible candidates off on his fingers, the dog yawned and resumed his nap. Not that Clarissa's prospects were any of Theo's business really, but he was consumed with curiosity all the same. If pressed, would Rowe confess the names? Theo instantly dismissed the inquiry as undignified and officious. Even though he looked upon Clarissa almost like a younger sister, such prying was beneath him...however sorely he was tempted.

A young voice rang out. "Lord Apollo, we're back!"

"I'm in the drawing room!" Theo chuckled. Six-year-old Myles was so enamored of his former stage moniker, the lad almost never called him anything else. The lad careened through the door as if a band of marauding pirates were after him. When he appeared, D'Artagnan jumped up and turned joyous circles. The boy dropped to his knees and gave the puppy a hug.

"Did you enjoy your outing?" Theo asked.

"Y-Yes." Myles's lower lip protruded. "I like Larken's house, but I don't want to leave Graceling Hall. Don't you want us here anymore?"

"Never think that, lad, not for a minute. In fact, I'd much prefer you stay. But you have to understand Wynstone Park is Larken's family home, and we must take her wishes into consideration."

The boy stroked the puppy's buttery-white fur. "Don't you like D'Artagnan?"

"I like your dog, too."

Myles gazed up at Theo with an earnest expression. "Maybe if you tell Mr. King and Larken that you want us to stay, it'll make a difference."

"I shall, but I can't promise it will do any good. Now why don't you take D'Artagnan with you to the nursery? It's nearly teatime, and I expect Ginny's waiting for you." He lowered his voice into a conspiratorial whisper. "I think there's cake."

A gasp. "I *adore* cake! Come on, D'Artagnan!"

The boy and the dog loped from the room just as Brandon and Larken appeared in the doorway.

"Where are you two going in such a hurry?" Larken asked.

"Cake!"

The fair-haired woman exchanged an amused glance with her husband, and the expression of love that passed between the two brought a wistful smile to Theo's lips.

"Hello!" he said. "Myles was telling me about your adventures today."

Larken sank down onto a chair. "He remains unconvinced about our move to Wynstone Park, I'm afraid."

Brandon took a seat. "He'll come around."

"Truth be told, I'm unconvinced as well." Theo leaned forward. "There's no reason for you to leave. Why not consider leasing Wynstone Park and remain here for the foreseeable future?"

Brandon shook his head. "We've talked about this, Theo. This is *your* estate, and I don't belong here any longer."

"Nonsense! We've more than enough room in Graceling Hall for two families. You take one wing and I'll take the other."

"Families?" Larken echoed.

"Rowe and Clarissa are determined to see me wed." Although Theo had no thoughts of marriage whatsoever, perhaps his supposed search for a bride would induce Brandon and Larken to stay. "After that, the King family will be one big jolly clan."

A glint of mischievousness appeared in Larken's eyes. "Have you any particular lady in mind?"

"No, but we must also find suitable marriage partners for Rowe and Clarissa at the same time, or everything will go lopsided."

Brandon chuckled. "Perhaps a mail-order spouse? The arrangement worked well for Larken and me."

She made a sound of protest. "No! If it weren't for Myles bringing us together, I don't think it would have worked out at all."

"I'm only joking." Brandon winked. "I thank God every day for my good and undeserved fortune in having you for my wife."

As the loving couple gazed at one another, Theo's wistful sensation returned. Given his history, he could never hope to achieve such happiness. With Mariah, he'd allowed himself to be so swayed by her reserved, untouchable beauty he never took the time to discover who she really was inside. Worse, he'd exercised extraordinarily poor judgment in interfering with her engagement to his brother. He'd been young and foolish then, but was he any wiser now? No, he would content himself with seeing Rowe and Clarissa happily wed and embrace the bachelor life. At least he'd be unlikely to make another mistake that way.

Chapter Three

The Colleen

As servants handed around trays of hot Lamb's Wool, the drawing room at Graceling Hall became scented with the aroma of hot apple cider and spices. Clarissa breathed a sigh of obvious pleasure. "I've always loved Lamb's Wool. It reminds me of All Hallows Eve or Twelfth Night."

Her brother gave her a teasing glance. "It's always reminded me of lamb's wool."

"The foamy surface looks similar, I grant you, but it tastes far better." She took an appreciative whiff. "Smells wonderful, too!"

Theo picked up his cup. "I propose a toast to Padraig Aengus Shields. If he hadn't suggested I become an actor, I might've become a bootblack. Then Larken would never have seen me on stage, and I wouldn't be here today."

Larken, Brandon, Rowe, and Clarissa raised their cups. "To Paddy."

The sweet beverage hit Theo's tongue, and he savored the flavor of apples, nutmeg, ginger, and sugar.

"Theo, do you miss the theater?" Larken asked.

"Not really. It barely paid my bills and I never really fit in with the troupe." He shrugged. "Whenever the director allowed me to play character roles, I suppose that was more enjoyable."

"Now you get to play the role of gentleman again. Let not too much time pass before we may also cast you in the role of bridegroom." Rowe gave him a wink.

"Speaking of which, did you know someone has been leaving flowers on your grave for years?" Brandon asked. "I think you've a secret admirer."

Theo frowned. "If I've been the cause of any heartache, I'm devastated."

"On the other hand, when the lady in question learns you're alive, she'll be overjoyed," Larken said.

"I wonder who it could be? I believe we've a mystery on our hands," Rowe said.

"The matter may never be resolved," Clarissa said.

"Indeed, it may not," Theo said. "I daresay no lovestruck ladies will ever show up on my doorstep."

A commotion in the entrance hall drew his attention just then as a young woman remonstrated with the butler to let her pass. Rowe gave Theo a startled glance. "Perhaps you spoke too soon?"

When the argument continued, Theo set down his cup. "It seems Seagate needs help." Before he could take more than a few steps, however, a dark-haired woman dashed through the doorway.

"Which one o' ye is Theodore King?" Her Irish brogue was thicker than the froth floating on top of the hot cider.

"Sorry, sir, but she wouldn't take no for an answer." The butler grabbed the woman by the arm.

"It's all right. Let her go, Seagate," Theo said.

"As you wish, sir."

The woman wrenched herself free from the butler's grasp and glared at him. "I've half a mind to slap ye for puttin' your hands on me, ye big galoot."

Theo caught Seagate's eye and dismissed him with a movement of his head. After the butler left, he bowed to the newcomer.

"Theodore King, at your service."

"Are ye nigh? My name is Megan Shields, and you're responsible for the death o' my brother."

Startled gasps came from the room's occupants.

Theo peered at her with dawning comprehension. "*You're* Paddy's younger sister?"

"That I am."

She'd been just thirteen five years ago, as he recalled, but she was a young woman now—and a very pretty one at that. Her black hair was swept up into a simple coiffeur, but curly locks had come free at the nape of her neck and at her temples. Her bottle-green gown was simple and frayed at the hem, but fitted her outstanding figure well, and her heart-shaped face drew attention to her dark green eyes. Megan was alarmingly drawn, however, and pale. As Theo peered at her, the woman swayed—as if exhausted beyond endurance.

"Forgive me, Miss Shields, but you look as if you're about to faint." He quickly offered her his arm and escorted her to a chair, into which she sank without protest.

"I suppose I am. I've been travelin' all day with nary a bite to eat, but I couldn't rest until I returned your money to ye." She produced several pound notes and laid them on a table. "I'll not be bought off for a few quid!"

Rowe bristled and set his cup down none too gently. "How dare you force your way in here and speak to Mr. King like that? He's behaved in a gentlemanly and kind fashion toward you, and you insult him?"

Brandon held up a quelling hand. "Rowe, please."

The earl would not be repressed. "Forgive me, but it's outrageous!"

"I'll tell ye what's outrageous!" Megan's eyes snapped with anger. "Mr. King brought robbers down on Paddy by dressin' him up as a toff! The police told me what happened, and I'm here to get satisfaction!"

Bewildered, Theo cocked his head. "You've passed judgment on me with very little evidence."

"None, I daresay," Rowe snapped.

Clarissa shot her brother a warning glance. "Hush, Jensen. Can't you see Miss Shields is upset?"

"And tired." Larken's expression was compassionate as she thrust a cup of hot cider into Megan's hands. "Please have something to drink."

"I thank ye." The young woman took a tentative sip and then a larger gulp.

Theo was hopeful the worst of Megan's emotional outburst was past. "Miss Shields, I sent that money to redeem a pocket watch Paddy purchased from me, and for no other reason. The money is yours, free and clear, without any strings or expectations. I should have made that more plain." He paused. "Will you stay for dinner?"

The woman lifted her chin. "Ye got my brother killed! I'll not break bread with the likes o' ye!"

Rowe groaned. "This is your brother's *wake*, Miss Shields. I should think you'd make an exception!"

Confusion settled on Megan's features. "What are ye goin' on about?"

"Theo recently received confirmation of Paddy's identity from the Liverpool authorities and asked us to gather here tonight in your brother's honor," Clarissa explained. "It seems your arrival is auspicious indeed."

Larken gave Megan an encouraging smile. "We mean to honor his memory. Please join us, I implore you."

Brandon nodded. "From what Theo has told us about your brother, I think he would be glad you've come. I understand Paddy was extraordinarily friendly."

Megan's eyes shimmered with emotion. "He never met a man he didn't like."

"Clearly, a quality not shared by his sister." Rowe grunted when Clarissa jabbed him in the ribs with an elbow.

"Miss Shields, Paddy and I spent a very amiable evening together the night he died," Theo said. "If you stay, I'll have the opportunity to tell you everything I remember."

A myriad of conflicting expressions crossed the young woman's face, but her famished condition seemed to edge her into acquiescence. In truth, Megan looked as if she hadn't eaten or slept well in a long time, and Theo couldn't blame her for a display of temper.

Finally, she nodded. "I'll stay. Truth be told, I'd likely drop dead o' hunger on your doorstep as soon as I set foot out the door, so I would."

After Theo introduced Brandon, Larken, Rowe, and Clarissa to Megan, he rang for the butler and asked him to have an extra place set at the table for their guest.

"I took the liberty of setting an extra place already," Seagate replied.

Megan flicked a guilty glance at the man. "I'm sorry for callin' ye a galoot. I'm sure ye were just doing your job."

The unflappable butler kept his countenance. "Thank you, miss." He nodded at Theo. "Dinner is served."

••••

The cook had prepared Irish colcannon, Irish stew, and Irish soda bread for the wake, along with Irish apple cake and a few other traditional Irish dishes. Guinness was available to drink, as well as water, tea, and wine.

Megan peered at her meal, clearly taken aback. "Is your cook Irish?"

Theo shook his head. "No, but I asked her to prepare Irish cuisine today in celebration of your brother's life. I hope it's to your liking."

Her face crumpled and tears pooled in her eyes. A wave of sympathy washed over Theo as he considered her plight; her brother had been missing for years, but she'd only just recently discovered he was dead. He probably couldn't do much to help her cope with her loss, but—like Larken—he could demonstrate compassion. Although Brandon, Larken, and Clarissa seemed solicitous toward the woman, Rowe was clearly wary. Theo appreciated his friend's protective posture, but he wished Rowe understood Megan Shields was no threat whatsoever. In fact, her appearance and dialect reminded Theo pleasantly of Paddy and triggered a few long-forgotten memories.

"Your brother and I had a few pints together at a dockside tavern that night. As I recall, he planned to stow away on a cargo ship bound for Ireland. He meant to surprise you on your birthday."

Megan became mulish once more. "Och aye, and if he hadn't been after wearin' your clothes, he would've succeeded."

Rowe sputtered. "You don't know that!"

"Paddy didn't have an enemy in the world!" Megan shot back. "He was murdered by someone looking to kill Mr. King."

"Preposterous!" Rowe set his glass of Guinness down with a thump. "Theo has no enemies, either!"

Clarissa smiled, but her tone was firm. "I have to agree with Jensen, Miss Shields. Although there's a natural tendency to grasp at straws when one tries to make sense of a tragedy, to assume Theo was the intended target defies logic."

"Does it nigh?" Megan's trembling lower lip betrayed her emotions.

"Has Sergeant O'Hara reopened the investigation?" Theo asked.

"Since my brother's death was so long ago, O'Hara said he has more important things to be worryin' about."

"That's a shame." Theo's eyebrows drew together. "Perhaps we could solve Paddy's murder ourselves? It won't bring him back, but it would at least give you closure."

"You're mad." Rowe shook his head. "Meddling in murder is a sure way to get yourself killed."

"I feel as if I have a moral duty to look into the matter."

"Paddy was killed in a robbery, so there's nothing to solve," Rowe said. "The killer was some random thief who will never be discovered."

"It wasn't ordinary theft, otherwise my timepiece would have been missing."

"But you said the police found no wallet," Rowe said.

"His wallet might have fallen from his pocket and sunk to the bottom of the river." As Theo's gaze settled on Megan, even more memories began to return. "Paddy told me he was employed as a driver for a rich fellow who'd grown fond of him. I'm sorry, but I don't remember the man's name."

"Old Mr. Osbourne," Megan said. "Paddy was always writin' home about him and the wise things he said. My brother looked up to the man like a grandfather."

"I believe Paddy and Mr. Osbourne were planning to find you a husband."

She made a sound of protest. "They were, were they? I wonder what gave Paddy the notion I was needin' his help in that area?"

Rowe cleared his throat. "Perhaps it was your extraordinarily sharp tongue?"

Megan scowled. "I've a half a mind to sharpen my tongue on ye, ye arrogant aristocrat! I know ye look down on me because I'm Irish."

"That's where you're wrong. In point of fact, my mother was Irish."

"You're half-Irish?" Megan sniffed. "Must be the part I can't see."

"Can't or won't?"

Larken bit her lip, as if trying to stifle laughter, and Theo exchanged an alarmed glance with Clarissa. Why did Rowe persist in baiting the woman?

Brandon spoke. "Miss Shields, can you tell us where Mr. Osbourne lived? We'll need much more if we're to proceed."

"Proceed?"

"I think we should contact the man and ask him if Paddy had any enemies," Theo said. "Mr. Osbourne might have an idea about who could have killed your brother."

"Or your nosiness may get you killed," Rowe said. "I suggest you let the authorities deal with the matter."

Megan ignored the earl. "I reckon Mr. Osbourne split his days between London and Hertfordshire, where he owned a vast sheep farm. Paddy sent me packets o' wool from the farm every so often." A ghost of a smile lit her features. "He sent me a wee sheepskin once, too. Paddy grew to love that farm very much. Said it reminded him o' Ireland."

"Theo, why don't you write Mr. Waite and set him on the case?" Brandon suggested. "He was instrumental in helping Larken regain her inheritance from those awful Howley people. I expect he could help Miss Shields find Osbourne straightaway."

"Oh, yes, do write him, Theo, so he can investigate as soon as may be," Larken said.

Theo nodded. "Miss Shields, Mr. Waite is a very good lawyer. Do I have your permission to contact him on your behalf?"

"You have, for all the good it'll do. I've no money to pay an expensive lawyer."

"Don't worry about that," Theo said. "Since I'd benefit from some answers as much as you would, I'm happy to pay his fee."

"Miss Shields, perhaps you could stay at Graceling Hall until we get this sorted out?" Brandon asked.

"Yes, you're very welcome here. We're giving a ball in ten days' time, and we'd love for you to attend," Larken added.

Megan shook her head. "I've not brought along a stitch to wear to a fancy party."

"If you didn't bring anything suitable, I've many gowns that will do quite well, I imagine," Clarissa said. "The ball will be great fun."

"Please say you'll stay," Larken said. "We'll furnish you anything you need."

Megan glanced around the table, seemingly mystified. "Why are ye bein' so kind to me?"

Theo opened his mouth to respond, but Rowe answered instead. "The King family is composed of extraordinary people who, despite having dealt with a myriad of their own personal tragedies, are always universally kind. I consider myself honored to be amongst their friends."

Theo nodded at him. "Thank you, Rowe."

"If I've misjudged ye, Mr. King, I apologize." Megan stared at her plate.

"No apology necessary."

Rowe's manufactured cough made Theo want to send the tip of his boot into the man's shin, but unfortunately he was on the far side of the table. From the way the earl flinched and scowled at Clarissa afterward, however, it was clear his sister had followed through on the same impulse. Theo smiled at her, and she gave him a surreptitious wink.

"Perhaps you can play for us after dinner tonight, Clarissa?" he said. "Do you know any Irish tunes?"

"I'm afraid not."

"Er...have ye a harp?" Megan asked.

"Yes, we do," Larken replied. "There was a beautiful harp stored in a corner of the attic, covered with a heavy cloth. I had it brought down to the ballroom last week and had it tuned."

Brandon gave Theo a bewildered glance. "I can't recall anyone in our family playing the harp."

"Perhaps you were too young to remember Grandmother Philippa? I'd quite forgotten about that harp." Theo smiled. "Thank you, Larken, for finding it."

"I spent a great deal of time in the attic when I first came to Graceling Hall," she replied. "I discovered all manner of treasures there."

"Including Lord Apollo's portrait." Brandon's smile was teasing.

"Who is Lord Apollo?" Megan asked.

"Me," Theo said.

"I didn't know ye were a lord."

"I'm not. Lord Apollo is the name I used when I was performing on stage in London."

"Well, Lord Apollo, I'll play a few Irish songs for ye after dinner—as a way of payin' for my supper, so to speak." Megan's cheeks were suddenly suffused with crimson. "If ye like."

"I'm sure we'd love to hear you play, Miss Shields," Theo said. "I'll have the harp brought into the drawing room."

••••

Even as Megan was warming up her fingers on the strings, Clarissa appreciated the woman's obvious skill as a harpist. Thereafter, the lovely, almost magical notes she coaxed from the instrument filled the room with music. Megan played "Bantry Bay," and "The Daughters of Erin." From her seat in the back of the room, Clarissa noticed everyone paying rapt attention. Even a few of the servants clustered near the doorway to listen.

To Clarissa's surprise, when Megan played "Pretty Maid Milking a Cow," Rowe began to sing the English lyrics in a clear, flawless tenor. He even managed the few Gaelic lines without any effort whatsoever. After the song faded away, he noticed everyone was staring.

"You needn't act so shocked. My mother played the harp, and that was her favorite song."

"I can't believe you remembered the words," Clarissa said. "It's been years since Mama sang it."

"As it so happens, it's my favorite song as well," he replied.

"It's enchanting," Larken said.

"Why have you never happened to sing for us before, Rowe?" Brandon asked. "I didn't even know you could sing!"

"Nor did I," Theo added.

Rowe shrugged. "There's rarely any reason for me to sing outside of church, particularly when beautiful ladies are available to exhibit their talents far more ably."

"Bravo, Miss Shields, and well done, Rowe," Theo said.

Even Megan was smiling. "Thank ye." She glanced at Rowe. "And I've ne'er heard a man sing better."

Rowe's complexion reddened at the praise. "Perhaps it was my Irish showing."

She laughed. "Perhaps 'twas."

"You play beautifully, and I enjoyed listening to you very much." Rowe slid a pointed glance in Clarissa's direction. "I think we must be going."

As Clarissa and Rowe drove away from Graceling Hall, she mulled over her brother's strange behavior that night. "Why were you so beastly to Miss Shields earlier?"

"Is that why you kicked me? You'd no call to assault my poor shin."

"Am I to have an answer to my question?"

"The woman stormed into the house and put Theo on the defensive with her wild allegations. He should have tossed her out immediately."

"Don't be absurd. He feels beholden to her brother."

"Pity."

"You're being perfectly horrid, Jensen. You're usually such a gentleman that I can't account for it, and I know Theo shares my bad opinion of you." Clarissa averted her gaze. "I urge you to rethink your behavior. He may have his eye on Miss Shields."

"You're joking."

"No, I'm not. You should have seen his expression when she was playing the harp."

"He enjoys music. You should see his expression when you play piano."

"There's a difference. Theo takes me for granted, while Miss Shields is new and different and...somewhat mesmerizing. If she's his choice, I shan't stand in his way, and neither should you."

A muscle worked in Rowe's jaw. "You're getting too far ahead of yourself, Clarissa. Theo was quite cordial to her, I grant you, but he's motivated by a sense of obligation. As for me, I find her manner to be extremely abrasive and off-putting. Nevertheless, I'll make an effort to curb my antipathy, for Theo's sake."

"See that you do. You don't want to put him in the position of having to choose between a lady and his friends. Such a conundrum wouldn't end well for any of us."

"You're awfully beneficent, all things considered."

"What do you mean?"

"If he forms an attachment to Miss Shields, you've the most to lose."

"I only want to see him happy."

"I do too, but not at the cost of your happiness."

"Don't start with that again."

Although Clarissa meant what she said, her throat swelled with suppressed emotion. Theo had looked so incredibly handsome that evening and his manners had been so ingratiating, Miss Shields could not fail to be captivated. Whether or not Theo had felt the same way toward her, only time would tell.

Suzanne G. Rogers

Chapter Four

Pride

Megan woke to find a young woman in her bedchamber, rummaging through her small carpetbag. She sat up in bed, clutching the covers to her chest. "Och, who are ye and what are ye doin' in here!"

The woman curtsied. "Forgive me for disturbing your rest, Miss Shields, but I'm to look after you during your stay at Graceling Hall. My name is Bess."

Megan's gaze fell to the garment in the maid's hands. "What are ye doin' with my dress?"

"I'm taking it downstairs for a quick sponge and press and then I'll be back." Bess smiled and gestured toward the screen in the corner. "I brought you hot water for your bath."

The maid turned to leave, and Megan felt a pang of remorse.

"Bess...I'm sorry for speakin' to ye so harsh. Ye startled me a bit."

"If a stranger was in my room, I'm sure I'd be startled as well. Please excuse me."

After the maid slipped out the door and shut it behind her, Megan left the bed. A small bathtub awaited behind the tall screen, with little curls of steam rising from the surface of the water. A smile crept onto her lips. A hot bath to herself and a maid to boot? The King family lived quite high indeed, and they'd all seemed cordial...except perhaps for the high-and-mighty Lord Rowe. He wasn't a member of the family, but he seemed a great favorite of theirs, unfortunately.

After draping her simple cotton nightshift over the screen, Megan eased herself into the tub, reveling in the heat that enveloped her body. A bar of perfumed, milled soap had been provided for her use, as well as a washcloth and a cup of raw egg yolk with which to cleanse her hair. After she'd massaged her scalp with the yolk, she washed it off and then soaked in the bath for a few more minutes.

A tap on the door heralded Bess's return. The young woman peeked around the screen with a pitcher in her hand. "Your dress is ready, and I brought you some rosemary water for a hair rinse."

"Did ye? I'm not used to such luxury."

A few minutes later, Megan sat in front of the vanity, clad in a wrapper, while the maid blotted the moisture from her hair with a towel and worked a comb through the tangles.

"Do ye like workin' at Graceling Hall, Bess?"

"Oh, yes. I haven't been here very long, but the family is ever so kind. I'm from an orphanage, and Mrs. King gave me my first position."

"That's a bit o' luck there. I'm an orphan too, but at least I had the good fortune to have a big brother to look after me. Paddy had to leave Ireland, but he found work in England right away and sent me something to live on every month. When I turned thirteen, his letters stopped comin,' and my letters were returned, unopened. I didn't find out what had happened to him until a few weeks ago."

Bess's eyes grew wide. "How did you survive all by yourself?"

"A distant cousin took me in. When I turned sixteen, I played my harp at a local pub for a coin or two."

"It's hard being without family."

"That it is." Megan bit her lip. "Do ye...do ye know anythin' about Lord Rowe?"

Bess giggled. "Half the maids are in love with him. The earl's always got a joke up his sleeve, and he dresses so elegant."

"Does he have himself a girl then?"

"I don't think so. If he does, she's not likely to be anyone below stairs."

"Why not?"

"His family lost their fortune a while back, and he must marry an heiress."

Megan nodded. "That's the way o' the world, so 'tis. A man can't live on thin air."

"None of us can."

As the maid continued unsnarling tangles, Megan became lost in thought. One thing she and Lord Rowe had in common was lack of money, although his clothes and those of his sister didn't look inexpensive. His impecunious circumstance was probably a relatively recent development, then. By contract, *her* past had been a constant struggle against poverty, and her future was just as bleak. An old friend—Riordan—had sought her out in Belfast a few weeks ago to ask if Paddy had ever made it home from Liverpool. After he'd related his conversation with her brother, she decided to take matters into her own hands. She'd sold her harp, packed her meager belongings, and booked passage to Liverpool to see if the police could help locate Paddy.

Ever since she'd discovered her brother was dead, a sick, panicked feeling had taken over her mind, body, and soul. The money Theo had sent to her during her stay in Liverpool was almost all the funds she had in the world now, and she'd been secretly relieved he'd refused to take it back. Although his lawyer would attempt to locate Paddy's employer, she'd no real faith Mr. Osbourne knew anything helpful. Furthermore, she couldn't reside at Graceling Hall forever. She said she'd stay for the ball, but then she'd have to leave.

She studied her reflection in the mirror, trying to decide if she could attract a wealthy English husband like Paddy had intended. Perhaps at the ball she would meet a rich young man who fancied her? For a brief moment, she allowed herself to daydream about falling madly in love with the handsome heir of a great fortune. In the next breath, however, she rejected the idea as hopelessly naïve. In English society, marriages were made to cement dynasties and shore up fortunes. No man of substance would marry an Irish girl—a colleen—especially not one without friends, property, or connections. A wealthy gentleman or aristocrat might seek to make her his mistress, but she'd have none of that! She might be without much in the way of material possessions, but she still had her virtue and her pride.

Although Megan's hair was still quite damp, the maid pinned it up loosely and helped her into the dress. As the maid tied the sash in back, Megan glanced at her reflection in the full-length mirror and winced inwardly at her gown. Although the maid had made the garment look as fresh as possible, it was still horribly plain, worn, and a trifle too short. Last night she'd been too hungry to be embarrassed about her attire, but this morning she felt differently.

"Would you like me to show you to the dining room?" Bess asked.

"I know my way, thank ye...but do ye think I could take my breakfast with the staff?"

"But you're a guest, Miss Shields! It wouldn't be proper."

The blood rushed to her cheeks. "I'm not fit to be dinin' with the family in this dress. None o' my clothes are suitable at all, I reckon."

"No one at Graceling Hall will judge you, I'm sure, but I can bring a tray up to your room, if you'd prefer."

"I don't want to make extra work for ye." She swallowed. "I'll just be goin' to the dinin' room then."

Downcast, she moved toward the door, but Bess stopped her. "Would you care to eat in the nursery with Myles?"

Megan brightened at the mention of a nursery. "There's a wee wain in the house?"

"Yes. Myles just turned six and he's a delightful lad. His nanny is abed with a cold, so he'll be alone this morning."

"Excuse me for sayin' so, but Mrs. King doesn't look old enough to have a wain that age."

"Myles is Mr. Brandon King's ward."

"Well, the nursery will suit me fine, right enough. If you'd be so kind as to let the family know, I'd be grateful."

"Certainly. Let me show you to the nursery then."

"Give me a moment." Megan reached up, pulled the pins from her hair, and let the dark mass fall to her waist. "I reckon it'll dry better this way."

She followed the maid from the room, down a long corridor, and around a corner. After another few yards, Bess gestured toward an open door.

"Why don't you wait for Myles, and I'll make sure the kitchen knows to set his breakfast cart for two people?"

"Thank ye, Bess."

The maid hastened off, and Megan stepped into the nursery. A table with six chairs was arranged in front of the fireplace. To her surprise, a top hat was dangling over the chair at the end. She slid into the seat underneath and reached up with a fingertip to set the hat swinging.

A young boy, clad in a sailor suit, appeared in the doorway. When he saw Megan, his eyebrows shot up and his eyes grew wide.

"You're sitting in Lord Topper's lap!"

"Am I?" With undue haste, she rose and stepped to one side. "I hope I wasn't after creasin' his trousers?"

Myles laughed. "Oh, no, he's used to people sitting in his lap by accident. Who are you?"

"My name is Megan, and I'm stayin' at Graceling Hall for a short while."

"I'm Myles." He wrinkled his nose. "You talk funny."

"I could say the same for ye. You're not English?"

"No, I'm from America. Where are you from?"

"The Emerald Isle. That's Ireland, so 'tis."

"Why do you call it the Emerald Isle? Are there a lot of emeralds there?"

"It's from a poem, 'When Erin First Rose.' Ireland is quite green, ye see."

"Like your eyes?"

"Ooh, aren't you a charmer!"

Myles giggled. "Maybe I'll visit there someday. Let me introduce you to my pretend friends. You've already met Lord Topper, of course." He patted a chair draped in a silk shawl. "This is Lady Peabody, who secretly used to be an actress." Next came a chair which held a parasol, an old pair of lace gloves, and a cluster of dried flowers. "And this is Miss Josie, who's a debutante."

Megan gave him a sidelong glance. "Are ye knowin' what a debutante is?"

"I think it means you go to parties and drink tea." He shrugged and pointed to the portrait hanging over the fireplace. "That's Lord Apollo, only this is where it gets confusing. He's really Mr. Brandon King, but Larken named him because he looks so much like his older brother, who really *is* Lord Apollo, the actor."

"Er…the King brothers do look alike, I'll grant ye."

Myles marched around to an unoccupied chair and pulled it out. "You may sit here, if you wish." He spoke in a grand fashion, as if he were a fully grown gentleman.

"I do, and ye have my thanks, sir."

Although Megan tried to be solemn as she took her seat, a giggle slipped out. Myles giggled, too. "You needn't call me sir. I'm only six."

A maid entered the room, pushing a cart laden with food and pots of hot chocolate and tea. "Good morning!" She began setting the food out on the table.

"Where is D'Artagnan?" Myles asked. "He's usually waiting for me by the fireplace."

The young woman smiled. "James is taking him for a long walk."

Megan gave Myles a quizzical glance.

"James is the carriage driver, and D'Artagnan is my puppy," Myles explained. "He's a golden retriever."

After the maid left, Myles used his spoon to push his oatmeal into a peak. As Megan watched, the lad hollowed out the center and poured milk inside until it spilled over the sides of the mountain.

"Ginny—she's my nanny—says I mustn't play with my food, but it's ever so much fun to make oatmeal into a volcano."

"I think so, too."

He cocked his head. "Why aren't you eating downstairs with the grown-ups?"

"I was invited, to be sure, but I declined because my clothes aren't very nice."

"When I first came here, Larken's clothes were terrible." He grimaced in disgust. "Then she bought new ones and looked so much prettier afterward. You can do the same thing."

"I haven't any money to buy new ones just nigh."

"Get married and then your husband can buy you new clothes."

The sweet child made it seem so simple when it was anything but. Megan gazed at the boy's earnest expression and smiled. "What a fine suggestion! That's just what I'll do."

••••

As his sister tucked into a breakfast of scrambled eggs and kippers, Rowe folded yet another piece of delectable bacon into his mouth, chewed, and swallowed.

"You were up early this morning." He reached for a piece of toast and the crock of butter.

Clarissa shrugged. "I was selecting a ball gown for Miss Shields, as well as a few other gowns for everyday wear. I don't think she arrived at Graceling Hall with an extensive wardrobe, so I packed a trunk. I had an extensive wardrobe for my Season, you know, so I can certainly spare a few things."

"You needn't go to such trouble. I'm certain Larken could furnish her some dresses."

"I believe my coloring is more similar to Miss Shields's, so my clothes will likely suit her better…even if they are a few years out of date."

"You're trying to push the girl at Theo, aren't you?"

"If she puts her best foot forward, he may discover her charms on his own."

Rowe regarded his sister with astonishment. "You're the most insanely kind and unselfish person imaginable."

"Not really. I'm sure Theo would do the same for me if he found a gentleman he thought I might like."

"It's not the same, as you're well aware. Besides which, Miss Shields is ill mannered and uncultured in the extreme. Theo would never consider her, and I can't think of anyone worth his salt who would."

"Her manners and temper will improve when she's eating more regularly. And as far as culture is concerned, even *you* were impressed with her accomplishments at the harp. Such talent, along with a pretty face and figure, goes a long way toward smoothing out any rough edges."

"I'd no idea you could be so calculating where men were concerned. You had poor Quinlan eating out of your hand yesterday at tea."

His sister merely smiled. "I've a pupil arriving for a piano lesson midmorning. Will you be a dear and take the trunk over to Graceling Hall?"

"Can't it wait until our dancing lesson with Larken this afternoon?"

"You don't understand a thing about women, do you? We're not happy unless we look our best."

"Apparently women have always been and will always be a mystery to me." He paused. "Do you want the last bit of bacon?"

"As long as you do as I ask, you may have it."

"All right." With a grin, he bit into the maple-flavored strip of bacon and savored the sweet, salty explosion of flavor on his tongue.

"And be polite to Miss Shields, should you happen to see her," Clarissa admonished. "Remember, she might be Theo's bride someday."

The bacon suddenly lost its appeal. "You've a knack for spoiling the moment."

••••

Theo joined Brandon in the dining room for breakfast, followed shortly thereafter by Larken.

"Bess informs me that Miss Shields is dining with Myles this morning," she said.

"Whatever for?" Theo gave her a bewildered glance. "Do you suppose she's still angry with me?"

Larken shook her head. "I don't believe it has anything to do with you. Bess indicated that Miss Shields feels self-conscious about her attire, and I'm not exactly sure how to proceed. It's one thing to furnish her a ball gown for a particular occasion, and quite another to offer her dresses and such. Her pride may prevent her from accepting our help."

"How perfectly ridiculous! Paddy Shields helped me in my time of need and I want to return the favor. Since he's no longer with us, I wish to help his sister instead." Theo sighed. "Perhaps I should go speak with her?"

"Leave it alone for now," Larken said. "I've an idea; why don't the three of us go riding with Myles this morning and give Miss Shields the opportunity to settle into her surroundings? Once Graceling Hall feels a little more familiar, she may be more open to our help."

Theo opened his mouth to protest, but Brandon held up his hand.

"Larken understands these things, Theo. As you may remember, when you first came back to Graceling Hall, you felt quite estranged from the place. Larken advised me to leave you alone, and eventually you came around admirably."

Theo's eyebrows rose. "I was managed, was I?" He laughed. "All right, we'll do it your way. In the end, however, I mean to help Miss Shields, whether she likes it or not."

••••

Rowe strapped the oversized, heavy trunk on the back of the gig and set off for Graceling Hall. Although the mid-October morning was warm, the changing color of the leaves was ample proof that fall was progressing. He felt somewhat contemplative as he drove underneath a long canopy of branches, listening to birds calling out to one another. It occurred to him that even the smallest of creatures yearned to feel part of a community. Over five years ago, his own community of dearest friends had been torn apart by a cold, self-serving woman by the name of Mariah Pettigrew. She'd come between the King brothers and had exacted a monstrous toll. Now that Brandon was happily settled with Larken, was it really so terrible to wish Theo would also put the past behind him once and for all and marry Clarissa? The close friendship between two families could continue that way and deepen as time went on.

Graceling Hall loomed into view, oddly welcoming for such an imposing structure. Built in the seventeenth century, its Jacobean architecture gave the home a formal appearance. Rowe and Clarissa had played there often as children, unaware that the future demise of their parents meant their own estate would have to be sold for taxes and most of the staff laid off. Rowe and his sister had moved into a cottage located at the edge of the property, and employed only a cook, maid, and part-time gardener now.

When Seagate opened the door, Rowe grinned. "Good morning. I've brought a trunk for Miss Shields." He gestured toward the gig parked nearby. "Would you have a servant take it to her room?"

"Certainly, milord. The family is not at home at the moment, but I'll tell them you called."

"That's all right; I'll return this afternoon." Rowe hesitated. "Er...is Miss Shields in?"

The butler stepped back so the earl could enter the house. "If you'll be so good as to wait in the drawing room, I'll see if she's available."

Rowe strolled into the drawing room, where the harp still stood. He sat down and tried to play a few chords, to poor results. When Megan entered the room, she seemed surprised to see him plucking the strings.

"Why...do ye play the harp, Lord Rowe?"

"Not really." He chuckled. "My mother tried to teach me to play when I was a child, but my fingers weren't terribly strong, and I didn't have the patience to stay with it. Sometimes I wish I had; harp music is so very soothing."

"That it is."

As Rowe stood, he noticed her mane hung down her back in a glossy, dark cloud. The reddish highlights revealed by a shaft of sunlight streaming through the window nearby drew his admiration.

"You've beautiful hair, if you don't mind me saying so." He regretted the words as soon as he spoke; he hadn't meant to puff the girl up with compliments.

She blushed. "I washed it this morning and it's only just now dried. I should've pinned it up before comin' down to see ye, but I forgot about it."

He cleared his throat and averted his gaze. "Er...I brought over a trunk filled with gowns my sister felt might suit you. A servant is putting it in your room right now."

Her chin jerked upward, and she stood with her arms akimbo. "So now ye reckon I'm a charity case, do ye? Ye can just take that trunk back home!"

"Not every act of kindness is meant as an insult!" Rowe tried to control his temper, but it was difficult. "My sister went to a great deal of effort to select dresses for you, Miss Shields, and I'll not have you throw them back in her face! She has little enough to give, and the least you can do is accept her generosity with grace." He grabbed his hat. "I'll let her know how delighted you were with her gift."

Furious, he strode from the room and out the front door without waiting for the butler to show him out. If Clarissa had witnessed Megan's ingratitude just now, she would have been crushed. He hoped his sister was wrong about Theo's interest in Megan Shields, because she was as prickly as a bramble bush and had the temperament of a wild boar.

As he reached the gig, he heard Megan's voice. "Lord Rowe, wait!"

For a moment he was sorely tempted to climb in and drive off, but he was too much of a gentleman to do so. He stood there with his arms folded across his chest and kept his gaze firmly fixed on a flock of sheep grazing in the grassy field some distance away.

Megan hastened down the steps and over to him.

"Forgive me, Your Lordship. I've grown cynical and mistrustful havin' to do for myself the past few years. Paddy would be disappointed if he could see what I've become, so he would. Please thank your sister for me and tell her I'm grateful for her takin' an interest."

Out of the corner of his eye, he could see her fists clenched at her side and she seemed to be fighting back tears. The strident quality he'd detected before was gone, replaced by a note of pleading. His anger dissipated somewhat, and he grudgingly met her gaze.

"Miss Shields, while you're at Graceling Hall, you're amongst kindred spirits—if you choose to accept our friendship."

A single tear ran down the side of her face, and she brushed it away. "I've nothin' to offer in return."

"Yes, you do. You're the key to everything."

She turned a silent, questioning gaze on him. "I'm not understandin' ye."

"There's much you don't comprehend about how Theo is feeling. He unwittingly allowed his family to believe he'd been killed, and he reproaches himself for causing them grief. Furthermore, he regrets your brother's death more than he can say. Unfortunately, he can't achieve peace without forgiveness. Your brother is gone, but if you can swallow your pride long enough to let us help *you*, Theo might begin to heal. That's a gift you can give him."

"I hadn't thought on it that way." She nodded. "In that case, I'll make an effort to be more agreeable from now on."

"Good." Rowe climbed into the gig. "Clarissa and I will be back this afternoon for Larken's dance lesson. She'd probably enjoy it if you'd wear one of your new gowns."

"Dance lesson?"

"Yes, my sister and I earn our living by giving piano and dance lessons." He tipped his hat. "Until then."

He turned the gig around and headed down the drive. Megan Shields was aggravating, but if nothing else she'd accepted Clarissa's gift and agreed to be more genial. That was something, he supposed.

Chapter Five

Fair Trade

Megan bit her lip with regret as she watched Rowe drive off without a backward glance. The earl thought her so despicable, he barely managed to hide it. Although he'd been blunt in his criticism, she gave him credit for having Theo's best interests at heart. When viewed from his perspective, she supposed she *had* behaved badly. Indeed, even though her pride had been wounded, she should've accepted Clarissa's gift with gratitude and humility. Now that the damage was done, however, she vowed to make the rest of her stay with the King family more pleasant for everyone involved.

And then what would become of her?

She returned to the drawing room and sat down at the harp. As she played a melancholy Irish folk tune, she thought about what sort of occupation she might pursue. After she heard what the lawyer discovered about Mr. Osbourne, she'd travel to London and look for employment. Although she'd prefer work as a governess or tutor, her heavy brogue would likely relegate her to a position as a maid-of-all-work—that is, assuming anyone would hire her without a reference. If only she spoke more like Larken or Clarissa, it would be far easier to stand out from the horde of other Irish souls desperate to find work.

Perhaps during her stay at Graceling Hall she could improve her speech by listening to the King family and their friends and trying to emulate the way they spoke? What better way to be accepted than to talk more like the English! Of course, it would be helpful if she had someone to give her elocution lessons. Would Clarissa be willing to take her on as a pupil, were she able to pay? Although she didn't have much money, it would only be a few lessons. Megan decided to ask Clarissa that afternoon if she'd be willing to be her tutor. If she could take the edge off her accent, she might aspire to be a governess after all.

Feeling somewhat more hopeful, Megan left the drawing room and mounted the stairs to the floor above. When she reached her room, she discovered Bess had already opened the trunk Rowe had delivered and was hanging up dresses in the wardrobe.

"Do you know where the trunk came from?" the maid asked.

"Lady Clarissa sent it, with her compliments. She's a real lady, she is."

"Yes, and she plays piano so very beautifully." Bess held up a gown of shimmering sapphire satin, with an off-the-shoulder bodice, dainty pleats around the bottom of the draped overskirt, and a wider pleat at the hem. "Look what she sent for you to wear at the ball!"

Megan gasped. "Lady Clarissa can't be meanin' to lend me that!"

"Of course she does." The maid brought Megan over to the mirror and held the dress in front of her to judge the effect. "With your dark hair and green eyes, you'll be stunning in it. There's a pair of gloves in the trunk too, as well as satin slippers. You and Lady Clarissa are the same height, so I'd wager everything will fit." She giggled. "Just don't bend over too deeply when you're wearing the ball gown. I think you're a bit fuller in the bust."

As Megan gazed at the magnificent dress, she shook her head in amazement. "Och, I've never seen anythin' so fine." She gave Bess a stricken glance. "I'm after forgettin'—I'm in mourning for my brother!"

The maid's eyebrows knit together. "I understood he died five years ago?"

"So he did, but I learned the truth o' the matter only a few weeks ago. I don't have a black dress to my name, but I'm not certain it's proper to wear something so bright."

Bess scratched her head. "I've never really thought about a situation like yours."

Megan gave the vibrantly colored gown a wistful glance. "I suppose Paddy would rather I be gettin' on with it, wouldn't he?" She sighed. "All right, then, I'll mourn in private and wear the dress."

"I'm glad, because there are a great many other dresses in the trunk and none of them suitable for mourning." Bess gave her a smile. "May I tell the footman to set a place at luncheon for you?"

A slow smile spread across Megan's lips. "Tell him he may."

••••

When Theo entered the dining room along with Larken and Brandon, he noticed the table was set for four. "Is it wishful thinking on my part or is Miss Shields to join us?"

"That she is." Megan stood in the doorway. "And properly clad this time."

Her attire was an elegant green-and-white striped afternoon gown, with the skirt caught up into a modest bustle in the back. Her dark curls had been twisted into a chignon, and she appeared to be every inch the lady.

Theo's surprise must have shown on his face because Megan laughed. "I've Lady Clarissa to thank for the use o' her clothes. She sent her brother over this morning to deliver a trunk filled with the most beautiful things I've ever seen."

"You look splendid, Miss Shields." Larken beamed. "I'm so glad!"

Brandon nodded. "As am I."

"Clarissa and Jensen are the best sort of people," Theo said. "I'm really quite fond of them both."

"You must let me know what else you need, Miss Shields," Larken said. "I'm more than happy to help."

Megan's smile lit her features. "I certainly will, Mrs. King."

They sat down to a lunch of sandwiches and a cold, sliced joint of beef.

"Miss Shields, Theo and Brandon will be taking Myles to the lake to fish this afternoon, but I'm staying here for a dance lesson in the ballroom," Larken said. "Perhaps you'd like to watch?"

"I would, thank ye."

The woman's attitude seemed quite pleasantly transformed, and Theo wondered what was responsible.

"Did you and Lord Rowe have the opportunity to visit?" he asked.

"Er...we did have a short visit, and a very gentlemanly fellow he is."

"It seems you and Rowe have heritage and music in common."

"That we do, as well as a great deal of admiration for his sister. Mr. King, I believe ye mentioned in your letter that Paddy is buried next to the church on the estate. Would ye mind if I walked there after lunch?"

"It's a rather long walk, but only a ten-minute journey by carriage. I'll have a gig brought around and we'll journey there together," Theo said.

"But you're to go fishin', aren't ye?"

"Not until two, so I'll be back in plenty of time."

"You're very thoughtful, sir. Paddy would be happy to know how hospitable ye've been to me."

Until then, Theo hadn't realized how much he'd longed to hear her say so. "I'm glad, Miss Shields." He paused. "I sent off a letter this morning to Mr. Waite, asking him to locate Mr. Osbourne. We'll see what he manages to discover."

"It's kind o' ye to remember, so 'tis."

"Before you leave for the church, Miss Shields, let me furnish you some flowers for Paddy's grave," Larken said.

"I'm grateful to ye, Mrs. King. I'd like that very much."

Theo exchanged pleased a glance with Brandon and Larken. So far, things with Megan were going better than he'd hoped.

••••

Megan held a fragrant basket of roses in her lap as Theo drove her toward the church in an open carriage. She wore a borrowed broad-brimmed hat to keep the sun off her skin and out of her eyes.

"It was very kind o' Mrs. King to lend me her hat, I reckon."

"Larken's more than happy to help, I'm sure." He glanced at her. "I hope you don't mind that Paddy's buried in our family plot. If you wish his body to be disinterred and sent to Ireland, I'll oblige you."

"If it's all the same to ye, I wouldn't like him disturbed, Mr. King."

"But...we're not Catholic."

"Nobody in my family is Catholic. We're Protestants, from Belfast."

His eyebrows rose. "I see. If Paddy's to stay, then I'd like to get a proper burial stone for him. Write the inscription out and I'll make sure it's done."

"You're a decent man, Mr. King, and I want ye to know I'm sorry for blamin' ye for my brother's death. I can see now it wasn't your fault. After I speak with your lawyer to see if he has any information for me, I'll be on my way and trouble ye no further."

"There's no rush. Will you return to Belfast?"

She shook her head. "I won't be returnin' to Ireland anytime soon. I'll be headin' to London to look for work."

"Forgive me if this seems an impertinent question, but what about marriage?"

"Och, a poor Irishwoman can't make a good match, Mr. King. Besides which, since my father was a drunk and not much o' a father or a husband to boot, I'm not so keen on marriage."

"I understand you completely. After being jilted, I've no wish to marry either."

She looked at him askance. "Come now...a gentleman such as yourself, turning your back on matrimony? I never heard o' such a thing. Ye ought to marry Lady Clarissa. She's a real beauty, that one."

"Clarissa's like a sister to me."

Megan's snort was unladylike. "Then you're blind *and* a fool...beggin' your pardon."

He chuckled. "No doubt you're right on both accounts."

They arrived at the church a few minutes later. Theo led Megan to the family plot, which was underneath the shade of a lovely tree. Although she'd thought she was emotionally prepared to see her brother's final resting place, despite her best efforts, her throat tightened and her vision blurred with tears.

While Theo stood at a discreet distance, she knelt next to the grave and arranged her flowers in the center of the plot.

"'Tis a fine place to sleep, Paddy, and you're finally rubbin' elbows with the gentry." Her smile faded. "I don't reckon I'll ever find out why you were killed, but I mean to try." She cleared her throat several times before she could speak again. "Just so ye know, I'll never forget ye and I'll never stop lovin' ye."

Megan rose, but when she turned away from the grave, she immediately dissolved into gut-wrenching sobs. Theo hastened over to envelop her into his comforting arms.

••••

As Rowe drove himself and Clarissa toward Graceling Hall, he noticed a familiar gig parked next to the church. "I wonder what Theo's doing here?"

"Perhaps we should stop."

After he'd driven past the church, the view of the graveyard revealed a man and a woman in an embrace. He stared in shock. "That's Theo and Miss Shields, isn't it?"

"Yes." Clarissa averted her eyes. "Drive on quickly, before they see us."

Rowe urged his horse to increase his pace. "Fast work on her part, I must say."

"You've been pushing Theo to wed, haven't you? Perhaps he's heeded your counsel."

"Yes, but I want him to wed *you*, not Miss Shields."

"Don't be ridiculous. Theo and Miss Shields make a fine couple."

"No they don't. They're as mismatched as a two-legged milk stool."

"That comparison makes no sense whatsoever, and it's none of our business anyway."

"Yes, it is! Theo's wife must be someone with whom we have something in common. Someone amiable, cultured, and pleasant. None of those qualities describe Miss Shields."

"Theo will select a wife for himself, not for us." She paused. "Life would be much simpler if we could choose to whom we're attracted."

"He's just returned to Graceling Hall and now he's about to ruin everything by forming an attachment to that woman!"

"And what do you propose to do?"

"I don't know yet, but there must be something."

His sister touched his arm to get his attention. "If that embrace we witnessed a few moments ago was any indication, it may already be too late. I beg you to take a different tack."

"Such as?"

"You can't expect Miss Shields to blossom under critical scrutiny. Pinpoint that which is admirable and praise her. Perhaps when you know her better, your opinion will improve. If Theo's relationship with her deepens, he'll thank you for being supportive."

"That's not a solution!"

"It's the high road, Jensen."

"That road is so high, I'm likely to get a nosebleed."

For the remainder of the journey, he grumbled inwardly. By the time the gig had reached Graceling Hall, however, he realized his sister was right. Voicing his objections to Miss Shields would earn him no approbation on Theo's part and would serve no good purpose except to appear churlish. It would be better to make the best of the situation around.

As he handed Clarissa down from the carriage, he gave her a tight smile.

"For what it's worth, I intend to heed your counsel...despite my feelings on the matter."

She nodded. "I knew you would. Deep down, you're an honorable gentleman."

"If that's so, why do I frequently feel like a swine?"

••••

Suddenly self-conscious, Megan stepped away from Theo. "Forgive me for cryin' on your shoulder, as it were."

He gave her the clean linen square from his pocket and a smile of sympathy. "I wish I had something more comforting to offer you than a handkerchief."

She shook her head. "You've been very kind, Mr. King, and I apologize for coming undone this way. Seein' my brother's grave made me realize I'll not see him in this life again, and it hit me hard."

"I understand. I'm not sure I've ever really accepted the loss of my parents. In your case, it's worse because Paddy was so young." Theo gestured toward the gig. "Are you ready to return to the house?"

"That I am. Thank ye for bringin' me here. 'Tis a lovely, peaceful place, and it sets my heart at ease to know Paddy is restin' in the shade o' such a beautiful tree."

Theo drove her back to Graceling Hall, where a gig was parked in front.

"I see Rowe and Clarissa have arrived for Larken's lesson," he said.

"I could use something cheerful to take my mind off my troubles." She blotted her eyes once more. "I'll have the maid launder this before returnin' it to ye."

After Theo handed the horse's reins off to a servant, he escorted Megan up the stairs and into the house. As soon as she stepped through the door, the sound of piano music lifted her spirits. "Is that Lady Clarissa? She plays very well."

"Yes, she does. Er...this is where I leave you. The ballroom is down the hall and to the left. Just follow the music and you can't miss it."

She curtsied. "Have a lovely time at the lake and give my regards to the wee wain."

"Thank you, I shall."

As Megan moved down the hall, she passed a framed wall mirror and paused to check her face and hair. Although her nose and eyes were still slightly reddened from her emotional outburst, the elegant gown she wore made her appear more sophisticated than she would have thought possible. Perhaps if she didn't open her mouth at the ball, she might even pass as a member of society. *Either that or a mute.* She stifled a giggle. Would Lord Rowe treat her any differently because of the way she was dressed, or would he continue to regard her with cool contempt?

In the spacious ballroom, Clarissa was seated at the gleaming black baby grand piano in the corner. Megan sank into one of the empty chairs in the corner. The lively music coming from the instrument made her want to tap her toes. Out on the polished, inlaid floor, Rowe was guiding Larken through the two-step. From the expression on her pretty face, the young, fair-haired woman was enjoying herself tremendously. Occasionally, Rowe would murmur something just before changing direction, and Larken managed to follow creditably. At the end of the song, Megan applauded.

"Ye looked magnificent, if ye don't mind me sayin' so!"

Larken's color was heightened from exercise. "I trod on my partner's toes several times, I'm afraid."

"If you did, it escaped my notice," he said.

"A pretty story, I think, but you're too gentlemanly to say otherwise. I'm going to ring for a servant to bring us some water. I'm simply parched!"

As Larken crossed toward the bell pull, Megan stole a quick glance at Rowe. To her dismay, he was blotting his forehead with a handkerchief and seemed not to notice her whatsoever. Crestfallen, she rose and crossed over to the piano.

"Thank ye for the loan o' your beautiful clothes, Lady Clarissa. I wish there was some way to repay your kindness."

"The gowns are a gift, not a loan, and there's no need to repay me," Clarissa replied.

"Och, you're far too generous!"

"Not at all. Perhaps the gowns will help you attract the right sort of attention, if you're interested in making a good marriage."

"With my Irish brogue as it is, I've no illusions about anything o' the sort. But now you've brought it up, I've been wonderin' if ye could give me speakin' lessons to improve my accent?"

"I think your accent charming!"

"Charmin' enough for below stairs and no doubt about it, but I'm hopin' to find work as a governess. Do ye suppose ye have the time to help me...in the mornings, perhaps?"

Clarissa's eyebrows drew together. "I've piano lessons every morning, from now until the ball."

Megan forced a smile. "Never ye mind. It was a silly notion, anyway."

"Actually, it's a very sensible notion. Some members of society are a rather superior lot, and it wouldn't hurt to soften your manner of speech a trifle." The woman glanced at her brother, who was standing several yards off. "I've an idea. My brother was president of the debate club at his university. I feel certain he could help."

Dismay made Megan's eyes widen. "I hadn't thought to bother—"

But it was too late; Clarissa was already beckoning him over. "Jensen, could we have a word?"

He closed the distance between himself and the piano in three strides. "Yes?"

"Miss Shields has need of elocution lessons, and my schedule is completely full with morning pupils. Would you be willing to work with her?"

Megan felt the blood rush to her cheeks. "I don't mean to impose on Your Lordship."

"It's no imposition," Clarissa said. "In fact, Jensen and I were just discussing how we could be as supportive of you as possible. Isn't that so?"

An unreadable expression flickered across Rowe's face. "Yes, that's true. I'm at your service, Miss Shields."

Megan gulped. She could refuse his offer, of course, but she desperately wanted the lessons. "I can pay ye, to make it worth your while."

"There's no need for that."

Her spine stiffened. "There's every need! I have a wee bit o' money and I insist on payin' for your tame!"

"Tame?"

"Tame is money, as they say."

"Aha. So they do." He pursed his lips, deep in thought. "I have a proposition for you. I'll help you improve your speech if you teach me to play the harp."

"Why...that seems an equitable trade," Clarissa said.

Megan bit her lip. "Do ye suppose the Kings will allow us the use o' their harp?"

"I've no doubt whatsoever."

Larken was returning from speaking with a servant about the water, and Rowe caught her eye. "Have you any objections to Miss Shields giving me harp lessons in your drawing room each morning?"

"Why...none at all! I dearly wish I could join you, actually, but preparations for the ball have me frightfully occupied."

Rowe turned his cool gaze on Megan. "It's settled, then. We'll begin tomorrow with the elocution lesson at nine o'clock, followed by a harp lesson the hour following."

Megan quailed inwardly under his scrutiny, but she truly needed his help. "I'll be ready."

••••

During the ride home, Jensen scowled at Clarissa. "Your schedule isn't at all full. What did you mean by tossing Miss Shields into my lap?"

"You're being purposely thick. With you and Miss Shields working together so closely, Theo will see you as competition for her affections. He will therefore be more motivated to pursue her. And if he's not, at least you'll be improving the girl for some other gentleman to take her off his hands."

"Ha! Truly, sister, you can be terribly devious."

"Not at all. I just know how the world works. By the way, Quinlan will be calling for me the night of the ball in his best carriage. There's room inside for you."

"I'll ride up top with the driver."

"You'll do no such thing."

"I don't like Quinlan!"

"There's no need to be so sour. Don't forget, Mr. Quinlan is fond of a pretty face; perhaps Miss Shields will catch his eye."

"If Miss Shields knew how freely you seem to be dispensing her favors hither and yon, I doubt she'd thank you."

"She'll thank me when she's happily settled."

"That's not likely, is it? And to be honest, I don't think you're being fair to Quinlan, giving him false hope where you're concerned. You've refused his proposals before, and he'll think you've changed your mind."

"Perhaps I have."

He made a sound of disgust. "A wretched notion, if ever I heard one."

A few minutes later, they noticed a man riding toward them on horseback.

"That's Sir Willard," Clarissa murmured.

As if he'd heard his name, the man lifted his hat, waved it about, and urged his horse to make haste. Rowe spoke out of the corner of his mouth. "Perhaps we can outrun him?"

"Behave."

Sighing inwardly, Rowe reined in his horse and waited for the man to pull alongside.

Clarissa nodded. "Good afternoon, Sir Willard."

"Good afternoon! I was just on my way to call on you, Lady Clarissa."

To Rowe's annoyance, Sir Willard stared directly at his sister's bodice as he spoke. He thrust a bouquet of wildflowers into her hands, which she accepted with a polite smile.

"How lovely, sir. Thank you."

"My pleasure. I was wondering if you had a conveyance to the upcoming King festivities? My brougham is at your disposal."

Rowe gritted his teeth, certain that the offer of a carriage also included the unwanted romantic attentions of the baronet.

"You're very gracious, but Jensen and I have already made other arrangements," Clarissa replied.

Annoyance flashed from the baronet's eyes. "I should've offered sooner, I see." He lifted his hat. "Good-bye, then."

Sir Willard wheeled his horse around and returned the way he'd come. Rowe waited to speak until he was out of earshot.

"I never thought I'd be grateful to Quinlan for anything."

"You should be grateful to *me*, don't you suppose? I'm the one who arranged his escort, after all. We could hardly have arrived at the ball in this gig."

"Theo would have been happy to send a carriage for us." Rowe curled his lip at the flowers in her hand. "Sir Willard lost interest in you after our money disappeared. I wonder why he's crawled out of the woodwork after so long?"

Clarissa shrugged. "I cannot say. I can assure you, however, I didn't encourage him back then and I won't encourage him now." She gave him a mischievous glance. "Of course, if I married him, I'd be mistress of our former home once more."

He sighed. "You're determined to vex me today, aren't you?"

She laughed. "Why should today be different from any other?"

Chapter Six

When in Newcastle

Clad in an ivy-print day dress with lace cuffs and underskirt, Megan joined Rowe in the drawing room precisely at nine o'clock. Although she had butterflies in her stomach, she tried to assume a pleasant demeanor. He was standing next to the window when she arrived, looking as cool, elegant, and sophisticated as usual.

"Good mornin', Lord Rowe. Thank ye for being on tame."

His right eyebrow rose. "That's the first thing we must fix. It's not tame, it's *time*—with a long I sound."

She swallowed. "Ti-aim."

He frowned. "This may be more challenging than I'd anticipated."

"I'm willin' to work hard." Her eyes fell to the book in his hand. "What's that?"

"A collection of poetry written by Alfred Tennyson. I thought we could use his poems to work on your diction, and then you can practice what you learned when you have a moment alone." He gestured toward the sofa. "Let's sit and read the first paragraph of 'Maud,' to see where we're at."

Over the next hour, Rowe listened to her read and then painstakingly corrected her pronunciation. There was so much to correct, however, they only managed to get halfway through the poem. Although the earl wasn't unkind, Megan's level of frustration was high.

"I can't understand how ye always pronounce the consonant at the end of a word like mornin'. Mornin-

guh. The word rolls off my tongue like a merchant ship's rusty anchor. People will think me daft!"

"Practice, repetition, and motivation are the keys. If nothing else, make an effort to say the word *you* properly."

"Yeh-oooo."

"Y-o-o-o." He sighed. "Practice, Miss Shields. Tomorrow we'll start from the beginning and see how much you've retained."

"I'll practice...all day, so I will." With a sense of relief, Megan closed the book. "And now, it's your turn. If you'll be seatin' yourself at the harp, I'll show *y-o-o-o* how to play a few simple chords."

••••

As Megan fought to enunciate the word "you" with an English accent, Rowe had the urge to kiss her pursed lips. *What an abominable thought!* He brushed away the startling impulse like he would an errant piece of lint which had deigned to light upon his sleeve. In the first place, he'd only agreed to the elocution lessons to groom her for Theo. And in the second place, he'd never consider courting Miss Shields, even if he did find her somewhat attractive. Perhaps Theo wasn't obliged to marry for money, but *he* most certainly was. Thirdly, she'd not given him any indication she would be interested in his advances. Was he losing his mind?

Megan peered at him. "Is somethin' amiss? You couldn't be frownin' any harder if a mule had kicked you in your backside with both hind legs."

"What a...colorful turn of phrase. No, my thoughts were elsewhere."

He shook off his unsettling notions and made his way to the harp. As he sat down behind the graceful instrument, he suddenly felt self-conscious. He'd devised the trade of lessons as a way to salve Megan's pride, but he hadn't really thought it through. Now he'd be obliged to make a fool of himself in front of one of the best harpists he'd ever heard.

Daunted, he stared at the instrument. "I'm quite apprehensive, actually."

"My offer o' payment still stands…if you're thinkin' the harp is too challengin' for you."

Her subtle dart found its mark and his dander rose. "Few things are too challenging for me. Let's proceed."

When her eyes danced with merriment, Rowe had the distinct impression she'd goaded him on purpose. He set his mind on the task nevertheless, and as she showed him how to hold his arms, hands, and fingers to best pluck the harp's strings, he braced himself for a stream of cutting remarks. To his surprise, her tone was encouraging and kind. The occasional touch of her hands sent waves of pleasure across his skin, and the nearness of her body made it difficult for him to concentrate. At the end of the lesson, however, he'd managed to play chords from the lower octave to the highest and to pluck out "Twinkle, Twinkle, Little Star."

"You're a good and patient teacher, Miss Shields," he admitted.

The mild look of surprise on her face gave way to a smile. "So are you, when it comes down to it. I did admire the way you encouraged Mrs. King on the dance floor yesterday."

Although her studied pronunciation was still quite forced, Rowe couldn't help but be impressed with Megan's efforts.

"You didn't sound half bad just now. Tell me, do you waltz?"

She shook her head. "I dance a jig well enough, but I've ne'er waltzed."

"After Larken's lesson this afternoon, I'll show you how. You can't be expected to attract a suitor at the ball if none of the gentlemen can appreciate your charms on the dance floor."

"A suitor? It seems you society folks can't think on anythin' but marriage."

"Oh, I don't know about that. Gentlemen might *think* on things other than marriage, but we don't act without the benefit of clergy."

He winked, and as the meaning of his suggestive quip sank in, Megan flushed bright red and became flustered. "You're a wee divil, right enough!"

"Quite possibly."

••••

Theo sought Larken out in the library, where she was dealing with correspondence regarding the ball. "I say, do we have a final guest list?" he asked.

"Yes." She looked through a sheaf of papers until she located the list. "There are always last minute adjustments, of course, but this should be close."

When he skimmed the names, he discovered Sir Willard on the list.

"Must we invite Sir Willard?"

"The invitations have long since gone out. Besides which, he's a neighbor, and it would seem churlish not to include him."

"I suppose you're right." Theo went back to the list. Although he didn't see Graham Quinlan listed, he did notice Lady Clarissa, plus one. His eyebrows rose.

"Clarissa is bringing a guest?"

"Yes, she mentioned an escort to me when we spoke last."

"She didn't happen to tell you his name, did she?"

"She mentioned it, but I can't recall what it was. We're not to have formal seating, so I didn't think it critical." Larken paused. "I believe Rowe is working with Miss Shields in the drawing room right now. He'd certainly know the name."

Theo waved his hand airily. "It's not important. Let Clarissa bring whomever she likes." He paused. "I didn't see Josie Wilkes on the list. Did you invite her?"

Larken pouted. "I sent her an invitation, but she had to decline. She's starring in a melodrama called *The Mademoiselle and the Mysterious Mystery*, and couldn't get away."

"What a shame." He put the list down. "You know, if Clarissa had wished to have an escort other than her brother, I'd have been happy to oblige. She didn't have to ask some Tom, Dick, or Harry to bring her."

"Wait a minute…" Larken screwed up her face, as if searching her memory. "I believe his name starts with a Q, but I can't be sure. Could it have been Quincy?"

"Quinlan?" *Blazes!*

"That might be it…or it might not. Do you know a Mr. Quinlan?"

"Unfortunately, I do."

"I imagine Clarissa assumed you'd be escorting Miss Shields."

He was taken aback. "Should I be?"

"Since she's a guest at Graceling Hall, it would be entirely appropriate."

Theo pondered the issue a moment before nodding. "Quite so, and thank you for suggesting it. I should have thought of it myself, but I'm rather out of practice with these things. I'll ask her right now, lest she consider herself neglected."

As he left the library, Theo felt peevish and generally out of sorts. Quinlan wasn't at all good enough for Clarissa—not by half. To be fair, he ought to reserve his final judgment until after he'd renewed his acquaintance with the man. Perhaps the preening idiot had improved in the five years since he'd known him...but Theo thought it highly unlikely.

••••

After Rowe returned to the cottage he shared with his sister, he went directly to his room to wash up before lunch. He almost wished he could beg off the midday meal and have some time alone to contemplate why his mood had turned so dark. He forced himself to smile as he entered the dining room and seated himself at the table.

"How was your morning, Clarissa?"

"A little tedious, I confess. Poor Miss Benning will never be an excellent pianist, I'm afraid, but her parents insist she continue with her study of music with dogged determination. They're convinced the girl must develop a talent to matriculate in society."

"That's probably true." He scowled at his potato soup and dipped his spoon into the fragrant mixture. "Some ladies are more talented than others."

His sister regarded him. "Your lesson with Miss Shields was disagreeable?"

"Not at all. Why do you ask?"

"Whenever things don't go your way, a blood vessel in your temple pulses."

"Well if you must know, your romantic intrigue appears to be working. Before I finished my harp lesson, Theo came into the drawing room to inquire if he could escort Miss Shields to the ball. She accepted with pleasure."

"Oh." Her response was almost a sigh. "Excellent."

The sober silence that followed allowed him to focus once more on his bad mood. Had he turned glum because he disapproved of Theo's interest in Miss Shields, or was something else troubling him?

"I'm to show Miss Shields how to waltz this afternoon," he muttered. "Since she's likely to be asked to dance at the ball, I thought it was important."

"Indeed, yes."

He dragged his gaze from his soup long enough to realize Clarissa seemed forlorn.

"I'm awfully sorry, Rissa. I didn't mean to upset you."

The corners of her mouth turned up slightly. "You didn't. Everything is going according to plan, so there's no need to be sorry. I'm hopeful Mr. Quinlan will propose again soon."

"There was somewhat of a rivalry between him, Theo, and Brandon when we were younger. They each created a stir amongst the ladies back then."

"You did, too."

"Perhaps." He chuckled. "And you created havoc amongst the men…until our fortune went away. Sir Willard dropped you entirely, but Quinlan wasn't dissuaded in the least."

"What a dreary reminder." Clarissa sighed and sat back in her chair. "It seems you and I are both in poor spirits at the moment." She stared at her soup. "I've rather lost my appetite."

"We'd best eat our lunch or Cook will quit yet again. You know how temperamental she can be."

"Good point."

They resumed their meal. Rowe broke off a piece of hot bread and slathered it with sweet butter. As he savored the delicious, yeasty flavor, he pondered his morning at Graceling Hall. Truth be told, he'd enjoyed the time he'd spent with the young Irish woman more than he had anticipated. It was curious she hadn't insisted on paying him for dance lessons like she had for the elocution lessons. Perhaps she'd found some enjoyment from their time together, too, and had begun to consider him a friend.

Were he and Miss Shields friends? His thinking had grown muddled about her. It was clear they were no longer at odds, but whether a friendship was developing between them remained to be seen.

Clarissa interrupted his reverie. "Did you enjoy your harp lesson with Miss Shields then?"

"Oh, er, well enough." He shrugged. "I've no interest in playing the harp, really, but it seemed to be the only way she'd accept my help."

"It was a clever idea, and I thought so at the time. Perhaps Theo will never know the extent of your sacrifice, but I admire your fortitude."

"Yes." A slight shiver traveled down his spine at the memory of Megan's gentle touch. "Indeed, a nobler sacrifice was never made."

His little joke seemed to fall on deaf ears. As Clarissa gamely ate her lunch, it suddenly hit Rowe how selfish he'd been. If he'd done his duty years ago and married a wealthy debutante or widow, his sister would be living a life of ease now. Her dowry would have been secured, and she could have had her pick of husbands. As it was, she was giving piano lessons to children who were probably no better musically than he'd been that morning with "Twinkle, Twinkle, Little Star." His generous, sweet, kind sister was obliged to work when he'd had the means all along to spare her. His shame forced him into a decision.

He cleared his throat. "I've changed my mind. You deserve better than this."

Clarissa looked up, puzzled. "The potato soup is perfectly delicious. I'm just not especially hungry."

"No, I'm speaking of our lives. I should have married years ago, but I suppose I had some stupid, romantic notion of falling in love. I'll pick a wealthy lady to wed and let the affection between us blossom afterward—if possible."

Her eyes widened. "Are you sure?"

"Absolutely. I'll do my best to be married by Christmas so that you may properly prepare for the London Season next year." He smiled. "As of this moment, I'm an earl in want of a wife."

••••

After lunch, Megan brought the book of Tennyson poems out to the garden gazebo, where she could practice aloud without being overheard. Although she felt as if she were wrestling with her tongue, she repeated her most problematic words over and over.

"Mornin-*guh*. Mornin...g. Morning. Beginnin-*guh*. Beginnin...g. Beginning."

Myles popped up from behind a nearby hedge. "What're you doing?"

"Och, ye startled me! I'm tryin' to speak more properly."

He came around to sit next to her. "Because I said you talked funny?" His eyebrows drew together and his head drooped. "I'm sorry."

"Don't ever think such a thing! I'm just tryin' to improve myself. Ye have to understand, some English people don't like my accent, and look dine on the Irish."

"Dine?"

"Ye know." Megan pointed her thumb at the ground. "Dine."

"*Oh*...down."

"D-own. Down."

"That's it!" He giggled. "Did you know your sentences always go up at the end?"

"Do they nigh?"

Another giggle. "*Now*."

"Now." Megan rolled her eyes. "Speakin' properly is a wee bit harder than speakin' normal. Speakin-*guh*, I mean."

"So why do English people look down on the Irish?"

"It has somethin' to do with history and politics, lad." She shrugged. "I'm well aware of the prejudice, but I try not to let it bother me."

"But you're changing the way you talk?"

"There's an old sayin' attributed to Saint Ambrose: 'When in Rome, do as the Romans do.' I'm in England now, so I want to speak more like the English."

He wrinkled his nose. "Do I have to speak like the English too?"

"Your American accent is perfectly charmin' the way it is." She craned her neck. "Is your nanny about?"

"Ginny told me to get some fresh air in the garden. She's still got the sniffles." He grinned and skipped off a few paces. "Don't get rid of *all* your Irish. I like it."

She laughed. "I don't think I could, even if I'd a mind to."

Myles sped off, calling for his dog.

Megan smiled to herself. "What a sweet wain...er, *child*. A sweet child." She bit her lip and went back to practicing. There was so much to know, and she wanted to demonstrate good progress when Lord Rowe arrived that afternoon.

Her concentration was such that she lost track of time. Worried she was late for Larken's dance lesson, she hastened into the house. As she passed by the library, she heard Rowe's voice through the half-open door.

"Has Theo heard from the attorney about Mr. Osbourne?"

Megan paused to hear the answer.

"Yes, but the investigation must be postponed a little while. Mr. Waite has been called away to Scotland for a week or two and will look into the matter when he returns," Brandon replied.

"I see."

When she heard the news, Megan's emotions were mixed. Although the delay was frustrating after a fashion, she was nevertheless relieved to stay at Graceling Hall a little while longer.

"Forgive me, Rowe, but I can't help notice you look like a man with something on his mind," Brandon said.

"I've come to a rather important decision, actually. Clarissa must have a dowry to make a good match, and I mean to secure one for her before year's end." The earl cleared his throat. "I've decided to search for a wealthy bride."

"Larken's guest list is right here," Brandon replied. "Let me see if there will be any prospects for you at the ball." A paper rustled. "Aha! Mrs. Aynsworth is attending. She's widowed now, but you might remember her as the former Miss Sylvia Trenton."

"Miss Trenton? Wasn't she the pretty little blonde we used to call The Nightingale because of her extraordinary voice?"

Brandon chuckled. "The very same. She married a rich, elderly businessman who obligingly dropped dead the following year."

"Not by her hand, I hope?"

"Since the man was in a Paris brothel at the time, I'd say not. It created quite a scandal, I must say, but she's lived it down."

"How do you know Mrs. Aynsworth?"

"I don't, really."

"What a strange coincidence, your inviting her to the ball just when there's been so much discussion of marriage amongst Theo, Clarissa, and myself."

"All right, I confess. I hope you don't mind my meddling a bit in your affairs, but I asked Larken to invite Mrs. Aynsworth with you in mind."

"She does seem a promising possibility, I grant you. I'm not sure how well I can ingratiate myself with her at one ball, but I'll do my best."

"Actually, I have another little confession to make. The woman lives in London year-round now, so we invited her to stay here at Graceling Hall for a few days. You can get better acquainted with her then."

"Splendid! Let's hope the merry widow is interested in becoming a countess."

Afraid she'd be caught eavesdropping, Megan tiptoed past the door and continued on toward the ballroom. Lord Rowe's marriage plans had nothing to do with her, so why was she was suffused with a vague sense of disappointment? Had wearing Lady Clarissa's beautiful clothes and working to acquire a more cultured accent put lofty notions in her head? Besides which, the earl was a judgmental prig, quick to anger, and argumentative to boot. He wasn't even as handsome as Theo or Brandon, if classical looks were the yardstick. And yet…almost from the start, she'd found something in his manner stirring. None of the burly, earnest men she'd known in Belfast had melted her inside the way Rowe did with his elegance, obvious intelligence, and innate charm. Her feelings mattered little in the face of reality, however. There was nothing between her and His Lordship and never could be.

"Might as well try to walk on the face of the sun," she murmured.

She slipped her book into a pocket and entered the ballroom, where Larken and Clarissa were exchanging pleasantries next to the piano. Megan crossed over to them, determined to try out her improved accent.

"How are you this afternoon, Lady Clarissa?" The question was slightly stilted, but Megan was pleased with her pronunciation.

"Why...I'm very well indeed, Miss Shields."

The word "indeed" struck her as sophisticated, so Megan vowed to use it at the first opportunity.

Clarissa continued, "I've heard from my brother that he's to teach you to waltz this afternoon?"

Megan cleared her throat. "*Indeed*, he is."

"The waltz was the first dance I learned," Larken said. "I think you'll enjoy it."

"Thank you." Megan gestured toward a chair. "I'll sit over here to watch your lesson."

She took a seat and tried to relax. Despite her best efforts, she'd sounded just now as if she were a little slow in her head. As Clarissa and Larken continued to chat, she took note of their posture, the way they smiled, and their composed expressions. If she could emulate their well-bred manners, would she be accepted by the guests at the ball? In the next moment, her self-confidence flagged. Under pressure, she'd never manage to keep up the pretense and was certain to make a fool of herself. How many times could she simper and say "indeed," before she was taken for a half-wit? Both Larken and Clarissa had been born to society and didn't have to think about pronunciation or couching their words in an acceptable way. If only Rowe's Irish mother were still alive, she could ask her advice about how best to fit in. Unfortunately, Megan was on her own.

Och, the only way she could hope to emerge from the ball with her dignity intact would be to avoid it altogether. Therefore, there was no reason to learn how to waltz. Megan rose, intending to make her escape, just as Rowe came through the door. When he caught sight of her, a broad smile lit his face.

"I'm so glad you're here. Larken and I will demonstrate the waltz so you can see how it's done. With your natural grace and cleverness, I expect you'll pick it up very quickly."

His brown eyes radiated sincerity, and she began to waver in her resolve.

"Well, I hadn't planned to...what I mean is, I..." She trailed off. "I-I'll try to pay close attention."

He moved past, and she sank into her chair once more. If the lesson went well for her, she really ought to attend the ball. Hadn't she'd told Myles she didn't let other people's opinions bother her? If she refused to go, the lad would think she'd been untruthful. At any rate, what was the worst that could happen? Since she was a friend of the Kings, their guests could hardly insult her to her face.

When the music began, Megan watched Rowe and Larken waltz across the floor like a fairy-tale couple. Could she really learn to dance like that? It would be the most wonderful sensation in the world, twirling around the ballroom with a man like Rowe. Perhaps it was pathetic, but she wanted to feel his arms around her just once before the arrival of the extraordinary Mrs. Aynsworth.

Chapter Seven

A Fool's Counsel

Theo stewed silently as he and Brandon rode their horses across the estate together. He didn't realize what poor company he'd been until after they had halted their horses next to a harrow stream and dismounted to let the animals rest and drink.

"Something seems to be troubling you," Brandon said. "You've said nothing since we left the stables, and your eyebrows are knitted up together like a pair of caterpillars. Does this have something to do with Mr. Waite's unavailability?"

"No. He's a diligent attorney, and I'm sure he'll search for Mr. Osbourne as soon as he returns to London."

"Then what on earth is amiss?"

Theo sighed. "Graham Quinlan is escorting Clarissa to the ball, and I don't approve."

Brandon looked appalled. "Why Quinlan of all people? The man thinks so well of himself I can't imagine a level-headed girl like Clarissa would find him appealing."

"Perhaps all this talk about marriage has made her think she must rush into something so as to not be left out."

"Has Rowe spoken to you then?"

"About what?"

"He's decided to take the plunge after all."

"With whom? Miss Shields?"

Brandon chuckled. "That's not likely, is it? They're as compatible as a mongoose and a cobra. Actually, I've suggested he pursue Mrs. Aynsworth."

"The former Miss Trenton?"

"The very same. She'll be arriving the day before the ball and staying with us a little while thereafter."

Theo nodded. "She might suit him quite well, if money is the measure. Should Rowe marry a wealthy woman, he could provide Clarissa a dowry. If that should occur, her prospects would improve immeasurably."

"That's the idea. Rowe wants to do the right thing by his sister."

"Good fellow." He paused. "I think I'll have a word with Clarissa about Quinlan and warn her off him. She ought to know he's a rake."

His brother winced. "She's not asked your opinion, Theo. Don't you think you'd be overstepping the mark?"

"Clarissa is a dear friend, and friends ought to look out for one another. I believe she'll welcome my counsel."

"Ha!" Brandon gave him a sidelong glance. "Believe that at your peril."

••••

During her brother's dance lesson with Larken that afternoon, Clarissa noticed he was in rare form. She wasn't entirely certain if his athletic, showy maneuvers were for Megan's benefit or whether he was just enjoying himself. Although Megan's expression revealed little of her opinion, Larken was certainly delighted by Rowe's antics.

After the lesson was over, the fair-haired beauty excused herself. "The ball will be here before I know it, and there's still so much to do. I hope you'll both stay for tea!"

She hastened from the room, looking like a dazzling ray of sunshine. Rowe crossed over to the piano, and Clarissa gave him a smile.

"Well done, Jensen! I don't think I've ever seen Larken laugh so much before."

"Has Mrs. King always been so cheerful?" Megan asked.

"Yes, but her sunny disposition has been hard won."

Rowe explained how Larken had been orphaned by a horrific train crash when she was fourteen and had been taken in by an abusive couple who'd tried to steal her inheritance. Megan listened, wide-eyed.

"It's amazin'—amazin*g*—to me how anyone could harm a child," she said finally. "Mrs. King must be a very strong lady."

"I think adversity has made Larken stronger. I quite admire her." Clarissa stood and stretched. "I think I've been sitting too long today."

"Why don't you take a break while I show Miss Shields the waltz footwork?"

"Actually, I'd like to stretch my legs a bit. I'll stroll outside for a few minutes and return directly."

Clarissa retrieved her hat, which was resting on the closed lid of the piano, and made her way from the house and into the garden. After strolling up and down the gravel paths for a few minutes, she decided to walk around the front of Graceling Hall. Just as she was admiring the view, Theo appeared, clad in riding clothes. Although he seemed deep in thought, when he noticed Clarissa, his expression became purposeful.

"Just the person I wished to see. Has the dance lesson concluded?"

"Jensen is working with Miss Shields at the moment, actually. I'm taking a short break."

"Hmm." He cleared his throat. "I understand Mr. Quinlan is to escort you to the ball."

She was taken aback. "Well...yes he is."

"You should know the man has a reputation as a rake."

Clarissa was unsure whether she should be astonished, annoyed, or both. "I'm not a dewy-eyed, naïve debutante, Theo."

"What does that have to do with anything?"

"I've long been aware of Mr. Quinlan's supposed reputation. Furthermore, I find your officious attitude exceedingly irksome. If you'll excuse me..."

He stepped into her path to prevent her from leaving. "I know what I said before about wanting to see both you and your brother properly settled, but you shouldn't feel pressured into making any rash decisions. I'll be watching Quinlan, and if he acts at all untoward or tries to take liberties, he'll regret it."

Her spine stiffened, and her flash of irritation became full blown anger. Theo had long since shown his disinterest where she was concerned, so why would he attempt interfere with her relationship with someone else?

"If I were going to make a rash decision regarding Mr. Quinlan, I would have done it long ago!"

Theo's nostrils flared. "So he asked you to marry him, did he?"

"That's none of your concern!"

"It jolly well *is* my concern, Clarissa. You're my friend—almost a sister, really—and I want to protect you."

"Protect me? Is that why you stayed gone so long?" To her dismay, she felt tears stinging the backs of her eyelids. "I find myself puzzled at your strange methods."

He flinched. "You *know* why I stayed away. After my disastrous relationship with Mariah Pettigrew, I thought I was unwelcome here!"

"Be that as it may, you can't walk back into my life and tell me how to act or with whom to associate. I've learned to take care of myself, and if I want to marry Mr. Quinlan, there's nothing you can say about it!"

Clarissa stepped around Theo and strode toward the entrance of Graceling Hall with her nose in the air. How dare he presume to tell her with whom she could socialize—or wed. If he had his way, she'd end up an old maid! If anything, his disapproval made her *more* inclined to like Graham Quinlan, not less. She'd continue to encourage him, and if he made her an offer, she'd accept. *That* would show Theo just how much she appreciated his interference, which was not at all.

••••

Although Megan had paid close attention to Rowe and Larken as they'd waltzed, and thought she knew the steps, it was quite a different matter when she attempted the dance for herself. While she and Rowe stood side-by-side, the rhythm and footwork was simple enough. When they stood face-to-face and he took her hand in his, however, her mind went blank. As he stepped out and she tried to follow, she felt stiff and clumsy.

"I'm sorry," she murmured. "I expect you think I've no natural grace now."

"Nobody could play the harp the way you do and not be graceful. Your hands are like poetry."

She blushed. "If only I could dance on my hands."

His laugh of appreciation for her joke relaxed her somewhat, and she laughed too. As they continued to move slowly through the waltz, she began to feel less awkward.

"How am I doing?"

"Quite well. As soon as my sister returns, we'll try it with music." He paused. "I can't tell you how impressed I am with your elocution. You've come a long way in just one lesson."

She flushed with pleasure. "I have to think about my pronunciation with every word. Did your mother ever lose her brogue?"

"My mother had an accent until the day she died. I think, however, it became quite a bit thicker when she was vexed with me. I was rather mischievous, so her vexation was a frequent occurrence."

"I can't imagine you being mischievous." Megan giggled. "Must have been your Irish showing."

"That's it, exactly. Clarissa was always far better behaved, and had a sweet nature. She was never out of sorts for long, as I recall. To this day, she has a very even temperament."

As if to prove her brother a liar, Clarissa stormed into the ballroom, her face a study in anger. She glanced neither right nor left, marching over to the piano as if she meant to strike it.

Rowe's eyes widened. "Is anything amiss?" he ventured.

"We won't be staying for tea." Her tone was clipped as she tossed her hat onto the piano lid. "Shall we start with a slow waltz?"

"Yes, thank you."

His tone was carefully polite, even as he exchanged a bewildered glance with Megan.

"It looks like your sister's Irish is showing," she whispered.

"Most decidedly so."

••••

Larken handed Theo a cup of freshly poured tea. "I'm sorry you and Clarissa have quarreled. I do hope it's resolved soon."

"Thank you." Theo sighed. "I don't understand why she lost her temper. I was only thinking of her welfare."

Brandon shook his head. "I did warn you not to interfere."

"I blame Rowe," Theo said. "He oughtn't to have given his permission for Quinlan to escort Clarissa. I don't know what he was thinking."

"Clarissa has never been one to concern herself overmuch with her brother's advice, has she?" Larken asked.

"Perhaps not. It's quite simple, really. I daresay he wishes for his sister to marry," Brandon said.

Theo scowled. "Then he's betting on the wrong horse."

"I've never met Mr. Quinlan," Larken said. "Is the man dastardly?"

"Yes," Theo said.

"No," Brandon spoke over him.

Theo peered at his brother in astonishment. "How can you say that? You've always disliked him as much as I did!"

"That was a long time ago. We were all strutting about like roosters back then, competing for attention. I daresay he's mellowed. Besides which, he made a point of attending your memorial service. He was quite solicitous toward Clarissa, who was distraught."

"Quinlan asked her to marry him once before, you know," Theo said. "Clarissa admitted there's a history between them."

"Storm in a teapot." Everyone turned to look at Megan, who'd been quietly listening. "Lady Clarissa didn't accept the fellow, did she? What makes you think she'll accept him now?"

"Although it pains me to say so, Quinlan is generally regarded as a good catch," Theo said. "What makes you think she won't?"

"You said it yourself; this Mr. Quinlan isn't the right horse. If I were you, I'd be wonderin' who is?"

Theo was slightly mollified. "You're suggesting Clarissa is feigning interest in Quinlan to arouse someone's jealousy?"

Megan gave him a crooked grin. "It wouldn't be the first time in history a girl resorted to such a ruse. Sometimes a man doesn't know his own mind until it's almost too late."

"Your point is a fair one." Theo stared off at nothing, deep in thought. "If you're right, the actual object of her affection will be in attendance at the ball. I'd like to have another look at that guest list."

"Let's not forget to invite Clarissa and Rowe for dinner the night before the ball. Mrs. Aynsworth will be here by then," Brandon said.

Larken nodded. "Of course. Have you a particular reason in mind?"

"Rowe wishes to reacquaint himself with Mrs. Aynsworth, and I've promised to help expedite the courtship in any way I can."

Megan shook her head. "Och, this courtship business is gettin' as complicated as an Irish reel."

••••

As they drove away from Graceling Hall, Rowe gave Clarissa a sidelong glance.

"What has you so perturbed that you didn't want to stay for tea?"

"Theo has taken it upon himself to disapprove of my escort to the ball. I can't believe he could be so spiteful!" She glared. "Did you mention Mr. Quinlan to him?"

"Why, no."

"He must have heard it from Larken, then." She made a sound of frustration. "I should have asked her to keep the name to herself."

"Was Theo only mildly disapproving or was he terribly put out?"

"I almost expected him to forbid Mr. Quinlan from entering his house."

"Well then, you should be happy. Your ploy succeeded."

"My ploy? What are you blathering on about?"

He shrugged. "Only that you asked Quinlan in order to provoke Theo, and it succeeded."

"That wasn't why I asked him!"

"Isn't it?"

"Stop it, Jensen."

Rowe chuckled. "You really ought to cheer up. Theo's reaction must mean he isn't as indifferent to you as he may like to suppose."

She stared straight ahead without making a response.

"Come now, Rissa. I'd think it a good thing if he finally begins to realize he may lose you."

"And so he may. I truly *am* giving Mr. Quinlan serious consideration."

"I hope Theo comes to his senses before then." He paused. "Are you acquainted with Mrs. Aynsworth?"

"Oh, yes. The former Miss Sylvia Trenton and I came out in the same Season, and were presented to Her Majesty on the same day." Clarissa's stony expression softened and became mischievous. "I trod upon her gown and tore her hem a few weeks later."

His eyes widened. "On purpose?"

"Absolutely. She'd been frightfully rude and deserved it. Thereafter, she tried to drop a piece of cake on my shoe, but I stepped aside in the nick of time. The cake landed on Lady Fitzwilliam instead, and she cut Sylvia socially the entire Season." Clarissa giggled at the memory.

"I thought such machinations beneath you."

"You've some exalted notion of my character, Jensen. I'm perfectly capable of knocking someone down a peg or two when the necessity arises. Why do you ask about the woman?"

He gulped. "Oh, er...I noticed her name on the guest list and rather wondered if you'd ever befriended her."

"I don't think she has any friends."

Inwardly, Rowe winced. *Oh, dear.*

••••

Having spent several days in a household of sophisticated English people, Megan's eyes had been opened to a world of ease and the pursuit of pleasure instead of constant toil and drudgery. She understood full well that few people in England were as wealthy, educated, and privileged as the Kings and she was fortunate to reside in their home for the time being. Her short stay in Liverpool, for example, had shown her a different class of hardscrabble English folks whose lives were much more like the one she'd left behind in Belfast. To which world was she more suited and where would she wind up? She was like an unmoored boat, struggling to navigate across rough seas to some unknown destination.

With her book of poetry in hand, Megan sat up in bed, doggedly practicing her elocution. Although every word she spoke required an effort, she believed her diligence would serve her well in the end. A reduced accent mightn't provide her a ready entrance into society, but it wouldn't hurt. Rowe had already praised her progress, and she didn't believe him to be a man given to flattery. When at last her lamp began to sputter for lack of oil, she finally blew out the flame and settled down for the night.

As she stared out into the darkness, she remembered how it had felt waltzing with Rowe that afternoon. Wistfulness settled around her like a soft woolen blanket as she replayed the encounter in her mind. Toward the end of the lesson, they'd managed to move together far more smoothly than before, and it had been...magic. The sensation of her hand in his had filled her with bliss, and she'd stood so close to him she'd even managed to catch faint traces of his fragrance. Why couldn't she harden her heart against the man, especially when it was abundantly clear her feelings were unrequited? If she didn't check herself, she was destined for heartbreak...if it wasn't already too late.

A tear rolled down her cheek and dampened the pillow beneath her head. Rowe was so different from any other man she'd ever known, and she could never have him. She'd treasure every day at Graceling Hall, however, until Mrs. Aynsworth arrived to capture his attention. Megan was determined to approve of the woman for Rowe's sake, and fervently hoped she was deserving of his ardor. Until then, she would enjoy her lessons with him...unless Theo opened his mouth and ruffled Clarissa's feathers so much she refused to set foot in the house. Why wouldn't Theo just admit he was in love with Clarissa? The besotted galoot had fetched the guest list after dinner and spent an hour combing through the names in a fruitless search for the mysterious object of her secret affections. *A bigger fool was never born,* she thought as she drifted off to sleep. *Unless that fool was me.*

Chapter Eight

Musical Hearts

Mrs. Aynsworth, née Sylvia Trenton, arrived at Graceling Hall late in the afternoon, the day before the ball. Megan didn't go downstairs with the Kings to welcome her, but instead, from an upstairs window overlooking the circular drive, she watched the entourage of two hansoms arrive. A footman handed the elegantly clad woman down from the first cab, and although Megan was eager to see Mrs. Aynsworth's face, it was largely obscured by a fancy, beplumed hat. The footman thereafter helped a pretty little girl around five or six years old climb down from the carriage. So the woman had a daughter? Megan had no trouble seeing the young lass's dainty features, which appeared to be set in porcelain. Her flaxen hair was arranged in bouncing corkscrew curls, and her lavender floral dress was trimmed in satin ribbons and snowy lace. If the daughter was any indication, the mother was a rare beauty. Megan swallowed her jealousy and told herself she was glad Rowe would have a beautiful wife by his side, and pretty step-daughter, too. A man was certainly entitled to be proud of his family.

After a second carriage arrived, disgorging a lady's maid and nanny, Megan moved away from the window and returned to her room to practice her enunciation. Her final elocution lesson with Rowe had taken place earlier in the day, but she wished to continue improving herself until dinner. Although Rowe and Clarissa were coming for dinner that night, the situation between Clarissa and Theo remained cool. Megan wished they'd resolve their argument before the ball, since Mr. Quinlan's presence would only complicate matters further.

Because Megan only knew how to dance the waltz, Larken had cleverly planned to mark her dance card beforehand so that only the waltzes could be claimed. Privately, Megan couldn't imagine any gentlemen would wish to dance with her at all, especially not after it became known she was Irish, poor, and not from a prominent family. Of course, she yearned to dance with Rowe at least once, but she couldn't count on him seeking her out when Mrs. Aynsworth was around.

During her stay at Graceling Hall, Megan had memorized a few bland phrases she could use to blend in. Things like, "Such beautiful weather we're having, don't you agree?" and "What a pleasure to meet you. Do you live in the neighborhood?" In the privacy of her room, she practiced being introduced to Mrs. Aynsworth and engaging her in small talk. If Megan could impress a woman like *her*, surely she could get through the ball the following evening without too much trouble.

••••

Myles was agog at the pretty little girl sitting on the sofa a few yards away. He wished he could stop staring, but it was impossible to tear his eyes away from her perfection. The girl's mother had said her name was Estella, and he'd never met such an exquisite creature before in his life. So intent was he on drinking in her loveliness, he didn't even hear Larken speaking to him.

"Myles!"

He snapped to attention. "Yes, Larken?"

"I said, why don't you take Estella upstairs and show her the sitting room and nursery while her nanny unpacks her things?"

A grin spread across his face. "All right."

He led Estella from the drawing room, remembering at the last second to pause and let her precede him out the door. As soon as they were alone, he felt only slightly more relaxed.

"This way." He gestured toward the stairs.

She marched alongside him. "Graceling Hall is too far from London."

Taken aback, he didn't know how to reply. "Er…it *is* a long way."

They mounted the steps together.

"Why do you call your mama by her first name?" Estella asked.

"Larken's not my mother, although sometimes I wish she were. I'm Mr. Brandon King's ward." He felt a sense of pride as he spoke.

Estella asked him a strange question then, using a word he'd never heard before. "Are you illegitimate?"

He hated to appear ignorant, but he had no choice. "Am I *what?*"

She repeated the word, but he still didn't know what it meant.

"Er…I don't think so," he replied. "I'm an American."

Her peals of laughter were so delightful, he joined in.

"No, stupid!" she said finally. "That means your mama wasn't married to your papa."

"Oh." The conversation had entered uncomfortable territory, so Myles tried to change the subject. "Have you ever been to America?"

"No. Mama says Americans are vulgar."

Having recently had a lesson on geography, Myles was on more comfortable grounds. "No, that's wrong. The Volga River is in Russia."

Estella shot him a peculiar look. When they arrived at his sitting room, she glanced around the place and frowned. "My playroom back home is twice this size."

"Well, this is just my sitting room. The playroom is across the hall." He moved over to the table and pulled a chair out for her. "Why don't you sit here?"

She ignored him and sat down on Lord Topper instead.

He giggled. "You can't sit there! That's Lord Topper's seat and you're creasing his trousers!"

Her expression was cool. "I'm a guest and I may sit wherever I like." She reached up to the top hat which was hanging by a string and set it swinging.

"Yes, of course, but I want to introduce you to my pretend friends."

"Mama says pretend friends are stupid."

Things were not going at all well, and Myles crossed his arms across his chest. "The pretend friends were Larken's idea and I think they're fun."

"Then Larken is stupid, too."

His eyes narrowed and his chest filled with righteous indignation. "You're horrible and I don't like you at all!"

Her lower lip trembled, and her blue eyes became flooded with tears. Without warning, Estella burst out into loud wailing sobs that brought Myles's nanny on the run.

"What's wrong, little lamb?" Ginny asked.

The young girl pointed an accusatory finger at Myles. "He says I'm horrible and he doesn't like me! I want to go home!"

"Go, then," Myles said. "It's an awfully long walk."

His nanny was seldom cross with him, but now was one of those times. "Myles, apologize to Miss Estella this instant!"

Unrepentant, he shook his head.

Ginny gasped. "If you don't apologize, it'll be bread and water for your dinner, lad."

Myles's stomach was grumbling, and his resolve wavered. One of his shoulders crept up as he muttered, "Sorry." Never before had he ever meant something less.

"That's better. Mind your manners, and I'll send a maid up directly with your tea." She gave Estella a smile and a pat on the head. "Your nanny is almost done unpacking your things, and she'll check on you soon."

The girl managed a weak "thank you."

As soon as the nanny left, Estella's tears dried up and she leveled a glare at Myles. "Don't cross me again."

Without a word, he flopped down into a chair and pinched himself on the arm as hard as he could.

Estella gaped. "What on earth are you doing?"

"Trying to wake up from this nightmare."

••••

Megan dressed in a pretty dinner gown of cream silk, with a white lace overskirt and trim. After Bess arranged her hair in a sleek chignon, Megan felt quite sophisticated. If she could only marshal her accent, there'd be no reason for Mrs. Aynsworth to suspect she was an outsider.

She met Bess's gaze in the mirror. "If I didn't know better, I'd think I was a society girl."

"I agree, Miss Shields. You've every right to feel confident."

Moments later, Megan descended the staircase and entered the drawing room, where the Kings had already assembled before dinner with Rowe and Clarissa. She was relieved to see Mrs. Aynsworth had not yet appeared.

"Good evening," Megan said. "I hope I'm not late."

"Not at all, Miss Shields," Larken said.

"Jensen and I have only just arrived ourselves," Clarissa said.

Megan met Rowe's gaze. He stared at her for several long seconds, gave her a half-smile, and then looked away. She felt a pang of discomfiture at his less than effusive greeting. Had she done something to offend him?

Clarissa cleared her throat. "Larken, I understand you have a guest staying at Graceling Hall?"

"Yes, Mrs. Aynsworth arrived this afternoon with her daughter. She should be down in a few minutes."

"Mrs. Aynsworth?"

"She's the former Miss Sylvia Trenton," Brandon said. "Are you acquainted with her, Clarissa?"

"We've met."

Clarissa cast an accusatory glance at Rowe. Megan had no time to wonder what was behind her ire, however, because Mrs. Aynsworth sailed into the drawing room at that moment, clad in a white lace dress. To Megan's dismay, the style and color of the gown were similar to the one *she* wore. The woman's fair tresses were arranged in an elaborate style, and a jeweled comb was nestled amongst the golden coils. Her features were handsome rather than pretty, and from the ostentatious way she'd swept into the room, Megan suspected Mrs. Aynsworth was used to being the center of attention. Megan's gaze slid over to Rowe to gauge his reaction—to no avail. His color had risen a bit, perhaps, but his expression was impossible to read.

When Theo introduced Mrs. Aynsworth to Megan, the woman was somewhat reserved. She became a little more animated when Theo introduced her to Rowe and Clarissa.

"I'm so delighted to see you both again!"

Clarissa's smile was polite. "It's been many years since we've had the pleasure of your company."

Rowe bowed. "I'm very happy to renew our association, Mrs. Aynsworth."

"As am I." The woman's gaze returned to Megan. "How have I escaped your acquaintance until now, Miss Shields?"

"We've not traveled in the same circles, I suspect. I've lived most of my life abroad."

"Paris, perhaps, or India?"

"Belfast."

"Oh, how lovely!" Mrs. Aynsworth turned her back to Megan, moved over to Theo, and batted her eyelashes. "I'd heard the most atrocious rumor you'd been killed, sir. I'm so relieved to discover the gossips were wrong."

"It was all a dreadful misunderstanding which has since been rectified. I've been working in London the past few years as an actor, but I'm retired from the profession now. I'm happy to be back in the bosom of my family."

"An actor? How droll!" Her lips curved into a smile. "I sense there's a bit of a tale to tell there, but I won't press you for details just now."

As the woman continued to flirt with Theo, Rowe appeared at Megan's elbow.

"Your accent was superb and you look every inch the lady," he murmured. "Perhaps it sounds silly, but I'm proud of you."

Megan was so touched by his sentiment that the insides of her eyelids began to sting with tears. "It's not silly at all, and I thank you." She took a moment to swallow the lump in her throat, and to remember she'd vowed to help Rowe woo his future bride. "Now, how are we to get Mrs. Aynsworth away from Mr. King long enough for you to court her?"

Rowe's expression of astonishment was almost comical. "How did you know I meant to court her?"

"A little bird, perhaps? I believe the woman may have mistaken an invitation to stay at Graceling Hall as an indication of romantic interest on Mr. King's part."

He sighed. "Undoubtedly so."

"I suggest you ask to escort her into dinner before she has the chance to drop hints in Mr. King's direction."

"Your thoughtfulness does you credit."

He bowed and left to join Theo and Mrs. Aynsworth. Moments later, Clarissa crossed over to Megan.

"My brother seems to be on a mission of some sort."

"He's on a campaign to woo Mrs. Aynsworth."

Clarissa's shoulders drooped. "That was what I was afraid of."

Megan was dismayed. "You dislike the woman?"

"We didn't get on well when we first met, but perhaps she's improved since then." Clarissa's gaze flickered toward Rowe. "I hope so, for my brother's sake. It seems, however, she has set her sights on Theo."

"Don't worry; I don't think Mr. King has any interest in her whatsoever."

"Me, worry?" Clarissa's sound of amusement was forced. "I'm not concerned with Theo's *amours* in the least."

Megan begged to differ, but she deliberately kept any note of irony from her response. "No, of course not."

••••

Although Clarissa pretended to be oblivious to Mrs. Aynsworth's conversation with Theo, she couldn't stop stealing glances in his direction. It didn't appear as if he was encouraging Mrs. Aynsworth overmuch, but then he mightn't wish to make his interest plain. When at last he left the elegant blonde with Rowe, he traversed the room toward her and Megan.

"I'm in a bit of a pickle, I'm afraid." Theo's voice was little more than a whisper.

"Regarding your guest?" Megan murmured.

He winced. "Unfortunately, yes. She may have the wrong idea about me altogether."

Clarissa hoped her relief wasn't obvious, but Theo was focused on Megan for the moment.

"Miss Shields, could I impose on you to engage in a little romantic deception—just long enough for Rowe to get his foot in the door with her, so to speak?"

Megan peered at him. "You want us to pretend to be a couple?"

"It would be only for a little while."

"Er...I'm happy to help, but might I suggest Lady Clarissa would be a far more credible choice?"

Clarissa's eyes widened with dismay. After all her kindness toward Megan, how could the girl put her in such an untenable position?

"I've only been in England for a few weeks, you see," Megan continued. "If Mrs. Aynsworth poses any probing questions at all, our relationship would be easily uncovered as a contrivance. I can't imagine the embarrassment you'd feel if the scheme was exposed."

Theo's eyebrows drew together. "I hadn't thought of that. Perhaps we ought not attempt it."

"No, I think it's brilliant—just so long as it involves you and Her Ladyship." Megan's glance at Clarissa seemed apologetic. "If you'll excuse me, I'll leave you two to work out the details."

She hastened off, and Clarissa was left face-to-face with Theo. He tugged on his collar and cleared his throat. "I apologize for my interference regarding Mr. Quinlan. It was officious and arrogant of me to assume you needed my advice."

Although she was tempted to reject his apology, she relented. Theo was obviously uncomfortable, but he seemed sincere.

"Thank you." She paused. "I'm sure you had my best interests at heart."

"Indeed, I did. Very much so." He averted his eyes. "H-Have you any objection to playing the part of my sweetheart? If anyone asks about it at the ball tomorrow, we can always say we've quarreled."

"For Jensen's sake, I'll go along with your scheme. But you must agree to be amiable to Mr. Quinlan tomorrow evening."

A muscle in Theo's jaw tightened. "I don't know if that's possible."

"In that case, best of luck fending off Mrs. Aynsworth's advances."

"Oh, all right. I'll be civil, but don't expect me to befriend the man."

"If I marry him, I expect you'll have to befriend him to a certain extent."

Theo peered at her. "Is it as serious as that?"

Clarissa shrugged. "I don't know yet...*sweetheart*."

With a simpering smile, she stepped closer to him than was strictly proper, long enough to attract Mrs. Aynsworth's notice. The deed was done.

••••

Theo tried to keep his countenance, but Clarissa's sudden, feigned affection caught him off guard. Although he knew she was performing a role for Mrs. Aynsworth's benefit, he was surprised how agreeable it felt to have her stand so near. Surely the surge of warmth in his chest was the natural result of having mended their relationship...and yet as he gazed at Clarissa's upturned face, he had no wish to look away. He'd never fully appreciated before how finely chiseled her cheekbones were, and how her large brown eyes seemed to draw him in. Graham Quinlan was a fortunate man indeed if he'd captured her heart. As Theo pictured Quinlan and Clarissa as a couple, a spiral of jealousy wrapped itself around his throat and gave a sharp tug.

Jealousy? No, he'd taken his protective posture toward her too far and he was simply confused. This was Clarissa, with whom he'd played as a child. He'd splashed her with mud when he was nine years old, and she'd retaliated by shoving him into the lake. If he even thought about courting her, she'd likely laugh and throw him under a carriage. Furthermore, Rowe would probably be offended beyond measure if he suspected Theo's feelings for Clarissa were tending toward the romantic. He vowed to control his thoughts and emotions before he did his friendships with Rowe and Clarissa an irreparable injury.

The butler arrived to announce dinner, and Theo offered Clarissa his arm. "May I escort you into dinner?"

"You may."

Her hand curled around his sleeve just above his elbow. Without thinking about it, he covered her fingers with his. Once again, a delicious sensation of warmth came over his entire body and his heart began to race. He stole a glance at her profile, and she met his gaze with a dazzling smile. His footsteps almost faltered, and he had to avert his eyes before he embarrassed himself. What had come over him tonight, and why? Perhaps his years away from home had changed him more than he knew. It was as if he were suddenly viewing Clarissa through someone else's gaze. Had his long absence possibly cast him in a new light as far as *she* was concerned, or was he still her elder brother's rather idiotic friend?

In the dining room, Theo was seated at the head of the table. Clarissa was seated to his right, affording him the opportunity to engage her in conversation over dinner. Although he reminded himself her affectionate manner was a pretense, as the meal progressed he found it quite easy to return her sentiment with sincerity. No matter how much he tried to hold himself back, he couldn't manage to do so—despite the frequent significant glances and raised eyebrows exchanged between Larken and Brandon.

Merciful heavens, had he fallen in love?

••••

During dinner, Megan relished the way Theo couldn't keep his eyes off Clarissa. Although the man had been an actor, surely no one could simulate the true affection radiating from his visage. Was he finally realizing how precious she was to him? Megan suspected Clarissa had given up on Theo long ago, so she hoped his sentiments hadn't come too late.

Her observations of Rowe and Mrs. Aynsworth gave her far less pleasure. Although she would do whatever she must to encourage their relationship, she felt forlorn and forsaken. Mrs. Aynsworth had turned from Theo to Rowe with little effort, and at present the two were immersed in an intimate conversation. How peculiar it was to hope they fell in love, and yet dread it at the same time! Her appetite gone, Megan pushed her food around on the plate and yearned for the evening to pass quickly.

She tried to say as little as possible at dinner, but over the lemon sherry syllabub meringue dessert, she found herself the focus of Mrs. Aynsworth's attention.

"Miss Shields, Lord Rowe tells me you play the harp very well indeed. I hope you'll play for us tonight."

Megan couldn't imagine a more exquisite torture than to play for Rowe's future bride.

"Oh, I suspect everyone here has had their fill of the harp, Mrs. Aynsworth." Sounds of protest ensued, but Megan pushed forward. "I'm sure we'd much rather listen to you sing. I understand your singing has earned you the name of The Nightingale."

The woman's laugh was throaty. "That was long ago, I'm afraid, but I'll be happy to sing for you."

"How marvelous. I doubt if Lord Rowe would have mentioned it, but he sings beautifully too," Megan said. "Perhaps you will treat us to a duet."

Mrs. Aynsworth gave Rowe an admiring smile. "You've hidden talents, sir? How delightful."

"Miss Shields has overstated my abilities, to be sure," he said.

"Not at all, Rowe," Brandon said. "I know I'd certainly enjoy hearing you sing again."

"As would I," Larken added.

"Well then, so you shall." Rowe gave Megan a nod and a surreptitious wink. "And thank you, Miss Shields, for the compliment."

Mrs. Aynsworth asked Brandon about his ward, Myles, and the conversation took a detour. Megan was relieved she'd managed to wriggle out of performing that evening and had given Rowe the opportunity to exhibit his abilities. Once Mrs. Aynsworth had heard Rowe sing, she'd definitely be smitten.

••••

Outwardly, Clarissa smiled and chatted over dinner, but her emotions were being tested as never before. If she didn't know better, she would've mistaken Theo's frequent, lingering glances for romantic affection. Surely his behavior had long since convinced Mrs. Aynsworth he was uninterested in courting her, so why did he continue his pretense with such zeal? She was obliged to remind herself more than once that his manners were not genuine, but as the evening wore on, his role of adoring suitor began to stir up feelings that had lain fallow. Two things were crystal clear: Theo King was a very, very clever actor...and her heart was still as malleable to his touch as the softest gold. She prayed that Graham Quinlan was up to the task of distracting her with his charm and good looks the following evening, otherwise she was very much in danger of becoming infatuated with Theo again.

Chapter Nine

Nightingale

Once dinner had concluded, the gentlemen stayed behind for drinks and cigars while the ladies went through to the drawing room. To Megan's surprise, Mrs. Aynsworth chose to walk with her. As they strolled down the hall behind Clarissa and Larken, the elegant blonde slipped her arm through hers and spoke in a conspiratorial tone.

"My dear, I couldn't help but notice you ate very little at dinner. I wouldn't worry *too* much about your figure. Some men love a plush frame. In my case, it's a mercy the bustle is so fashionable."

Embarrassment caused blood to warm Megan's cheeks. She'd never before considered her figure might be less than attractive, but Mrs. Aynsworth seemed to suggest otherwise. It was true the woman's waist was smaller than hers, but she was also several inches shorter in stature. Could Megan's figure really be described as "plush"? Back home in Belfast, she'd been the frequent target of whistles and appreciative comments. In England, perhaps a more slender silhouette was the ideal. Megan instantly vowed to walk more often and eschew sweets at tea.

"A full glass of water before meals might be just the thing you need," Mrs. Aynsworth said. "My housekeeper swears by it, and she's Irish, like you."

"Thank you," Megan managed. "I'm grateful for your advice."

"I asked Lord Rowe what your plans were, and he seemed to think you might be heading to London after you leave Graceling Hall."

"I am."

"If there's anything I can do for you, let me know."

Megan was touched. "How kind of you to offer."

"It's no trouble at all, my dear. I often hear from my friends about vacancies suitable for girls like yourself. If you're looking for a position as a maid, I can always put in a good word."

The woman's presumptuousness sent Megan's temperature soaring, and she took several deep breaths to avoid answering in a rash manner she'd most certainly regret.

"Why do you assume I wish to be a maid?" Her tone was carefully conversational...and contained not a trace of a brogue.

"Every Irish girl I've ever met works below stairs."

"Many do, but not every colleen aspires to work in service."

"Quite so. I've a marvelous Irish seamstress who does beautiful embroidery on my petticoats and undergarments. If you're good with a needle, you can earn a decent living that way, too."

So despite Megan's cultured accent and ladylike wardrobe, Mrs. Aynsworth thought her fit only to empty chamber pots or stitch underclothes? Megan was disappointed beyond measure. She'd had such high hopes, but the woman was the worst sort of elitist imaginable. With a smile, Megan took her arm back and stepped away.

"Forgive me, but I believe you've taken my measure too quickly. In fact, I have friends who wish to sponsor me for a London Season." The assertion was a falsehood, but there would be no way for the woman to disprove it.

Mrs. Aynsworth's tinkling laugh was an icy weapon. "You've heard the proverb 'you can't make a silk purse out of a sow's ear,' haven't you? I've taken your measure accurately, Miss Shields, but you're certainly free to prove me wrong."

Megan's eyes narrowed and her spine stiffened. "And so I shall." A bluff of the worst sort, admittedly, but it was the only defense she had.

••••

As the two children ate their dinner in Myles's sitting room, they glared at each other in frosty disdain. Myles was still nursing a grudge over having to apologize to the girl, and her arrogant, superior attitude continued to irk him to no end. By the time the nanny cleared their plates and brought desserts of chocolate custard, he'd run the gamut of emotions. When Ginny left the nursery carrying a tray of dishes, Myles planned his revenge. He angled a spoonful of custard toward Estella and launched a brown glob in the air. It landed in the center of her pink silk bodice with a satisfying splat.

She stared down at her dress in shock. "You've ruined my gown!"

"Sorry, that was a mistake. I meant to hit your face."

Her blue eyes narrowed. "You evil boy!"

She flung a spoonful of custard at him, which he was able to dodge. The custard hit the back of his chair, and he sat up, laughing. "Ha, ha, you missed!"

In the next moment, another spoonful of Estella's custard hit him between his eyes and slid down to the tip of his nose. In a fury, he stood up and flung glob after glob of custard at her. She shrieked, and followed suit. Only when the custard was completely gone did the battle pause. At that point, Myles and Estella were both decorated with splotches, and a large quantity had fallen to the floor and on the table. Myles's chest was heaving in indignation, but when he caught sight of Estella's messy face and hair, he suddenly burst out laughing.

"You look like you've rolled around in a mud puddle!"

Her seething anger gave way to a giggle. "You look disgusting! I'm never going to be able to eat custard again."

Ginny entered the nursery to retrieve the last of the dishes. When she saw the mess, she shrieked in horror. "What on earth!" Her arms akimbo, she glared at Myles. "Is this your doing?"

Estella cleared her throat. "Er…no. It was a dreadful accident."

The nanny looked at her askance. "I find that hard to believe."

"It's like she said. We had an accident." Myles glanced at the carpet and grimaced. "If you give me a tea towel, I'll clean it up."

Estella nodded. "I'll help."

Ginny scowled as she gave them the towels. "Accident or not, see that you clean up every last splotch or I'll report this to Mrs. King and Mrs. Aynsworth."

Myles hung his head. "Thank you, Ginny."

"Yes, thank you," Estella echoed.

The two dropped to their hands and knees to sop up the custard. Estella met Myles's gaze under the table and gave him a tiny smile.

••••

While the ladies waited for the gentlemen to join them in the drawing room, Larken asked Megan to give her a quick lesson on the harp. To Clarissa's dismay, Mrs. Aynsworth settled next to her on the sofa for some conversation. As she glanced at the elegant woman, Clarissa was reminded of a sleek, self-satisfied Persian cat.

"I'm so glad we can visit together privately, Lady Clarissa. It's been far too long since we've seen one another."

"Indeed, it has." Clarissa covered her active dislike with a smile. "I was very sorry to hear about Mr. Aynsworth's passing. Losing him must have been a blow."

"Yes it was, but I'm grateful to him for giving me Estella as well as a sizable inheritance. Fortunately, I'm young enough to seek another husband."

"That *is* fortunate."

"You and Mr. Theodore King are great friends?"

"Perhaps more than friends." Clarissa pretended to blush. "We grew up in the same neighborhood, you see, and it's natural we should be drawn to one another."

"I enjoyed conversing with your brother at dinner. He asked to escort me into the ball tomorrow night, and I accepted. It's sad I never had the pleasure of making his acquaintance before now. He's absolutely delightful."

"Jensen is always well-liked wherever he goes."

"He has much praise for Miss Shields, and she for him." Mrs. Aynsworth's eyes slid toward Megan. "Tell me, have they known each other long?"

"Not at all, but she made an instant impression, I think."

A flicker of a frown crossed Mrs. Aynsworth's countenance. "Well, she's a lovely girl, and better spoken than most of her..." She trailed off at the arrival of Theo, Brandon, and Rowe. "Oh, here we are, and sooner than expected!"

Rowe's smile radiated charm. "We couldn't stay away long, not with The Nightingale here to sing for us. Perhaps my sister will accompany you?"

"As I recall, wasn't your signature piece, 'Wilt Thou Be Gone, Love,' by Stephen Foster?" Clarissa asked.

Mrs. Aynsworth laughed. "I'm flattered you remembered."

"I recall it quite well, since Mr. Graham Quinlan usually sang it with you." Out of the corner of Clarissa's eye, she noticed Theo cross his arms over his chest. "Do you know the song, Jensen?"

He nodded. "I used to sing a version of it in Glee Club at university."

Clarissa rose and moved toward the piano. "It's settled then. We'll sing a duet."

••••

Despite her desire to hear Rowe sing again, Megan had mixed feelings about listening to Mrs. Aynsworth. She wanted as little as possible to do with the horrible woman, and feared her dislike would show in her expression. Fortunately, Mrs. Aynsworth's clear soprano was so beautiful, Megan had no trouble maintaining a smile. The elegant blonde sang the opening of the song by herself, and when Rowe finally joined in, Megan's pleasure blossomed. The duo's voices blended and soared as if they were birds lifted up by a warm zephyr. When Rowe and Mrs. Aynsworth exchanged glances during the song, Megan's throat closed up with emotion. The two made a handsome couple and were suited to one another in ways she and Rowe could never be. Even if he didn't wed Mrs. Aynsworth, he would ultimately marry someone just like her—not a poor Irish girl from Belfast.

As the song continued, Megan glanced around the room, trying to memorize the faces of the people she'd come to care about. Tonight would be the last occasion she would have to spend time alone with them. She'd decided to depart for London the day after tomorrow. Mr. Waite would return to his office sooner or later, and she'd call upon him to inquire about Mr. Osbourne. In the meantime, she'd join the hordes of her fellow countrymen who were seeking employment. Although she resented Mrs. Aynsworth's assumptions, Megan might have to work as a maid after all.

When the song came to an end, enthusiastic applause followed.

Mrs. Aynsworth glanced at Megan and laughed. "We should be flattered, Lord Rowe. I do believe we've moved Miss Shields to tears."

Annoyed, Megan brushed away the moisture underneath her eyes—tears which had been for an entirely different reason than the woman supposed. Rowe hastened over to press his handkerchief into her hands. After a murmured thanks, she blotted the moisture away.

"Oh, there's no shame in being sensitive, Miss Shields," Mrs. Aynsworth said. "I'm so happy I was able to touch your heart."

Megan wanted to gag. The woman was so conceited and vain as to defy belief. *How soon can I beg fatigue and retire for the evening?*

"You sang beautifully, Mrs. Aynsworth. I believe Lord Rowe's voice and Lady Clarissa's accompaniment made you sound your best," she managed.

"Thank you, dear."

"Can I convince you to change your mind, Miss Shields?" Rowe asked. "I'd love to hear you play the harp."

As Megan gazed into the earl's earnest, handsome face, she decided she would accede to his request—not for Mrs. Aynsworth, but for him alone. "Only because *you* asked, Lord Rowe, I shall."

She rose, returned the moistened handkerchief to him, and moved toward the harp.

Mrs. Aynsworth clasped her hands together as if in the throes of ecstasy. "So we're to have music from Miss Shields after all? I couldn't be more delighted."

Megan slid a glance at Clarissa, to gauge her reaction. When the woman surreptitiously rolled her eyes, Megan had to bite her lip to keep from laughing. It seemed clear that she and Clarissa shared an ill opinion of the Kings' guest.

"I'll play 'Carolan's Dream.'" Megan seated herself at the harp. "It was my brother's favorite."

When she'd finished the lovely, lilting melody, everyone was smiling—although Mrs. Aynsworth's enthusiasm was rather contained.

"A pretty little tune," she said. "So very...Irish. Who was Carol Ann?"

"The song was composed by a blind harpist named O'Carolan," Megan said. "He's quite famous."

Mrs. Aynsworth tittered. "He couldn't be that famous if I've never met him."

"He lived during the last century," Megan said.

"I see." Her color deepened. "Then I wouldn't have met him, would I?"

Megan could take it no longer. "I'll bid you all good-night." She picked up the book of Tennyson from a table where she'd left it and extended it to Rowe. "I should return this to you now."

He stared at the tome, but made no effort to reach for it. "I wish you'd keep the book, as my gift."

"Thank you, Lord Rowe. Many folks could learn a thing or two about generosity from you and your sister."

With the book clutched in her hands, Megan left the room...but her heart remained behind.

••••

As Clarissa and Rowe drove away from Graceling Hall, he gave his sister an inquiring glance.

"You and Theo seem to be forming an attachment. I couldn't be more pleased."

She sighed. "Don't be misled by our behavior tonight. We were attempting to discourage Mrs. Aynsworth from pursuing Theo and turn her attentions to you instead. If I'm not greatly mistaken, it did the trick."

He detected a harsh note in her reply. "You disapprove of her?"

"Jensen, it's not for me to approve or disapprove."

"It's too soon to decide, of course, but she *would* make me a suitable wife."

"Indeed."

"You must admit, she has a lovely voice."

She shrugged. "I freely admit it."

"But you don't like her." Rowe paused. "I'm not sure I do either, but she's exceedingly wealthy."

"Mr. Quinlan would probably take me without a penny. Sadly, Theo doesn't approve of him, either." She glanced at Rowe. "Do you?"

"If he makes you happy, I won't stand in your way."

"Hardly a ringing endorsement."

"Sorry, but it's the best I can muster."

She shook her head. "What a ghastly state of affairs. None of us like the other's candidate for a spouse."

"Perhaps tomorrow night's festivities will change everything."

"More likely than not, it will complicate everything." She paused. "I wish you'd marry Miss Shields."

Rowe's stomach lurched. "H-How would that help you?"

"Is helping me your only concern? I should dearly love to have her as a sister-in-law, that's how."

He felt her eyes on his profile, but didn't dare meet her gaze.

Clarissa peered at him. "Have you no protests to make? There was a time when you would have had a litany of insults to lay at her door."

"I've nothing to say whatsoever."

She gasped. "Why...you've come to admire Miss Shields, haven't you!"

"Perhaps, but she doesn't like *me*."

"She didn't care for you at first, admittedly, but you've been thrown together so much I suspect she's come to like you too."

His heart gave a great leap. "Do you really think so?"

"Although she hasn't confided her feelings to me, her entire demeanor changes when you're near. Truly, I think the time you've spent together has improved her opinion of you entirely."

"I wish..." He trailed off. "No, it doesn't matter what I wish. I don't have enough money to support a poor wife, and that's the end of it."

"I'll marry Mr. Quinlan and you two can reside with us."

"I *won't* have you marry where you don't love, Clarissa."

"I won't have you marry where you don't love, either!"

Rowe gnashed his teeth in frustration. Despite all efforts to the contrary, everything had become as tangled as a lump of wool, and there seemed to be no way to make it smooth again.

••••

Myles glanced at Estella over a breakfast of toast, stewed apples, bacon, and eggs.

"I'm still not sure if I like you. You were mean to me yesterday."

Estella's lower lip pouted. "I helped you clean up the custard, when it was really all your fault."

"You made me mad!"

"You can't go tossing custard about just because you're mad."

"Well I did last night, didn't I?"

"I suppose so." She piled a spoonful of apples onto a piece of toast and ate it.

"Why are you at Graceling Hall, anyway?" he asked. "Are you here just for the party?"

"Mama told me on the train that she was hoping to marry Mr. Theodore King."

"I don't think she will. He's sweet on Lady Clarissa."

"She figured that out already. Now she's hoping to marry Lord Rowe."

"I don't think she'll marry him, either. He's sweet on Miss Shields."

"How do you know that?"

"Sometimes people do and say things when they don't realize I'm around."

She shrugged. "Maybe Mama won't marry anyone. I'd rather she didn't, actually. I don't remember my papa, but I don't think I want another one."

"Marriage is stupid."

Estella laughed. "I think so, too."

"I'm never going to get married."

"Me neither." She gave Myles a sidelong glance. "What do I have to do to get you to like me?"

He crossed his arms over his chest. "If I dare you to do something, would you do it?"

"Depends on what it was."

"You have to agree ahead of time, or it's not a proper dare."

A flicker of apprehension crossed her face. "Will I get into trouble?"

Myles thought a moment. "I don't know for certain. Maybe."

Her chin lifted. "Well, what's the dare?"

"Cut off a lock of your hair and give it to me."

"Is that all?" She glanced around the room. "Have you any shears?"

He jumped up from the table, retrieved a pair of shears from atop a small bookcase, and put them on the table with a smirk. "You won't do it."

"I'll do it, but you have to give me something in return."

"Like what?"

Her eyes turned mischievous. "A kiss."

He recoiled, and his face suddenly felt as if it had been lit on fire. "What do you want me to do *that* for?"

She tossed her head. "It's a dare. You won't do it, either."

His spine straightened. "I will so."

Estella turned her face toward him, closed her eyes, and puckered her dainty pink lips. Myles winced, held his breath, and dove forward until his lips met hers. Afterward, he straightened.

"Now it's your turn."

Estella laughed and pushed the shears away. "Fooled you, didn't I?"

He gasped at her betrayal and took a step back. "I...I-I *hate* you."

Wiping the kiss off his lips with his sleeve, he stomped out of the sitting room, went across the hall into his playroom, and threw himself down on the carpet. Estella Aynsworth was a horrible girl, and he was stupid to have trusted her. If he'd had a bowl of custard, he would have dumped it on her head and not felt bad about it whatsoever. Thank goodness the ball was tonight. Maybe her mother would take her away tomorrow and he'd never have to see her again.

A rustling noise meant Estella had followed him into the playroom. A long, silvery blond spiral curl came into his field of vision, and when she let it go, the lock of hair formed a coil on the carpet.

"There," she said. "Do you still hate me?"

He picked up the shining lock of hair as if it were a precious baby chick, and glanced up. From his vantage point, Estella's corkscrew curls didn't look any different.

"Where'd you cut it from?"

"In the back, at the nape of my neck. My nanny won't ever know, I don't think." She smiled. "And if she does, I don't care."

"Why'd you tease me like that?"

Her shoulders moved up and down. "It's fun to make you mad."

"Don't make me mad anymore."

"All right."

He glanced down at the golden coil in the palm of his hand. "In that case...I guess I don't hate you."

"Good." She sat cross-legged in front of him. "Let's go outside and play tag."

"All right." Myles got up, crossed over to a small, lidded porcelain box sitting on a shelf, and dropped the lock of hair inside. He turned back to Estella, with a grin. "You're it."

Chapter Ten
Mixed Up

Graceling Hall was abuzz with activity as servants prepared the home for the ball. Carpets were rolled up and hauled off, elaborate floral displays were set out, and breakable objects were put away. The banquet hall was arranged with buffet stations for food, and dozens of dining tables were draped with white linen. The floor of the ballroom had already been polished with beeswax the week prior, but extra chairs were grouped in the corners and alcoves.

When Megan went down for breakfast that morning, she was relieved to discover Mrs. Aynsworth was absent, having ordered a breakfast tray sent to her room. The last thing Megan needed was any impertinent remarks about her figure, or more advice about seeking a position as a maid-of-all-work. She was pensive and in no mood to talk, but fortunately Brandon and Larken had plenty to discuss regarding the impending festivities and didn't notice. Theo, on the other hand, also appeared to be preoccupied.

Megan waited until the meal was almost over to broach the topic of her departure. "May I say something?"

Theo, Larken, and Brandon gave her their attention.

"Now that we have a few minutes to ourselves, I want to thank each one of you for your kindness to me. When I think how I barged in here ten days ago, making accusations and such..." She trailed off. "Well, it pains me to remember it."

Larken's eyebrows drew together. "You speak as if you're leaving us."

"Indeed, I am. I've trespassed on your hospitality long enough, and after tonight there's no reason for me to stay. I'll travel on to London so I can seek some sort of employment."

"But Mr. Waite hasn't returned to his office yet," Brandon said. "Can't you delay your departure until then?"

"I think it's best I get on with my life. I'm planning to call on Mr. Waite myself when he returns."

Theo shook his head. "If you insist on traveling to town, Miss Shields, I'll escort you. It's not safe for a young woman to walk around London unprotected."

"And after you hear what Mr. Waite has discovered, I urge you to hasten your return," Larken said. "We've grown fond of you, and you're welcome to reside with us as long as you like."

"Thank you, Mrs. King, but since I'm not a member of the family or staff, I wouldn't feel right living here at Graceling Hall." Megan gave Theo a crooked smile. "And although I'm not society, I'm properly brought up enough to know traveling with a man who's not my husband would be a scandal."

"That's true, but you must have an escort," Larken said. "I can't get away just now, but you and Theo could take Bess along. Or perhaps Clarissa would enjoy visiting town for a day or two."

Theo cleared his throat. "Not Clarissa. She has piano lessons, surely."

"She might be willing to rearrange her schedule," Brandon said.

"I feel certain she would," Larken said. "Rowe should go as well. He and Clarissa don't get to town often enough, I wager."

"Not Lord Rowe." Megan stared at her plate. "He's occupied with courting Mrs. Aynsworth at present, and it wouldn't be fair to take him away."

"Oh, dear." Larken sighed. "Well, we don't have to decide anything right now, do we? Let's discuss this again tomorrow and see what we can come up with then."

"Thank you, Mrs. King. My time here has truly been a blessing."

Megan was glad she'd finished eating, because she would never have been able to choke down another morsel with the lump in her throat.

••••

Theo rode to the lake after breakfast, removed his jacket, and climbed into the rowboat moored to the dock. He rowed across the wide, smooth expanse of water as if pursued by the devil, glad for some rote exercise to take his mind off his troubles. By the time he reached the far side of the lake, he was almost convinced that he'd misinterpreted his feelings for Clarissa the previous evening. He turned the boat around and rowed back toward the dock at a more leisurely pace. All the county's most eligible beauties would be in attendance at the ball tonight, and he would likely have his pick. The image brought a smile to his lips…until he thought about all the bachelors who'd surely be flocking around Clarissa like a pack of wolves. Amongst them would be Graham Quinlan. How would he feel if Clarissa accepted Quinlan's proposal of marriage? He gritted his teeth and pulled for the dock—a lion sprinting toward its prey.

By the time he reached the short wooden pier, perspiration was rolling down his face and moistening the shirt on his back. As he climbed from the boat, he finally admitted the truth: he was smitten with Clarissa. He loved her; he was *in* love with her, and it was only by the grace of God she was unmarried still.

If he declared himself, he might risk losing her friendship—and that of her brother. If he did nothing, however, Clarissa would marry someone else and he'd have to stand aside and live with yet another hideous mistake.

It was time to act.

Theo tied the boat to the dock, mounted his horse, and rode toward the stables. As he handed the horse off to the stable boy, he asked for a fresh horse to be made ready in an hour. Before returning to the house, he detoured into the garden to cut roses with his pocketknife. As he sheared off the thorns and collected the flowers into a bouquet, two children ran past, shrieking with laughter.

The boy caught sight of Theo and paused. "Lord Apollo! What are you doing there?"

The girl skidded to a stop next to Myles. "Good morning, Mr. King."

Theo nodded. "Good morning, Miss Estella. Good morning, Myles." He glanced down at the bouquet in his hand. "I'm cutting flowers to give to a lady."

Myles exchanged a knowing smirk with Estella.

"Lady Clarissa?" he asked.

Theo was taken aback. "Why, yes. How did you guess?"

The lad puffed out his chest. "I see things." He paused. "Too bad you don't have any yellow flowers to give her." He burst out into inexplicable laughter, as if he'd told the funniest joke imaginable.

"I'm afraid we haven't got any yellow flowers growing in our garden," Theo said, mystified.

"Yes, I know!"

"I don't understand."

Myles snickered behind his hand. Theo sighed and cocked his head. "Well...carry on, then."

As the children darted off, he chuckled. Was he ever that silly when he was younger?

An hour later, Theo had freshened up, changed into a clean suit, and was riding to the Rowe cottage with his bouquet resting against the pommel. During the ride, he tried to devise what to say to Clarissa. Nervous energy swirled in his stomach and his palms grew moist as he pictured her face. Surely when she saw the flowers she'd ask about them, and her inquiry would give him the opening he needed to confess what was on his mind. With stiffened resolve, he raised his chin and urged his horse into a trot.

As he drew near the cottage, a man emerged from the house and untied a handsome dapple gray from a fencepost. When the fellow mounted his horse and turned toward the road, Theo recognized him.

"Hello, Quinlan. It's been a long time."

"If it isn't Theo King! A few years back, I heard the most dreadful rumor you were dead." The man's grin revealed his straight, white teeth. "Unless you're a ghost, I can see you're alive and well."

"I'm not a ghost, and I can't imagine how these silly rumors get started." Theo forced a laugh. "I've been living in London the past few years, but now I'm back."

"So you are." Quinlan gave him an appraising look. "I'm to escort Lady Clarissa to the ball tonight."

"She mentioned that to me, yes."

"I'm looking forward to it very much." Quinlan touched the brim of his hat. "I'll see you later, then."

He rode off with a flick of his horse's tail. So the man had just paid Clarissa a call, had he? *It seems my visit is in the nick of time.* Theo dismounted, brushed the dust off his clothes and tugged his waistcoat into place. With his bouquet in hand, he knocked on the door and waited for the housekeeper to open it. When she showed him into the front parlor, Clarissa and Rowe were there. From the atmosphere in the room, Theo gathered he'd interrupted an argument of some kind. Clarissa was pale, and Rowe's cheekbones were mottled red.

"I'm glad you're here, Theo. Perhaps you can talk some sense into my sister!"

"What seems to be the trouble?"

Clarissa averted her eyes. "Graham Quinlan has asked me to marry him, and I've accepted."

Theo felt as if he were falling into a bottomless, black well. "Ah." He nodded. "You have my best wishes for a happy marriage." His lips had become so numb, he was surprised he could form words.

Rowe flinched. "Is that all? Tell her she's making a mistake!"

Theo swallowed the bile creeping up his throat and fixed his gaze on a bowl of yellow flowers sitting on the upright piano in the corner. "I've no right to say anything of the sort, I'm afraid." *However much I might want to.*

Rowe made a sound of disgust, but Clarissa met his gaze and gave him a half-smile.

"Thank you, Theo. We're to keep our engagement private until a week or so after the ball. I certainly don't want to complicate matters as far as Mrs. Aynsworth is concerned."

"Very thoughtful of you, I'm sure."

"Have you brought us flowers?" Rowe asked.

Theo suddenly remembered the bouquet in his hand. "N-No. Miss Shields asked me to take them to her brother's grave while I was out." He cast about for another excuse to explain his presence. "Actually, I came by to tell you she wishes to leave for London soon. I'm to escort her, and was wondering if you'd like to come with us."

The color in Rowe's face disappeared. "Miss Shields isn't leaving permanently, is she?"

"I believe she intends to stay in town and seek employment."

"Why? You've no objection to her staying on at Graceling Hall, do you, Theo?" Rowe asked.

"None whatsoever. We've asked Miss Shields to stay, but I think she feels she's imposing." He forced himself to smile. "You know how stubborn she can be."

Rowe paced. "This won't do at all. She *can't* leave just now!"

Clarissa's laugh sounded slightly bitter. "Find a way to make her stay, Jensen."

"I can't sacrifice your happiness for mine!" Rowe's eyes looked wild. "I won't!"

"If Miss Shields slips through your fingers, I can't be held responsible."

Confused, Theo glanced between them. "Am I missing something?"

"My brother has grown very fond of Miss Shields, and the one impediment preventing him from pursuing her has just been removed." Clarissa glared at Rowe. "So pursue her!"

"If I thought you really liked Quinlan, I might be convinced," Rowe said.

She advanced on him. "I adore him, and always have. I only refused him before because I thought you didn't like him!"

Theo felt as if his heart had been ripped from his chest and thrown into the fireplace to sizzle on the coals. "Forgive me for intruding. I'll see myself out."

He fled the house, mounted his horse, and galloped off, stopping at the church long enough to lay the bouquet of roses on Paddy's grave.

"I waited too long to know my own mind, Padraig Shields." The grass at Theo's feet blurred as he blinked away tears. "I might as well be in that grave along with you."

••••

After Theo left the parlor and slammed the front door in his wake, Clarissa's brother scowled at her. "Now you've gone and done it."

"What are you talking about?"

"If you think those roses were actually for Paddy, you're sorely misguided. Theo brought them for you."

"Don't be absurd."

"And he was wearing his best waistcoat, if you didn't notice."

"What does that signify?"

"He meant to ask you to marry him. The way he was behaving with you last night was not an act!"

Her insides twisted up into a knot. "I know you're angry with me, but there's no need to be cruel."

Rowe raked his hair back with his fingers, as if frustrated beyond measure. "I'm in love with Miss Shields, who thinks I'm despicable. You're in love with Theo, but you're convinced he's indifferent. He's in love with you, but now he believes you care only for Quinlan. This is the stupidest, most mixed-up tangle imaginable. "

"If you ask Theo about his feelings, I'm sure he'll tell you that you're wrong."

"I'm not wrong. Didn't you see his face just now? When you lied about adoring Quinlan...well, I've never seen a man go so pale before."

"I didn't lie." The pretense was making Clarissa's temples throb. "I'm going upstairs to take a headache powder and rest, otherwise I'll never be able to attend the ball tonight."

"Wait." Rowe pulled her into an embrace. "You're a brave girl, and a wonderful sister. I thank you for sacrificing yourself on my behalf, but I'm not ready to give up hope that you and Theo will end up together."

She buried her face in his lapel. "It's hopeless for Theo and me, Jensen, but not for you and Miss Shields."

He gave her one last squeeze before he let her go. "We'll see."

••••

When Megan went down for afternoon tea, she noticed musicians milling outside the ballroom down the hall with their instruments. A sense of excitement filled her with anticipation. She'd never been to a society party before and would likely never attend one again, so she planned to enjoy the splendor, music, food, and dancing as much as possible. Perhaps everyone else might take the festivities in stride, but she felt extraordinarily fortunate to be a part of things.

She joined Larken, Brandon, and Mrs. Aynsworth in the drawing room, but Theo had not yet arrived.

"Will Mr. King be joining us?" Megan asked.

"He's decided to take tea in his room," Brandon replied. "He has a headache."

Larken gave her husband a worried glance. "I hope he feels well enough to attend the ball."

"I'm sure he'll be fine," he replied. "We've several hours yet until it's time to dress."

As the tea cart came around, Megan deliberately took cake, to twit Mrs. Aynsworth. Despite the odious woman's presence, her mood was elevated.

"I almost feel like it's Christmas Eve. I can't wait to see what all the ladies are wearing."

Mrs. Aynsworth smirked. "Did you bring a gown from Belfast? I can hardly wait to see what the fashions are in that part of the world."

Megan was sick of the woman's superior attitude. "My gown was made in London and delivered to Graceling Hall just last week. I'm very pleased with it."

Larken's eyes danced with merriment at Megan's artful reply. "I had my gown made locally. We have some fine seamstresses in Newcastle."

"Perhaps, but the seamstresses in Paris are incomparable," Mrs. Aynsworth said. "When I remarry, I'm going to have all my wedding clothes made there."

As the woman rattled on about fashion, Megan reflected on the evening ahead. If she waltzed with Rowe just once, her expectations would be exceeded. Just as she'd settled into a lovely daydream about their dance, Mrs. Aynsworth interrupted her train of thought.

"Miss Shields, you spoke of the London Season last night. Does that mean you intend to marry?"

"My future is unclear at the moment, so it is," Megan said. "If my older brother had lived, I might have had more choices."

"What happened to him?"

Brandon answered on Megan's behalf. "Padraig Shields met with an accident, I'm afraid. He and Theo were quite close at one point, and we look upon Miss Shields as almost a member of the family."

Tears stung Megan's eyes. "What a lovely sentiment, Mr. King. I've grown terribly fond of you...and your friends."

"I do so admire loyalty." Mrs. Aynsworth set her tea cup and saucer down. "If you'll excuse me, I'm going to retire to my room now. I must have repose if I'm to look my best at the ball." She hastened from the room.

Megan lingered awhile longer, to make certain Mrs. Aynsworth was gone. "I suppose I should go as well."

"Before you do, let me give you your dance card now so I don't forget about it later." Larken moved over to the desk, where a basket was filled with folded cards and pencils attached by strings. She retrieved Megan's card and handed it to her. "I've already marked it like we discussed. Only the waltzes are unclaimed."

"You're so terribly thoughtful, Mrs. King. Er...this is my first dance card. What do I do with it exactly?"

"This loop goes around your wrist, like so." Larken demonstrated. "The dances are listed in order, and when a gentleman wishes to reserve one, he writes his name down on your card with this pencil. At the end of the night, you have a souvenir of the evening."

"Isn't that clever! I can't tell you how much I'm looking forward to the party."

Fearful of creasing the pretty card, she left the drawing room carrying it between her thumb and forefinger. Although she'd delayed her departure from the drawing room long enough to successfully avoid Mrs. Aynsworth, the woman was waiting outside the door of her bedchamber.

"Miss Shields, I need your help. You admire Lord Rowe, do you not?"

"There are few people who would not admire him."

Mrs. Aynsworth gave her a level glance. "Let's be frank with one another. Lord Rowe must marry wealth. I've more than enough money to last several lifetimes, and I need a father for my daughter. If he and I wed, many people will benefit from our union."

"I don't know how I could possibly help or hinder you in securing His Lordship."

The woman's insincere laugh grated on Megan's nerves.

"Surely you're not that naïve, Miss Shields? It's obvious Lord Rowe admires you tremendously. Should he be selfish enough to pursue his inclination for you, his life will be ruined, and his friends will be tainted by association."

"Selfish isn't a word I'd ever associate with Lord Rowe."

"He has no money, and no estate. Don't you realize marriage to an Irish nobody will damage him socially? You'll be ignored by the Upper Ten Thousand, and your children will be obliged to marry their inferiors…all because you refused to see reason."

If Mrs. Aynsworth had slapped Megan across the face, she couldn't have been more shocked. The woman gave her a pitying glance. "I'm sorry to be the one to tell you this, but I feel certain your regard for him will guide your actions."

"Do you now? Excuse me."

Megan swept past, slipped into her room, and shut the door. Mrs. Aynsworth's words had felt like a bucket of water tossed in her face, and she felt thoroughly chilled. As much as she hated to admit it, however, there was a kernel of truth inside the woman's assertions. If Rowe truly *did* have an inclination for her, only disaster could come from it.

He couldn't support a poor wife, even if he wished to, and would be forced to rely on his friends. How much affection would survive between them after a few years of privation, especially after they had more mouths to feed? Poverty wasn't unfamiliar or necessarily shameful to *her*, but an earl would see it differently.

No, if Megan cared about Lord Rowe, she'd have to do the right thing and remove herself from his life. As she pulled her carpetbag from the wardrobe, however, she dissolved into tears. Leaving Graceling Hall and her new friends was going to be so much more difficult than she could ever have imagined.

••••

The two children shrank back into the shadows as Estella's mother approached. After the woman strode past and disappeared into her room, they scrambled out from underneath the hallway bench. Myles paused at Megan's door long enough to hear sobs coming from the other side, and then tiptoed off. He motioned Estella to follow, and once they'd turned the corner, they sped down the corridor and ducked into the nursery.

"Poor Miss Shields," Myles said. "I hope Lord Rowe marries her anyway, even if he's poor."

"How can he? He hasn't any money."

"If Apollo marries Lady Clarissa, and Lord Rowe marries Miss Shields, they can all live at Graceling Hall!"

"I don't think Mr. King *will* marry Lady Clarissa. Didn't you see how sad he was when he returned from bringing her flowers? And anyway, where will that leave Mama?"

"Sorry, but she'll have to find someone else to marry."

Myles expected Estella to argue, but she merely shrugged her shoulders. "I suppose. Still, it's too bad Mama can't marry Mr. King. If she did, then I could live at Graceling Hall with you."

"It's a bit like musical chairs, I'm afraid. In the end, somebody always gets left out."

"But that someone will be Mama—and me." To Myles's shock, Estella threw her arms around his shoulders and buried her face in his shirt. "I don't want to go home to London. Even if you're a vulgar American, I like you."

Feeling strangely pleased at the left-handed compliment, he patted her back. "Don't worry. Years from now, when it's our turn to go to parties in London, we'll see each other again."

"You'll forget about me."

"I won't. I've got a lock of your hair to remember you by."

"That's true."

"Besides which…you're the prettiest girl I've ever met."

"Do you really think so?" Estella stepped away, but she was smiling. "See that you don't forget me or I'll dump custard down your front when we meet again."

Ginny appeared in the doorway. "I'm a bit late with your tea, duckies, but it's ready now."

Myles grinned, grabbed Estella's hand, and tugged her along. "Let's hurry before my imaginary friends eat up all the clotted cream!"

Chapter Eleven

Secrets

Clarissa's gown was not new, but she'd never worn it in public before. Her London Season had been interrupted by the death of her father, and the ensuing financial disaster had meant she couldn't return to London the following year. The bodice was pleated gold brocade, off the shoulder, and the full skirt was a mesmerizing combination of gold and white tulle. Most of her jewels had long since been sold, but her thick, dark hair had been arranged in a fetching waterfall display of curls enhanced by a single yellow bloom from her garden. Quinlan's reaction to her appearance when he came to pick her up had been gratifying...but it was Theo's admiration she craved.

As Clarissa waited in the receiving queue at Graceling Hall, she tugged nervously on her elbow-length gloves and tried to calm her racing pulse. She glanced up ahead at Theo, while he welcomed his guests alongside Brandon and a radiant Larken. When she reached Theo at last, and offered him her hand, he bent to brush his lips against her glove.

"Welcome to Graceling Hall, Lady Clarissa. I hope you enjoy the evening."

His greeting could only be characterized as perfunctory, and her heart sank.

"Thank you."

Clarissa continued on into the entrance hall, but when she cast a look back, she caught him staring at her with a sad expression. If he only knew how she truly felt and why she'd become engaged to Quinlan, he'd understand her actions more fully! As it was, she might indeed lose his friendship forever.

After Rowe and Quinlan had passed through the receiving line, they joined her.

"I've never seen Theo King more downcast." Quinlan chuckled. "Perhaps some lady has crossed him in love."

Rowe gave Clarissa a meaningful glance. "I daresay you're onto something there."

Inwardly, she sighed. "Why don't you gentlemen find the smoking room and get yourselves a drink?"

"A capital idea." Quinlan beamed. "Care to join me, Rowe?"

"Not just now. I'd like to find Miss Shields first."

Quinlan's eyebrows rose. "I thought you said you were escorting Mrs. Aynsworth?"

Clarissa came to the rescue. "Indeed he is, but Miss Shields is a particular friend of ours and new here. We've promised to introduce her around and make sure she feels at home."

"There you are!" Mrs. Aynsworth slid her hand around Rowe's arm. "You must have just arrived."

"Ah, yes," he replied. "I understand you're acquainted with Mr. Graham Quinlan?"

As Quinlan and Mrs. Aynsworth exchanged pleasantries, Clarissa noticed Sir Willard just beginning to make his way through the receiving line. To her dismay, he was casting lingering glances in her direction. How unpleasant it would be if he tried to monopolize her time! Myles and Estella were watching the crowd through the balustrade on the second floor. Clarissa seized on an excuse to absent herself for a little while.

"If you'll excuse me, Jensen, I'm going to say hello to the children."

She traversed the entryway and ascended the stairs before Sir Willard could hail her. As she approached, Myles and Estella jumped to their feet.

"Don't you look splendid!" Myles said.

"Why, thank you!"

"Who was the man you came in with?" Myles asked. "I've never seen him before."

"Mr. Graham Quinlan."

"Is he angry with Lord Apollo?"

"Not at all. What would make you think that?"

Myles shrugged. "As he shook Lord Apollo's hand, his expression was quite strange."

"I can't imagine what you mean."

"Lady Clarissa, didn't you like Mr. King's flowers today?" Estella asked.

She was confused. "Sorry?"

"Lord Apollo was awfully sad when he came back this afternoon." Myles exchanged a glance with Estella. "We thought perhaps you didn't care for red roses."

Clarissa flashed back to the bouquet Theo had with him when he visited the cottage. "Oh...*those* flowers were for Miss Shields's brother's grave."

Myles shook his head. "No, they weren't. Lord Apollo told us he was bringing them to you." He snickered.

"Mr. King said so, right in front of me," Estella added. "He's sweet on you!"

"I think you overstate the case. We're just friends." Despite her words, Clarissa was taken aback. Had Theo really meant to bring her flowers and possibly even propose as her brother had suggested? No, that was wishful thinking on her part. Myles and

Estella had simply gotten Theo's words twisted up somehow...or had they?

Myles peered at her, concerned. "I hope I wasn't wrong to tell you."

She found her tongue. "N-No, not at all. Has Miss Shields passed this way?"

Estella's flaxen curls danced as she shook her head. "She was crying earlier, because of something Mama said. I don't think she's come out of her room since then, but I'm not sure."

"Oh, dear. I'll go see how she's doing."

••••

Theo watched Clarissa climb the stairs, the yellow rosebud in her hair shining like a star within her dark, coiled tresses. She looked so exquisite—and yet so utterly unattainable. He suddenly yearned to retreat to a darkened room with a bottle of brandy and drown his sorrows. No, that would be to give in to one of his moods. It would be far better to go after Clarissa, tell her how he felt, and beg her to marry him instead of that buffoon, Quinlan. He'd actually taken a half-step forward before he stopped himself. If Clarissa truly adored the man, he had no right to interfere.

With a leaden heart, he turned back to the receiving line. As he welcomed the last of his guests to Graceling Hall, Clarissa's floral hair ornament lingered in his mind. Hadn't Myles mentioned something about her preferring yellow flowers? A bowl of similar blossoms had been resting on her piano that afternoon, so obviously her garden must be full of them. Since Theo was certain Myles had never been to Clarissa's cottage, it was curious the child knew such a thing.

After Sir Willard had passed through the queue, Theo turned toward Larken and Brandon.

"Unless we have latecomers, I believe everyone's here."

"We should circulate amongst our guests until it's time to start the dancing," Brandon said. "Seagate can admit any latecomers."

Larken's brow furrowed. "Have either of you happened to see Miss Shields?"

"No," Brandon said. "I don't think she's come down yet."

Theo cocked his thumb toward the staircase. "Clarissa went up a few moments ago. I suspect she's gone to fetch her."

"I'm sure all is well, but if I don't see both of them in the next few minutes, I'll go check on them myself," Larken said.

As she and Brandon headed down the hall to mingle with the crowd, Theo noticed Myles and Estella peering through the balusters on the gallery level. He waved and mounted the stairs to join them. "Hullo! Where did Lady Clarissa disappear to?"

Myles nodded. "She went to Miss Shields's room."

"I'd guessed as much. Do you two want me to send a servant up with a plate of treats from the banquet room?"

"No, thank you, Mr. King," Estella said. "Ginny and Bess already brought us all sorts of pastries." She giggled. "They were delicious."

"Good." Theo paused. "Myles, I was wondering how you happened to know Lady Clarissa enjoyed yellow flowers?"

The lad grinned, looking very pleased with himself. "When I first came here, back when everyone thought you were dead, I'd go exploring. I used to climb the tree near the church and pretend it was a ship and I was the captain."

Estella wrinkled her nose. "How can anyone think a tree is like a ship? It doesn't go anywhere, and it's not surrounded by water."

The boy sighed with exasperation. "You just have to use your imagination! Anyway, Lady Clarissa would bring bunches of yellow flowers to your grave and cry a little. I'm glad she doesn't have to do that anymore."

Estella tugged on Myles's sleeve. "Let's go back to the nursery and play a game."

He chortled, "Too bad we can't play musical chairs!"

The children sped off down the hall, laughing together as if they had just shared some sort of private joke. Theo sat on the uppermost step, confused, as Brandon's words came back to haunt him. *Did you know someone was leaving flowers on your grave regularly? You've a secret admirer.* Of course, just because Clarissa had brought flowers to his grave wasn't proof she'd been in love with him. Besides which, if she *had* cared for him that much, she wouldn't have accepted Quinlan's offer of marriage, would she? Wait...what if he was the actual object of her affection and she accepted Quinlan only to make him jealous? Theo scratched his head at the idea. Certainly, the pieces of the puzzle seemed to fit together, but it wouldn't be wise to jump to conclusions. He'd have to force her to admit her feelings for him—but how?

A rustling in the hallway made him look up. To his surprise, Clarissa was hastening toward him with a note in her hand and a strained expression on her face.

He stood. "Are you all right?"

"I'm well, but Miss Shields has gone!"

••••

Rowe nursed a glass of port in the smoking room, alongside Quinlan. Mrs. Aynsworth had become so engrossed in a conversation about Paris with another Francophile, Lady Beatrice, that he and Quinlan had excused themselves for a moment of repose and spirits. Moments later, a dour-looking Sir Willard entered the room. Fortunately, he took his glass of whisky and joined another group in the corner.

Although Rowe wished to enjoy his drink in silence, Quinlan intruded on his thoughts with an enthusiastic declaration.

"I'm hoping Clarissa and I may marry as soon as possible. I trust you have no objection to a Christmas wedding?"

Unimpressed, Rowe gave the man a level glance. "You understand my sister has no dowry, don't you?"

"That's not important." He shrugged. "I love her. I think I loved Clarissa from the moment I saw her."

"There are a great many women you've loved from the moment you saw them. I'd like to believe my sister is unique."

Quinlan's grin was unrepentant. "And so she is! I worship the ground she walks on, I can assure you."

"And yet, I'm not reassured." Rowe drained his port.

Theo entered the smoking room and rested his hand on Rowe's shoulder. "Forgive me for the interruption, but I must have a word with you, in private."

The strain in his friend's voice caught Rowe's attention right away. "Certainly. Excuse me a moment, Quinlan."

He followed Theo into the hall, waiting until they were alone before asking what was wrong.

"Miss Shields has slipped away, and Clarissa believes she's heading for the train station," Theo said. "She's bound for London tonight."

A thread of panic wrapped itself around Rowe's chest. "I'll go after her!"

"Not alone; Clarissa and I are going with you. A carriage is being brought around now. Meet us out front."

"I'll be there straightaway."

Rowe ducked back into the smoking room to speak with Quinlan.

"Look, old chap, something critically important has come up. Will you escort Mrs. Aynsworth into the ballroom for me, and be sure to give her my most sincere regrets?"

Quinlan was taken aback. "What about Clarissa?"

"She'll be detained for a while as well, I'm afraid. You'll have to carry on without her."

As Rowe rushed from the room, he tried to keep his worry from showing on his face. What had possessed Megan to leave so suddenly, and why? The hour was too late for a young woman to be on the road at night, alone and without protection. He prayed they could find her before she ran afoul of any danger.

••••

Clad in her old green dress, Megan bribed one of the drivers relaxing in the courtyard to take her to the Gateshead train station. He put out his cigarette, tossed her carpetbag in the boot, and gave her a hand up into the driver's seat. Although she'd rather ride in the carriage itself, she was hardly in a position to object.

They drove in silence for a little while before the driver gave her a sidelong glance. "Ye get the sack, did ye? What a shame."

His Irish brogue almost made her homesick.

"Nothing like that. I've just been called away on an urgent matter."

"Durin' a grand party? Sure." He chuckled and shrugged his shoulders. "None o' my business, I reckon."

"You won't get in trouble for driving me to the station, will you?"

He shook his head. "I'll ne'er be missed at all. My employer will be at it till the wee hours, along with them other rich folk. Dancin' and eatin' enough food to feed half o' Dublin."

"That's where you're from, then? I was born in Belfast."

"Must've left when ye were a wain. Not much o' Belfast in your voice. Ye sound right genteel, in fact."

"Thank you."

When the carriage passed the church graveyard where Paddy was buried, Megan's eyes and throat burned with unshed tears. She was leaving her brother behind, and there was no way to know if she'd ever be back.

"I'm thinkin' ye've missed the last train tonight," the driver said. "Are ye sure ye can't stay here till the morrow?"

"I really must go, but please don't worry about me. If I've missed the last train, I'll sit on a bench and wait until morning. It won't be the first time I've spent the night out of doors."

"At least ye've got a warm night for it. Been a mild October, so it has."

"Who is your employer, if you don't mind me asking?"

"Mr. Graham Quinlan. He's just this day become engaged to a friend o' the King family, Lady Clarissa Alderforth. Her brother's the Earl of Rowe."

Megan's eyes widened and her jaw dropped slightly. "Lady Clarissa is…engaged?"

He nodded. "She's a nice woman, she is, and a pretty little thing. I hope he settles down proper, for her sake. Mr. Quinlan has always had an eye for the ladies, if ye don't mind me sayin' so."

"I should hope he's in love with her!"

"On that score, ye needn't worry. He's been carryin' a torch for years, I reckon. I shouldn't have said anythin' since their engagement is supposed to be secret, but I don't imagine you'll be tellin' anyone."

"I won't be telling a soul."

The road was quiet, with little traffic, and the train station came into view at last. The driver pulled to a stop and retrieved her bag. After she gave him the sum they'd agreed upon, he helped her down and lifted his hat.

"May the road rise up to meet ye, lass."

"Same to you."

As it turned out, the station was locked up for the night. Megan carried her bag around to the back of the building and settled herself on a bench with a view of the tracks. Although the place was deserted, gas lamps in the street lifted the darkness somewhat. Now that she was alone, she'd all the time in the world to wonder if she'd done the right thing by leaving Graceling Hall. Since Clarissa had become engaged to a gentleman of means, had she left Rowe's side too soon? No, she still had nothing to offer the man, so her reasons for leaving were unchanged. Furthermore, even if she regretted her actions, it was too late to go back; surely her absence had been noted by now. She'd tried to express her appreciation in the letter she'd left on her pillow, but the Kings would likely consider her precipitous departure to be rude. Once she was settled, she'd send another letter of apology and hope the family would forgive her someday.

Overwhelmed with emotion, Megan leaned forward, covered her face with her hands, and let the tears flow.

••••

The driver, James, stood next to a four-seat landau, which had its soft folding-top down. Theo and Clarissa were seated inside, facing one another. Rowe practically leaped inside and sat next to his sister.

"Drive on, James," Theo said.

As the horses surged forward, Rowe almost felt sick to his stomach. "Tell me everything, Clarissa. How did you discover Miss Shields was missing?"

"She hadn't come down yet, so I went to her room. When there was no answer to my knock, I entered and noticed her ball gown draped across the bed, along with all the other clothes I'd given her." Clarissa held up a crumpled piece of paper. "This note was addressed to Mr. and Mrs. King, but I took the liberty of reading it."

"Did she say anything about me?"

"She wrote that she was grateful for all our kindnesses but she felt it was time to move on. Her maid, Bess, said she'd sworn her to silence before slipping out the servants' entrance."

"What on earth could have precipitated Miss Shields's abrupt departure?" Rowe asked.

"I don't know, exactly, but Estella told me Miss Shields had been hurt by something Mrs. Aynsworth had said earlier today," Clarissa said. "The children heard her crying."

The image of Megan's tears added more fuel to Rowe's worry. "Blast Mrs. Aynsworth! I sensed she was unkind, but I didn't want to believe it."

"Perhaps this is just a horrible misunderstanding." Clarissa glared at Theo. "There's a great deal of that going around."

Theo returned her piercing look with one of his own. "Truer words were never spoken. I'd like to think close friends could be open and honest with one another."

"One would like to *think* so, but I've recently discovered such isn't always the case."

"A great deal of trouble could have be avoided with a bit of frank disclosure."

"Ha! And what would you know of frank disclosure except how best to avoid it?"

Bewildered, Rowe glanced from Clarissa to Theo. "What does this have to do with Miss Shields?"

Theo ignored him. "Clarissa, let's put our cards on the table, once and for all. I know you're the person who's been leaving flowers on my grave."

She gasped and glared at Rowe, who held his hands up in a defensive posture.

"Don't look at me that way, Clarissa. I didn't say a word!"

It was Theo's turn to glare at him. "No, you didn't, Rowe, which is less than I would have expected from a friend!"

"What?" Rowe exclaimed. "Don't drag me into this argument!"

"That's right, Theo! Leave my brother out of it. This isn't his fault."

"Not entirely, but if your brother had dropped a hint about the flowers, we could've avoided this donnybrook!"

"Oh, merciful heavens." Rowe slid down in his seat, wishing he were elsewhere.

Clarissa lifted her chin. "I freely admit I left flowers on your grave."

Theo wagged his finger in the air. "Now we're getting somewhere!"

"The flowers signified nothing more than one friend missing another. I hope you'd have done the same for me."

"Some people seem to think the flowers had a more particular significance."

"And some other people are conceited, vain, and hypocritical!"

Theo's eyes narrowed. "Hypocritical? What have you to accuse me of?"

"A bouquet of flowers meant to find its way to *me* today, somehow took a mysterious and inexplicable turn toward the graveyard. A certain person misrepresented the case entirely."

With a grimace, Rowe shrank down into his seat further.

"As if I would have given them to you after finding out you'd thrown yourself away on a rake like Quinlan!"

"About that..." Rowe began

"Shh!" Theo and Clarissa spoke at the same time.

Having had enough, Rowe cleared his throat. "James, will you stop the carriage a moment?"

Since Theo and Clarissa were bickering with one another, they barely noticed when Rowe climbed up to sit with the driver—who was grinning from ear to ear.

"Don't say a word, James." Rowe flicked his fingers toward the road. "Let's make tracks."

Five minutes later, when another carriage approached, Rowe stood and waved his arms to get it to stop. To his surprise, he recognized Graham Quinlan's driver.

"Fergus?"

The man was taken aback. "Lord Rowe? What are ye doin' all the way out here?"

"Did you take a young woman to the train station just now?"

"That I did. I was feelin' right sorry for the lass, gettin' the sack and all on a night like tonight."

"Did you see her get on a train?"

Fergus shook his head. "The last one had already come and gone by the time we'd arrived. She insisted on waitin', and I expect she's still there."

Rowe sat, only slightly relieved. "Thank you, Fergus."

The man touched the brim of his hat and continued on his way. Rowe glanced at James.

"Let's get to the train station with all due haste."

••••

At the sound of an approaching carriage, Megan tried to compose herself. She hoped the carriage would pass the station and keep going, but unfortunately the hoof beats stopped out front. Muffled conversation ensued, followed by footsteps.

"Miss Shields, are you here?"

Lord Rowe? She shot to her feet, gasping in dismay. Moments later, the earl appeared around the side of the building and strode toward her.

"Miss Shields! Thank heavens you're all right."

"What are you doing here? Have you come to say goodbye?"

"I've come to bring you back."

Theo and Clarissa joined Rowe.

"Oh, dear!" Megan exclaimed. "Why aren't you all at the party?"

Clarissa gave her a concerned smile. "We're not at the party because you're not at the party, Miss Shields."

"We're not leaving without you," Theo said.

Rowe picked up her carpetbag. "You're coming back to Graceling Hall, and that's final."

Her eyes widened. "I can't!"

"You can and you must," Clarissa said.

"When you finally travel to London, the three of us will accompany you," Rowe said.

"And we'll stay in my townhouse," Theo added.

She looked at the three of them. "I don't deserve your kindness."

"Miss Shields, I don't know what Mrs. Aynsworth might have said to hurt you today, but I wouldn't give it another thought," Rowe said. "She's beneath your notice."

Megan was taken aback. "How do you know about that?"

"The children overheard your conversation and told me about it," Clarissa said.

Humiliation hit Megan like a blast of hot air from a bread oven.

"Lord Rowe, whatever Mrs. Aynsworth said regarding your feelings for me was only because she wishes to secure you. I never gave her assertions any credence whatsoever."

Rowe looked puzzled. "What?"

Megan glanced at Clarissa in confusion. "I'm sorry, didn't you say—"

"The children didn't repeat the conversation verbatim," Clarissa murmured. "Only that Mrs. Aynsworth said something hurtful."

"Oh."

In the silence that followed, Megan stared at the tips of her shoes.

"If Mrs. Aynsworth has accurately divined my most tender sentiments, she's shrewder than I'd supposed," Rowe said.

His declaration was so soft, Megan was forced to look at him to make sure she'd heard correctly.

"Would you consider marrying me, Miss Shields?"

Megan's cheekbones burned, and she stifled the impulse to throw herself into his arms.

"W-What're ye goin' on about, Your Lordship! I could no sooner marry an earl than a sheepdog."

"I find the comparison oddly flattering, although I should hope I smell better," Rowe said. "I admire you greatly, Miss Shields, and I beg you to give me a chance."

Tears welled up in her eyes. "I can't do that to ye...I mean *you*. I haven't a penny to my name."

"I don't either, but that didn't stop Mr. Quinlan," Clarissa said.

"Your situation is entirely different, Lady Clarissa, if you don't mind me saying so. In marrying me, your brother would be marrying down so far he wouldn't be able to see daylight."

Rowe gasped. "You can't believe that!"

"Your view of the situation is far too harsh, Miss Shields," Theo said.

"I agree," Clarissa said. "You ought not think of yourself so meanly."

"I suspect this is Mrs. Aynsworth's opinion and not your own," Rowe said.

"Perhaps, but there can be no other opinion on the subject." Megan didn't have the heart to argue any longer. "I'll go back to Graceling Hall with you tonight."

A broad smile lit Rowe's face. "Thank you."

He reached for her hand, but she pulled away. "Forgive me, Lord Rowe, but I can never marry you. We'd have no money at all, and you're not the type of man to live off the charity of others."

"I'll get regular employment, perhaps in the banking industry or some such." His voice had a strangled quality. "We'll make it work."

Her heart broke into a million pieces. "My answer is no. And that's my final word."

Chapter Twelve
The Ball

Megan's stunning rejection of his marriage proposal sent Rowe spinning into the depths of despair and frustration. How could he convince her to change her mind—especially when she was perfectly right in her refusal? Could he swallow his pride, move into Graceling Hall, and live off the kindness of the King family? He'd no doubt Theo would welcome him and Megan wholeheartedly and perhaps even give him whatever allowance he asked. Nevertheless, he could never repay the man's generosity.

Not for the first time did Rowe resent the way his father had wasted away the estate after their mother's death. Although he and Clarissa never spoke of it, they'd both been aware of their father's gambling habit. When he had examined the books after his funeral, he'd discovered then that his father had even squandered the sum set aside for Clarissa's dowry. It was of little consequence now, since all the resentment in the world—however justified—wouldn't help him support a wife in the style she deserved.

He rode back to Graceling Hall in the carriage alongside Megan, but took scant solace from her nearness. No argument he could devise would overcome her objections, so he said nothing. Theo and Clarissa had stopped arguing, therefore the drive took place in almost complete silence. Only after the carriage stopped in the courtyard did Theo finally speak.

"James, please take Miss Shields's bag to her room straightaway. You can deal with the carriage when you return."

"Yes, sir."

The driver set the brake, helped the ladies step down from the carriage, and disappeared with the carpetbag. Rowe and Theo accompanied Megan and Clarissa into the house, where music flowed from the ballroom and ebullient guests were clustered in the hallway, chatting.

Clarissa beckoned Megan toward the stairs. "Come quickly. We must get you ready for the ball."

Before she could move, Rowe touched her arm. "Please reserve at least one waltz for me, Miss Shields."

Megan nodded. "That I will."

The two ladies ascended the steps, while Theo and Rowe lingered in the entrance hall. Servants were scurrying to and fro with trays of drinks and hors d'oeuvres. Rowe accepted a glass of champagne and held up the glass toward Theo, as if making a toast.

"Here's to you and my sister settling your differences." He drank half the glass in one gulp.

"It hasn't happened yet."

Rowe drained the glass. "I hope you manage to bridge the gap without further ado."

Theo peered at him. "Are you going to be all right?"

"No."

"You might explain to Miss Shields that you and your bride would always have a home here at Graceling Hall."

Rowe gave him a crooked smile. "I knew you'd say that, and I have the utmost regard for your generosity, Theo. But I have the feeling it's not what she wants."

"What will you do?"

He shook his head. "I'm not exactly sure. When I'm in London, I'll make a few inquiries about employment."

"But, Rowe—"

"I understand full well the implications, I can assure you. Joining the working class will make me a pariah amongst society...but then a lack of funds these past few years has rather cramped my popularity as it is. Perhaps once I've established myself, Miss Shields might reconsider my offer...if she's not married to someone else by then."

"I don't know what to say."

"Neither do I, really." He paused. "Actually, I have one bit of advice. Tell my sister you're in love with her."

"Is it that obvious?"

"To a blind man."

Theo peered at him. "So...you don't mind?"

Rowe managed to laugh. "Mind? I'd far rather have *you* for a brother-in-law than anyone else of my acquaintance."

"Thank you." Theo gulped. "Are you absolutely sure my attentions won't be unwanted?"

"At the risk of exposing myself to Clarissa's wrath for revealing a confidence, I can assure you that your attentions will be quite welcome—and long overdue."

His friend's expression brightened. "You're not just saying that to spare my feelings?"

Rowe rolled his eyes. "Are you choosing to ignore my 'dropped hint' now?"

Theo had the grace to blush. "I don't mean to seem ungrateful."

"In that case, take the hint."

"What about Quinlan?"

"I'll deal with him. In fact, it would be my pleasure to do so."

Theo grabbed his hand and shook it with enthusiasm. "I'm in your debt. I'll talk to Clarissa tonight. I confess, it won't be easy for me to find the right moment."

"Love is never easy." Rowe jerked his head toward the ballroom. "We should go in. You must circulate amongst your guests, and I suppose I should learn what has happened to Mrs. Aynsworth. I would feel rather badly about leading her on, but having learned her true nature, I count myself fortunate to have escaped her clutches."

Theo clapped him on the shoulder. "Cheer up. Everything might turn out all right in the end for us both."

Rowe deposited his empty glass on a passing servant's tray. "So say you."

Once inside the ballroom, Theo went off to speak with Brandon, and Rowe searched for Mrs. Aynsworth. She was on the dance floor in the arms of Sir Willard, seemingly enjoying herself. Rowe was relieved that his neglect had not been injurious to the woman. Although he didn't give two figs for her now, he wouldn't like to be accused of ungentlemanly behavior.

Quinlan hastened over with an expectant look on his face. "Has Clarissa returned?"

"She'll be along directly. I trust Mrs. Aynsworth wasn't too put out with me for my unexpected absence?"

"Perhaps a little, but not for long. She and I have always gotten along well. Extraordinarily beautiful woman, I must say, and a first-rate dancer."

The man's effusive praise gave Rowe the idea to nudge Quinlan in Mrs. Aynsworth's direction.

"I understand she's quite keen to remarry."

"Oh?" As the blonde beauty twirled past, a flicker of interest lit Quinlan's face. "She'll make some fortunate man very, very happy, I daresay."

"And wealthy too, since she's inherited the entirety of her late husband's estate. Do you enjoy children? She has a young daughter."

"I adore children, actually. Whenever my nieces and nephews come to visit, we get along splendidly."

"Marvelous. Say, why don't you escort Mrs. Aynsworth into dinner this evening and deepen your acquaintance?"

He chuckled. "Thanks ever so, but I'm to escort Clarissa."

"I'm afraid not. You see, I've withdrawn my permission for her to marry you."

Quinlan's eyes grew wide and his jaw dropped. "On what grounds?"

"Because she's in love with someone else."

••••

Clarissa accompanied Megan to her bedchamber and rang for Bess.

"While we're waiting for your maid, let's get you out of this dress, Miss Shields. You've no time to waste."

Megan laughed. "It may be that giving piano lessons has made you a wee bit bossy."

"Undoubtedly, but it's for a good cause. There are still several dances left before the dinner break, and I don't want you to miss anything more than you already have."

"You've such a good heart." Megan turned around and let Clarissa unfasten the buttons on the back of her dress. "I wish your brother hadn't been so downcast when I refused him. I never meant to cause him any pain."

"Naturally, Jensen is disappointed. He cares for you a great deal."

Wistfulness settled around Megan's shoulders like a mantle. "I care for him more than I can say, but surely you can see it's an impossible situation."

"Oh, I don't know. Sometimes miracles can occur."

"Can they now? I think the world of your brother, but he has as much pride as I do. He and I might be happy together—at first. But over the years, he'd come to realize how foolish he'd been to throw his future away on a fancy. I couldn't bear to watch his affection turn to resentment."

Clarissa frowned. "You underestimate Jensen's character...but I can't deny that he has pride."

Bess arrived shortly thereafter. "Oh, I'm so glad you've come back, Miss Shields!"

"Thank you, Bess."

The maid blushed. "I'm sorry for not keeping your confidence, but when Lady Clarissa came to me so worried, I had to say something."

"You did the right thing," Clarissa said.

Megan smiled. "I agree. I can see now that it's better to leave Graceling Hall through the front door and in the proper way."

Bess's grin was sheepish. "I'm certainly glad I don't have to explain your absence to the Kings in the morning."

She helped Megan don her ball gown and arranged her hair with impossible speed. When Megan was finally ready to go down to the party, however, her midsection suddenly turned to jelly and her palms became moist. As she and Clarissa descended the stairs to the ground floor, she tried—and failed—to emulate the woman's serene expression.

"How do you stay so calm?"

"Practice, I think. During my first London Season, I was so nervous before every ball I almost made myself sick. Jensen, Theo, and Brandon were almost always around to make me feel better, fortunately."

"I'm not meaning to be an interfering busybody, but you and Mr. Theo King are well suited to one another."

"I'm engaged to Mr. Quinlan!"

"True enough, but it's not too late to change your mind. I don't know why Mr. King hasn't proposed to you before now. I'm beginning to wonder if he has rocks where his brain is supposed to be."

Clarissa sighed. "Just between you and me, so do I."

As they approached the ballroom, she took Megan by the arm. "Stay close, so I may introduce you properly to everyone."

As soon as Megan entered the ballroom, music, motion, and the delicate fragrance of expensive perfume filled her senses. Couples were twirling on the dance floor, the orchestra was playing, and guests were chatting on the periphery. Megan tried not to gape like a bumpkin at all the exquisite gowns and copious jewels on display.

"What am I supposed to talk about, Lady Clarissa? I've nothing in common with anyone!"

"The ladies just want you to admire their gowns, and the gentlemen want to talk about themselves. Smile and nod, and you'll do splendidly."

••••

Quinlan bristled at Rowe's announcement. "I'm afraid I don't appreciate your humor!"

"I'm not in a joking mood, I assure you."

The man squared his chiseled chin. "If she's not in love with me, who *has* caught her fancy?"

"I'm not at liberty to say."

"But that's not fair! Am I not to know the name of my competition?"

"Life isn't fair, and many people—myself included—have been crossed in love. In your case, however, I'm sure your distress will be of short duration."

His eyes flashed. "I won't believe this until I hear it from Clarissa's lips."

"And so you shall, if you insist."

The music concluded. As the couples on the floor applauded, Quinlan stood scowling with his arms crossed over his chest. "If she throws me over, she'll be known as a jilt!"

"Not if you step aside like a gentleman. Since the engagement hasn't been formally announced, no one need be the wiser."

"Your attitude is uncommonly callous."

Rowe lost his patience. "Be practical! There are a half-dozen young women on the dance floor, including Mrs. Aynsworth, who'd be more than receptive to your charms."

Quinlan did a double take over Rowe's shoulder, and his lips curved into a smile. "Well, well, well...who have we here?"

When Rowe followed the man's gaze, his mouth went dry. Megan had entered the ballroom arm-in-arm with Clarissa. The colleen was a rare vision, clad in a head-turning peacock blue gown. Her lush figure was displayed to its best advantage, and Rowe felt his pulse quicken. Unfortunately, his was not the only pulse similarly affected. Quinlan's eyes gleamed with undisguised interest as he smoothed his mustache with his index and forefinger.

"Pardon me while I meet your sister's extraordinary friend. Perhaps my distress will be short-lived after all."

The man strode off with a purposeful gait, and Rowe nearly groaned out loud. He'd hoped to steer Quinlan toward Mrs. Aynsworth, but he'd forgotten how competitive the man could be. He should have expressed *more* interest in Mrs. Aynsworth, not less, if he meant to encourage him. He'd botched the matter entirely, and now Quinlan had Megan in his sights.

As Clarissa introduced him to Megan, the rake immediately reached for her dance card and wrote his name on it several times. Almost as if someone had rung a dinner bell, Megan and Clarissa were surrounded by gentlemen asking to be introduced to the fresh new face. *Blast it!* All Megan's dances might be spoken for if he didn't get over there quickly.

Before he took more than a few steps, however, Mrs. Aynsworth stepped into his path.

"There you are, Lord Rowe! I trust your little emergency was managed?"

"Ah...yes. All is well, and please accept my apologies."

"I've been absolutely desolate without you." She dangled her dance card by its string and gave him a pretty pout. "I've still a few dances available, if you'd like to reserve one or two."

"Of course." His frustration at the delay mounted as he scribbled his name on her card.

"I see Miss Shields has finally deigned to arrive. Such bad manners to be so late."

Rowe peered at her. "I understand you had an argument with her earlier today?"

"What would Miss Shields and I have to argue about?" Her trilling laugh sounded forced. "If she says anything to the contrary, I wouldn't give it credence." Her voice lowered to a whisper. "The Irish aren't known to be particularly trustworthy, I'm afraid."

He leaned forward, as if to impart a secret. "Perhaps I should tell you that my own dear, departed mother was full-blooded Irish."

Her eyes widened, and a crimson blush stained her pale skin all the way up to her hairline. "I-I didn't mean any offense," she managed.

"I didn't think you had." He smiled. "Now, if you'll excuse me, I'd like to claim one of Miss Shields's dances before I'm crowded out."

••••

Although Megan had been worried about being ignored by the Kings' guests, she and Clarissa seemed to create a stir almost as soon as they entered the ballroom. Only a few seconds passed before a very good-looking man hastened over and sketched a bow.

"Will you introduce me to this beautiful creature, Clarissa?" He fixed Megan with an admiring gaze.

"Of course. Miss Shields, allow me to present Graham Quinlan," Clarissa said.

So this is Lady Clarissa's fiancé? Why does he look at me as if I were an eclair? Megan curtsied. "It's a pleasure to meet you, sir."

"Miss Shields has been visiting the King family," Clarissa said. "We've grown quite close."

"I see." Quinlan's smile was dazzling. "May I reserve a dance, Miss Shields?"

"You may." Feeling awkward, Megan removed her dance card from around her wrist and handed it to him. As he scribbled his name on the card in several different spots, Clarissa gave Megan a sidelong glance and an encouraging smile. When several other gentlemen clustered around at once, however, Megan began to feel overwhelmed. While Clarissa made introductions, Megan lost track of her dance card. Faces and names blurred together, and she knew she'd never remember them all. Fortunately, the dance card finally made its way back into her hands, and she looped it around her wrist once more. At least she could refer to the card if she forgot someone's name.

Finally a familiar face appeared, pushing his way through the crowd. Megan drew a breath of relief. "Lord Rowe!"

He bowed. "May I claim a dance, Miss Shields?"

She gave him her card, wishing she could anchor herself to his side for the remainder of the night. When he glanced down at the card, a crease appeared in between his eyebrows.

"It appears I'm already too late."

"What?"

He handed the card back. "Every dance has been spoken for."

Although she was crestfallen, she tried to control her countenance. It would be horribly rude to express disappointment, especially since Quinlan was hovering at her elbow.

"Forgive me, Lord Rowe. I did promise to save you a dance, but it wasn't possible."

Clarissa reached for the card and studied it. "Jensen, are you available for the final waltz before the dinner break?"

"Why, yes."

"Since Graham has claimed three of Miss Shields's waltzes, he won't mind if you take his place, will you, Graham?" Clarissa crossed out the name and put in her brother's instead.

Quinlan bristled. "I jolly well—"

"Oh, *thank* you," Clarissa interrupted. "I knew I could count on you to be a gentleman." She gave Megan a surreptitious wink.

"What a lovely gesture, Mr. Quinlan." Megan returned the card to her wrist. "I believe the next dance is yours?"

The man's disgruntlement seemingly faded as he offered Megan his arm. "I'm the most fortunate of men."

As Megan accompanied Quinlan toward the dance floor, she gave Rowe a tender smile. Perhaps they couldn't have a future together, but at least they would have one waltz.

••••

As Megan and Quinlan took their places on the dance floor, Rowe was filled with consternation, and more than a little jealousy. It was too soon to tell if Megan was receiving the man's attentions with pleasure, but admittedly he *was* charming, handsome, and rich. What if she preferred Quinlan to him?

"I think I managed that quite well, don't you?" Clarissa asked.

Rowe dragged his attention away from Megan and Quinlan. "What?"

She made a sound of exasperation. "You acquired a dance with Miss Shields because of me."

"Oh, yes. I'm grateful for that."

"It wasn't Miss Shields's fault she didn't save you a dance. There were so many gentleman passing her card between them, it became impossible to manage.

Graham should never have taken three dances for himself in the first place. It was rather selfish."

"I wish you hadn't introduced Miss Shields to him. I suspect he'll make a nuisance of himself now."

"I should be insulted at his interest in her, I suppose, now that we're engaged."

"Don't bother being insulted. I told him the engagement is off."

Clarissa bristled. "Are you mad? Why would you do such a thing without consulting me?"

"To clear the field for a far worthier candidate. And don't pretend you don't know who I mean."

She ignored his remark, but her color visibly deepened. "How did Graham take the news?"

"Like a temperamental little puppy—until he caught sight of Miss Shields, of course. Then he turned into a hungry wolf." He sighed. "I'm to collect Mrs. Aynsworth for the next dance. Did you know she had the audacity to insult Miss Shields's Irish heritage?"

"I'm not surprised. You never did ask me why I stepped on her dress all those years ago."

"Do tell."

"When she and I were at Lady Frampton's soirée, I overheard her make a nasty remark about a woman's Irish brogue. Her prejudice toward the Irish vexed me greatly."

He peered at her in alarm. "Why didn't you tell me this before?"

She rolled her eyes. "Nobody can ever tell you anything, Jensen. You were so intent on marrying Mrs. Aynsworth, nothing I said would have dissuaded you. You needed to discover her character on your own."

"And what if I hadn't!"

"Despite your bad beginning, you came to appreciate Miss Shields's charms, didn't you? I felt certain you'd learn Mrs. Aynsworth fell short of the mark sooner rather than later."

Theo approached and sketched a bow. "May I have this dance, Clarissa?"

"Y-You may."

As Theo offered Clarissa his arm, Rowe gave him a pointed look. Hopefully, his friend would find the courage to say what was on his mind at last.

Chapter Thirteen
Ripples

As Megan waltzed with Quinlan, he gave her a wink. "I absolutely forbid you to feel sorry for me, you know."

"I'm not understanding you?"

"You see, until a few minutes ago I was engaged to Lady Clarissa."

"Are you not still engaged to her then?"

"I'm afraid not. Her brother has withdrawn his permission for us to marry, on the grounds that her affections lay elsewhere." His laugh revealed deep dimples, straight white teeth, and a twinkle in his hazel eyes.

"You don't seem terribly distraught."

"That's why you mustn't feel sorry for me. I adore Clarissa and always have, so I want her to be happy. I know she wants the same thing for me."

"Your resilient attitude is remarkable."

"I believe your presence tonight may have something to do with it. Are you Scottish, Miss Shields? I detect a slight lilt in your voice."

"I'm from Belfast."

"Even better! I've been to the Emerald Isle and found it charming."

Quinlan was doing his best to put her at ease, and Megan felt herself relaxing more and more.

"Er…tell me about yourself, sir," she said, mindful of Clarissa's advice.

"Perhaps later. Right now, I'd like to hear how such a beautiful colleen came to stay with the Kings."

"It's a rather long story."

"Let me escort you into dinner tonight, and you can tell me the entire tale."

"Aren't you to escort Lady Clarissa?"

"I rather think she'd prefer the company of her future bridegroom, don't you? Do you suppose you could arrange it?"

"It can be easily arranged, to be sure. Mr. Theo King was to escort me, so I'm sure he'll be more than happy to escort Lady Clarissa instead."

A ripple of anger crossed Quinlan's face, but it was gone so quickly Megan thought perhaps she'd imagined it.

"Theo's such a reasonable fellow, I'm sure it can be managed." He paused. "Why don't you ask him when you get the chance, and I'll speak with Clarissa?"

Megan nodded. "That I will."

••••

As Theo moved around the dance floor with Clarissa, she wore an uneasy expression which he suspected mirrored his own. Although he tried to find the right moment to confess his feelings, he couldn't seem to find the words. Finally she broke the silence between them.

"Jensen told Graham he revoked his permission for us to marry." Clarissa met his gaze, as if to gauge his response, and then looked away.

"Ah...good. I-I trust you're not too disappointed."

"I suppose not, although I would have preferred Jensen tell me about it first." Her shoulders moved up and down in a slight shrug. "I'd hoped my engagement to Graham would have encouraged Miss Shields to accept my brother's proposal, but she had other ideas."

He stared at her, incredulous. "Do you mean to say you would have married Quinlan only to help your brother?"

"Naturally. Is that so very wrong?"

"Of course it is!"

"Why? Jensen intended to marry Mrs. Aynsworth to help *me*."

"That's different. Men ought to make sacrifices for their sisters."

Megan and Quinlan danced past, seemingly enjoying each other's company.

"I daresay some people wouldn't consider marriage to Graham to be a sacrifice," Clarissa said.

"So you *do* have strong feelings for him?"

"I like him, yes."

Theo ground his teeth together in frustration. "Do you love him?"

"I hardly think it's any of your business."

"And what if I choose to make it my business?"

He'd meant the question to be tender, but when her eyes widened, he realized it had sounded arrogant. Why had all his stage training deserted him just when he needed it most?

"Are you trying to interfere in my life again?"

"No!" He felt a trickle of perspiration roll down the middle of his back. "What I meant is, your brother and I were discussing your prospects, and he seemed to think it would be a good idea if you and I were to marry."

As soon as he spoke, he realized he'd blundered. Clarissa's eyes shone with unshed tears and her skin grew pale.

"He did, did he? Well, I wouldn't like to see you make a sacrifice either, Theo. You should marry where your heart leads you, and not for the convenience of others." She pulled away. "Excuse me, but I must have some fresh air."

Disappointed in himself, Theo watched her leave. What was wrong with him that he couldn't tell the woman of his dreams how much he loved her? He'd made it seem as if his marriage proposal was Rowe's idea, when it had been *his* all along. Vowing to rectify his mistake, he made his way off the dance floor and followed Clarissa toward the double doors. When he caught up to her, he would blurt out his feelings, no matter what.

In the hallway outside the ballroom, however, she was nowhere to be found. Theo sped toward the front of the house, but saw no sign of her there, either. She'd mentioned needing fresh air, so he concluded she must have gone to the garden for a walk. He retraced his steps, passed the ballroom, and went outside. The patio was lit by oil lamps and a nearly full moon, but he didn't see Clarissa there, either.

There was no answer when he called out her name, but he didn't really expect one. She probably wished he would crawl under a rock, not to be heard from for a fortnight. If she wanted to be alone, she would more than likely head for the gazebo. He took one of the oil lamps down off its hook and left the patio behind.

••••

From the middle of the dance floor, Megan watched Clarissa break away from Theo, clearly distressed. To Megan's dismay, Clarissa left the ballroom, followed a short while later by Theo.

Quinlan chuckled with delight. "Lover's quarrel?"

He seemed to find a mean-spirited amusement in the misfortune of others, and Megan was taken aback.

"If so, I'm certain it will be soon mended," she replied. "Lady Clarissa and Mr. King care for one another deeply."

A small muscle quivered in Quinlan's cheek. "I'm sure you're perfectly right."

The song ended shortly thereafter, and he bent to kiss her hand. "Thank you, Miss Shields. I've seldom danced with a more charming partner."

As soon as he turned away, Megan hastened from the ballroom as quickly as decorum would allow. The man was well-mannered, but underneath the charm was an unpleasant undercurrent. She'd seen the same sort of gentleman before, in Ireland. Such men usually aspired to politics—or crime. Her own father had possessed a similar outward charm, but had been capable of cruelty to his wife.

She stepped into the ladies' sitting room down the hall. Clarissa, clearly upset, was perched on a chair in the corner, pretending to fiddle with the buttons on her glove. Megan sank into the nearest chair and gave her a sympathetic smile.

"Are you well, milady?"

Clarissa shook her head. "A pox on all men, including my brother! Did you know he's been working on Theo's sympathies, trying to get him to propose?"

"I can scarcely believe that."

"Theo as much as said so just now."

"Something's got twisted around, then. Mr. King needs no further inducement to marry you than his own feelings."

"He's not spoken to me about his feelings, Miss Shields, and I'm beginning to think he has none."

"Not every gentleman is capable of expressing himself as glibly as Mr. Quinlan." Megan gave her a sidelong glance. "Perhaps a little flirtation on your part will loosen Mr. King's tongue?"

"I can't imagine flirting with him. Last night was just a pretense."

"I believe when you pretended to be in love, it was then Mr. King finally realized how he really felt. He needs to know you care for him more than just as a friend."

A myriad of expressions crossed Clarissa's face, culminating with a soft smile. "I suppose it couldn't hurt."

"Let Mr. King escort you into dinner, and you can flirt with him then."

"But Graham—"

"I'll dine with Mr. Quinlan in your stead." She tried to keep the distaste from her voice. "Now, if you'll excuse me, I must return to the ballroom. The next waltz is your brother's."

"I'll come too." As Clarissa stood, she caught Megan's hand. "Thank you, Miss Shields. You've been more help to me than you can imagine."

••••

Myles crept into his darkened sitting room, jacket in hand. "Estella?" His whisper received no reply. He moved over to the moonlit window to get a glimpse of the garden below. An abrupt noise near the doorway made him jump.

"Estella?"

"Yes."

"What are you doing?"

"I bumped into the doorframe. I can't see anything."

She joined him at the window, clad in a pinafore dress. The ends of her sash were dragging on the floor, and her golden ringlets formed a loose halo around her shoulders.

"Can you tie my sash in back?" she whispered.

He grimaced. "I can't tie a bow very well yet."

"How did you tie your shoes?"

With a shrug, he bent one of his knees to show her the flopping laces on his boot. "I didn't."

Estella made a sound of exasperation. "You're going to fall flat on your face like that." She dragged a chair into the light. "Put your foot there and I'll show you how to tie a proper bow."

After a bit of trial and error, Myles managed to get the hang of it. Thereafter, he tied Estella's sash.

"It doesn't look very nice," he admitted afterward.

"Never mind. Nobody will see it."

"Did you have any trouble sneaking out of your room?"

"No, my nanny was eager to get downstairs because the servants are having a celebration, too." Her eyes sparkled in the light from the window. "So what are we going to do now?"

"I thought we could spy on people in the garden."

"What if we get caught?"

"Are you afraid?"

"Ha! Never." She paused. "How do we get down there? I'm not climbing out the window."

"No, silly. We sneak out the servants' entrance when nobody's looking." He grabbed her hand. "Follow me."

"You've done this before...haven't you?"

"Loads of times," he lied.

More easily than Myles would have imagined, he and Estella managed to slip from the house undetected. The strains of orchestra music spilled out from the open windows of the ballroom nearby, and they edged closer to take a peek.

Estella pointed. "Oh, look, there's Mama! She's the one in the pink satin dress."

"She looks very pretty."

A man came out onto the patio just then, and Myles yanked Estella down so she wouldn't be seen.

"Clarissa?" a man's voice rang out.

"That's Lord Apollo!" Myles whispered. "Quick, let's get into the garden before we're caught!"

Bent almost double, they sped down the path until they neared the gazebo, then crouched in between several decorative boxwood bushes and a tall hedge. He and Estella collapsed in a fit of giggles.

"That was close," Myles said.

"Shh! Someone's coming!"

Gravel crunched underneath Theo's feet as he approached, lantern held high. "Clarissa, are you out here? Please let me talk to you."

Myles held his breath, and Estella clapped her hand over her mouth. Myles stole a glance around the side of the boxwood and watched Theo pause only a few feet away. The man peered into the empty gazebo, sighed, and lowered the lantern. Seemingly out of nowhere, a second man crept up from behind, brandishing a poker. *Quinlan!* Before Myles could shout out a warning, the man swung his weapon at Theo's head, where it connected with a dull thud. Theo dropped his lantern with a crash and crumpled to the ground.

"If you'd just *stayed* dead when I killed you five years ago, Clarissa would have been mine!" Quinlan exclaimed. "It was the wretched fog that threw me off then, but I have the right man this time."

He held the poker like a spear and thrust it into the boxwood, as if sheathing it into a scabbard. When the metal tip protruded out the other side—a scant inch away from Estella's face—she screamed and fell backward. Quinlan, who'd been reaching both hands toward Theo's neck, pulled back.

"Who's there?"

Moments later, Quinlan grabbed Estella by the hair, and yanked her upright.

"Hasn't anyone ever told you spying can be deadly?"

As Estella shrieked in horror, Myles extricated the poker from the bush and swung it in a downward arc at the man's arm.

"You let her go!"

The man howled in pain and his grip loosened. Estella managed to twist out of his grasp.

"Run, Estella!" Myles yelled. "Hide!"

Screaming like a siren, the little girl sprinted off into the darkness. Although Quinlan lunged forward to stop her, Myles swung the poker again, striking the man on the back. With a curse and a snarl, Quinlan rounded on the boy, wrested the weapon from his grip, and slapped him across the face. Myles fell to the ground, stunned. The man lifted the poker high overhead, preparing to strike. Cornered, the lad had nowhere to run and no means to escape. He cringed and braced himself for the blow...but then a bleeding Theo lurched to his feet.

"Don't touch that boy!"

With a visceral growl, Theo tackled Quinlan to the ground, sending the poker flying. As the two men began to grapple in a fierce battle, Myles sped toward the house to get help.

••••

When Clarissa entered the ballroom with Megan, her brother hastened toward them immediately. The vulnerable expression on Rowe's face made Clarissa ache for him.

"Miss Shields, I was worried you'd be late for our waltz."

"I wouldn't have missed it for anything, Lord Rowe."

Couples were beginning to assemble on the dance floor, and Rowe offered her his arm. "Shall we?"

Before Megan could move, Myles shot into the ballroom, grabbed Rowe by the sleeve, and began to tug him toward the door.

"There was a man in the garden with a poker—Mr. Quinlan—and he hit Lord Apollo with it over the head! Now they're fighting, but Apollo is bleeding something terrible! You've got to help him!"

Clarissa turned icy cold from the inside out and a strangled sound emerged from deep in her throat.

"Find Brandon and ask him to come," Rowe told her. "I'll go with Myles."

The two darted off, but Clarissa's feet seemed to be rooted to the spot. Megan peered into her face. "Go on with Lord Rowe and Myles, and I'll find Mr. Brandon King."

"Bless you!"

Heedless of propriety, Clarissa picked up her skirts and sped down the hall, pausing only long enough to pick up one of the oil lanterns illuminating the patio. Apparently Rowe had done the same thing, since a bobbling light was proceeding her up ahead. She practically leaped down the stairs into the garden, dodging around rose beds and short, decorative hedges. When she reached Rowe, he was bent over a prone figure. Estella and Myles stood several feet away. Although Estella looked wretched, Myles had a black eye and his features were contorted with grief.

Clarissa gulped. "Theo? Is he—"

Rowe straightened, and she nearly fainted. Theo was lying on the ground, motionless. Rivulets of crimson streaked down his forehead and cheeks, staining his white shirt collar. Her brother was staring at him, as if in shock.

"No!" Aghast, Clarissa stepped over Theo's body and knelt by his side. "I never told him I loved him!" She bent forward and laid her cheek against his chest. "I love you, Theo. I've always loved you, ever since I can remember."

Broken-hearted, she sobbed. A few moments later, she felt a hand stroking her back. She pulled away, startled. Theo's eyes were half-open, and a soft smile curved his lips.

"I love you too, Clarissa."

"You're not dead!"

"Not yet, though it wasn't for lack of trying." Theo glanced at Rowe, who seemed to be struck dumb. "Help me to sit up, would you?"

As gently as Rowe could manage, he lifted his friend into a sitting position.

Theo winced. "I'm bleeding like a stuck pig. Have you a handkerchief, old boy?"

"Yes, of course."

When Rowe produced a linen square from his pocket, Clarissa took it from him. "I'll do it." She pressed the cloth over the gash on Theo's scalp and he inhaled sharply.

"Should I stop?" she exclaimed.

"No, it must be done or I'll bleed to death. It just hurts like the dickens."

Brandon arrived, along with Megan, Larken, and several servants. As Brandon knelt by his brother, his eyes grew wide. "Who did this to you?"

"Quinlan. I believe he meant to finish the job he started five years ago."

Everyone gasped.

"Apparently he followed me to Liverpool that night in order to do me in, but because of the fog, he killed the wrong man." He glanced up at Megan. "I'm sorry, Miss Shields, but I *am* responsible for the death of your brother after all."

With a soft keening noise, she crumpled to the ground.

Chapter Fourteen
Wishes

When Megan swam to consciousness, she was lying on her bed with a cold compress on her forehead. Bess was hovering nearby with a worried expression.

"How are you feeling, Miss Shields?"

"I don't know, really."

"Can't say I blame you for that. The attack in the garden has the staff in a tizzy."

When Megan made an attempt to sit up, she was quite woozy. In addition, a tender knot was swelling on the back of her head.

"How long have I been unconscious?"

"For a good while. The surgeon said you hit your head when you fainted."

"I fainted, did I? Och, I'm not usually so fragile, but I'd never seen so much blood before. How does Mr. King fare?"

"Lord Rowe will know more about that than I do. He's been pacing outside in the hallway, waiting to come in. With your permission, I'll let him answer your questions."

"Do I...do I look all right?" After everything that had happened, Megan knew the question was silly, but she couldn't help herself.

"Let me tidy your hair. You picked up a stray leaf or two when you were on the ground."

After a bit of fussing, Bess propped Megan up with extra pillows and pronounced her fit for company. When the maid opened the door, Rowe hastened inside with a concerned expression.

"How are you, Miss Shields?" He carried a straight-backed chair over to Megan's bedside and sat down.

"Well enough, I suppose. How is Mr. King?"

"He has a nasty gash, but the surgeon is attending him now."

"The light wasn't very good in the garden, but Myles also looked injured?"

"Quinlan backhanded him, Myles said."

"Good heavens!"

"Yes, Quinlan is truly a villain of the lowest sort. He tried to do Theo in with a poker tonight, and if Myles and Estella hadn't interrupted the assault, he might have succeeded."

"Why would Mr. Quinlan resort to murder?"

"Because of a long-standing grudge. I believe Quinlan has always been obsessed with Clarissa. He knew she was in love with Theo, and wanted him out of the way. Years ago, when Theo went to Liverpool to stop Mariah Pettigrew from going to America, Quinlan planned to kill him then. Unfortunately, he followed the wrong man in the fog and killed your brother instead."

Megan squeezed her eyes shut for a long moment, wishing desperately she could blot the image from her mind. "Poor Paddy."

"Theo is devastated to learn the truth, I assure you. He thinks you'll never forgive him."

"Not too long ago, he would have been right. Now that I've become acquainted with him and his family, however, I hold him blameless."

"He'll be extraordinarily relieved to hear that."

"Has Mr. Quinlan been caught yet?"

"We've contacted the local constable, and he's on the case. I can't imagine Quinlan will evade capture for long. All the train stations and ports will be watched."

"At least I finally know what really happened to my brother."

"I hope closure brings you peace."

"Perhaps it will, in time." She sighed. "I suppose there's no reason for Mr. Waite to search for Mr. Osbourne, now that we know the truth."

"You sound sad. Was there some other reason you wished to speak with him?"

"I'd hoped he might want to know what had happened to Paddy. I would have liked to tell Mr. Osbourne how much he'd meant to my brother."

"Maybe he would like to hear from you."

Megan shook her head. "It's a silly notion. Paddy was only his driver, after all. I expect Mr. Osbourne has forgotten about him by now."

"Well, there's one other happy circumstance to be gleaned from tonight. Theo and Clarissa have finally professed their feelings for one another."

Megan smiled. "Have they now? I'm glad of it."

••••

The surgeon finished wrapping a bandage around Theo's head. "I hope that's not too tight?"

The throbbing in Theo's brain made him frown. "The bandage is the least of my worries. I've not had such a bad headache since overindulging during my university days."

"A drop or two of laudanum in a glass of water should alleviate your suffering."

Clarissa had been quietly standing by during the physician's ministrations. "I'll get it."

"Thank you, Clarissa." Theo watched the doctor pack his bag. "Have you had a look at Myles and Miss Shields?"

"The lad has a blackened eye which will improve with time. Miss Shields is resting comfortably and should be well by morning." The man smiled. "I'll come back tomorrow to change that bandage."

After the doctor took his leave, Clarissa brought Theo water with laudanum and helped him sip it.

"Bless you for that," he murmured.

As she put the glass down on his bedside table, however, he suddenly remembered the ball. "Oh, no! What about the party?"

She laughed. "Brandon, Larken, and a household full of well-trained servants are tending to your guests, none of whom are aware of what transpired in the garden. The children have been properly tucked into bed, and I understand Mrs. Aynsworth is being ably looked after by Sir Willard."

Theo managed to chuckle. "If she marries *him*, she's apt to be a young widow twice over."

"I'm sure such a thing would set tongues to wagging."

"Indeed it would." He paused. "Myles played quite the hero tonight...even if he *was* out of bed after hours."

"Your brother wouldn't dream of punishing him for that, would he?"

"Heavens, no. I'll have to think of a treat to reward the lad."

"He's brave, just like you and Brandon."

Theo gazed into Clarissa's beautiful eyes. "If you can find an unbruised spot anywhere, I'd dearly love a kiss."

She sat on his bed, bent forward, and pressed her lips gently to his. Even in his wretched condition, he felt his blood stir. When she pulled back, he felt bereft.

"I love you, Clarissa Alderforth. I wish I'd found a more romantic way to tell you, other than when I was lying on the ground and covered with blood."

He was alarmed to see tears moistening her lashes, but she gave him a smile. "I was so afraid I'd lost you again."

"Never."

Clarissa melted against him once more, and he held her nestled in the crook of one arm.

"I can't get down on bended knee at the moment, but would you consider marrying me at the soonest possible opportunity? In fact, I believe the vicar is downstairs."

She giggled. "Yes he is, but we haven't a license."

"Hang the license."

"Some formalities must be observed. I think Christmas will do."

The laudanum was taking effect, and he was drifting off to sleep. "Christmas it is."

••••

Rowe regarded his sister as she spread marmalade on her morning toast. "I'm giving the servants a few days off."

"What are we to do in the meantime?"

"I'd like you to pack some things and move into Graceling Hall. I've already sent a message, so the Kings will be expecting you."

Clarissa's eyebrows rose. "I've no objection, but what about you?"

"I've business in London, and I don't want you to stay here alone while Quinlan is at large."

She peered at him. "What business could you possibly have in London?"

"You're not to breathe a word to Miss Shields, but I intend to locate Mr. Osbourne. I believe she feels a bit of nostalgia where he is concerned, and I think it worthwhile to discover if he wishes to speak with her."

"And you'd like to spare her pain if he has no interest in doing so?"

"Yes. I don't really know what sort of man he is, so there's always the distinct possibility he won't."

Clarissa nodded her approval. "It's a very thoughtful gesture on your part, but what if Miss Shields wishes to leave Graceling Hall?"

"Beg her to delay until after your wedding. Surely, she can't object to another two months, especially after Mrs. Aynsworth is no longer around to bedevil her."

"Fair enough, but where shall I say you've gone?"

"Say only that I've gone to town to see about employment. That much is true enough. You have my permission to disclose the other, more pressing reason to Brandon, Theo, and Larken in private."

"Do you really intend to seek employment? Now that I'm to marry Theo, it's wholly unnecessary."

"After I locate Osbourne, I'll be making inquiries while I'm in town. I'd do anything to convince Miss Shields I can support her without relying on my friends." He paused. "If she agrees to marry me, would I have your blessing?"

"Wholeheartedly. I've grown to care about her very much. In fact, I believe she's the only woman I've ever met who can keep you in line…besides myself, of course."

Rowe pretended to take offense. "I needn't be kept in line!"

Clarissa laughed. "You're wrong about that, but let's not quarrel. I'll pack my things, and we'll drive over to Graceling Hall. You can leave the gig there and have James take you to the station."

"While I'm gone, I'd rather you not come back to the cottage."

"Don't be silly! I still have piano lessons to give. But don't worry, I won't come alone."

"See that you don't." He shook his head. "I won't rest easy until Quinlan is caught."

••••

In the drawing room, Megan was helping Larken sort through the large quantity of thank you notes from the morning post. The blond woman's hair was lit by sunlight from the window, which gave her an angelic aura.

"I'm so glad you're feeling better this morning, Miss Shields."

"Och aye, I'm perfectly fine. It's Mr. Theo King who has my concern."

"The physician is checking his wound right now." Larken shook her head. "I could never have imagined Mr. Quinlan was capable of such violence. I only spoke with him in the receiving line last night, of course, but he seemed rather lighthearted."

"His charm was only on the surface, I'm thinking. I had a lengthy conversation with the man and I found him to be mean-spirited."

Larken shuddered. "I wouldn't be at all surprised to learn he's fled the country to escape punishment for his crimes. By the way, Clarissa is coming around noon, to stay with us a few days. Rowe has business in

London, and he didn't want her to stay in the cottage by herself."

Megan felt a pang of guilt. "I expect he's gone to look for employment." She sighed. "He's a wonderful gentleman and deserves better."

"There are far worse things than a man earning an honest living."

"I agree, but Lord Rowe is so educated, refined, and elegant. I hate to think of him toiling away in an office, especially when it means he'll no longer be a proper member of society."

"Forgive me for prying, but I can see you care for him a great deal."

"That I do, but tender feelings don't put bread on the table. I wish His Lordship would wait for the London Season and find himself a pretty heiress to wed." She swallowed the emotions that threatened to overwhelm her. "I'm quite certain he'd have his pick of ladies who could make him happy." Despite her best efforts, her voice wavered.

Larken reached out a comforting hand. "Rowe will find happiness, no matter what his financial circumstance." She smiled. "He made a narrow escape from Mrs. Aynsworth, at least. She's gone riding with Sir Willard this morning."

"I suppose it's too much to hope that her horse throws her into the lake?"

Larken's laugh sounded like music. "One should never give up hope."

••••

Estella, clad in a traveling cloak and hat, peered at Myles's face. "Your bruise is terribly ugly now. It's turning green and yellow."

Despite her unflattering comment, he was still rather proud of his black eye. "I think it's interesting."

She giggled. "I wish I could stay a few more days to see what color it turns next." Her smile faded. "Mama thinks she's going to marry a baronet called Sir Willard."

"So she wasn't left out of musical chairs after all. Do you like the fellow?"

"I haven't met him yet. He's coming to London in a few days, to take us to the theater."

"The theater should be fun."

"I expect it will be."

"Your mother wasn't angry about the other night in the garden, was she?"

"She doesn't know I was there, actually. If I told the truth, my nanny would get the sack for neglecting me, and that would be unfair. Did you get punished?"

"No. Lord Apollo said he didn't approve of my sneaking out at night, but he said I saved his life. I'm to think of a reward and let him know what I want." Myles dug something out from his pocket. "The credit is half yours, really, so this is for you." He dropped a clear glass marble with swirled metal flecks into Estella's waiting palm. "It's my favorite one."

Her pink mouth formed an O. "I love it! And thank you for saving my life, too. I've never seen anyone act so brave."

Myles puffed out his chest a little. "It wasn't anything special. I mean, that's just what the King family gentlemen do."

She darted forward and planted a kiss on his lips. "I hope I see you again someday. You won't forget me, will you?"

Dazzled at the kiss, he could barely shake his head. "Never."

The golden retriever sitting at Myles's feet wagged his tail, as if the puppy could sense his master's mood. A few moments later, Ginny appeared in the sitting room doorway.

"Come along, lambs! James has brought the carriage around and it's time for Miss Estella to leave for the train station with her mama. Myles, you're to come downstairs and see our guests off."

Myles whistled for D'Artagnan to follow, and the trio trooped downstairs. Brandon, Larken, Megan, Clarissa, and Theo had assembled with Estella's mother in the courtyard, along with the staff and two hansoms. When they arrived, Estella's nanny and the lady's maid were just climbing into the trailing carriage.

To Myles's surprise, Mrs. Aynsworth beamed at him. "I heard about your bravery in saving Mr. King from that dreadful Mr. Quinlan! Thank you for being a good influence on my daughter. She seems quite transformed over the course of her visit."

"Thank you, Mrs. Aynsworth."

Myles met Estella's mischievous gaze and had to bite his lip to keep from giggling. James helped the two Aynsworth ladies into the first carriage, and as the convoy departed, D'Artagnan barked. Estella waved to Myles through the window, and he waved back as furiously as if his hand were on fire. When the carriage was out of view, a slight sadness descended. Myles swallowed his emotions and tried not to cry.

After Theo ushered everyone back inside and into the drawing room, Brandon patted Myles on the back. "I'm glad you made a new friend."

"Estella and I didn't like each other in the beginning. In fact, I hated her. But we finally worked things out."

Myles sat down on the carpet, next to his puppy, and contented himself with stroking the dog's fur.

A chuckle escaped Brandon's lips. "There can be many pitfalls where ladies are concerned. Congratulations on escaping from your first encounter unscathed."

"I agree," Theo said. "Congratulations are in order." Several days had passed since the party, so he was sporting only a light bandage now. "Have you decided yet what you'd like as your reward?"

"Yes...I want us all to live here at Graceling Hall, forever."

Theo winced. "It's not within my power to grant you that particular wish."

The boy made no attempt to hide his disappointment.

"Don't be unhappy, Myles," Larken said. "We aren't going anywhere for a little while." She exchanged a shy glance with Brandon. "It's early days yet to know for sure, but we believe we'll be here for the better part of seven months at the very least."

Clarissa gasped. "Oh, Larken!" She gave Larken a hug.

Myles was confused. "Why seven months?"

"That's how much longer it will take for the baby to arrive." Brandon put his arms around Larken and kissed her on the forehead.

Megan exclaimed with delight. "A wee wain? Och aye, I'm so happy for you both!"

Theo sat down abruptly, as if someone had shoved him backward. "I'm to be an uncle?"

Larken laughed. "Shall I ring for the smelling salts?"

"I'll be fine in a minute. What with the blow to my head, your news made me a little dizzy." Theo looked up at her, stricken, before springing to his feet. "Are you all right? Perhaps you should sit down."

She waved him away. "I'm perfectly fine. In fact, I've never felt better."

Although the adults seemed to know what was going on, Myles was still confused. "A baby's coming here in seven months? I don't understand. It only took two weeks for me to sail to England from America."

"I'm in the family way." Larken was beaming. "Brandon and I are going to have a child."

Myles wasn't at all sure how he felt about a new baby. "Well...if a baby means we'll be staying at Graceling Hall, I'll put up with ten of them!"

••••

Exhausted and footsore, Rowe finally arrived at a luxurious Mayfair address—the home of Mr. Osbourne. When the butler answered the door, Rowe offered him his calling card.

"Is Mr. Osbourne at home?"

The butler peered at his card. "Wait here, please, milord."

As the door shut, Rowe drew a deep breath and said a quiet prayer that his quest had not been in vain. He'd spent days visiting every gentlemen's club in town, asking doormen if they were acquainted with a Mr. Osbourne from Hertfordshire. Finally, he managed to obtain an address...but whether the gentleman would receive him remained to be seen.

Several minutes later the door opened, and the butler ushered him into the drawing room. A tall, silver-haired gentleman stood as he entered, and Rowe bowed.

"Thank you for seeing me, Mr. Osbourne."

The elderly man gestured toward a sofa. "Please have a seat. Are we acquainted, Lord Rowe?"

"Not at all, but I have some news for you. I understand you had Paddy Shields in your employ as a driver at one time?"

Osbourne's eyebrows rose, and he appeared momentarily confused. "Why yes, I did. Shields went off to Ireland on an errand five years ago, and he never returned or sent word of his whereabouts. I've never been so disappointed in someone in my entire life."

"There's no gentle way to tell you his fate, I'm afraid. He didn't return because he was attacked and killed in Liverpool before he could leave England."

"Merciful heavens!" The gentleman's lined face became parchment white, and he gripped the arms of his chair with his hands.

Rowe became worried. "I can see you've had a shock. Shall I summon help?"

"No." Osbourne closed his eyes for several moments, and a spasm of pain crossed his features. When he opened his eyes, he looked older than before. "I *am* shocked...and grieved. Furthermore, I'm mortified I could have thought ill of the lad." He shook his head. "We'd grown so close, I should have known he'd never abandon me voluntarily."

"I never met him, unfortunately, but I *am* acquainted with his sister."

"Megan, wasn't she called?"

"Yes. Let me start from the beginning..."

Rowe told Osbourne everything he knew, from the fateful evening Paddy and Theo met each other in Liverpool, up to Quinlan's attack on Theo two nights ago.

"And so now Miss Shields is staying at Graceling Hall, but how long we can convince her to remain is anyone's guess. She's exceedingly independent."

Osbourne chuckled. "Shields used to tell me stories about his younger sister and her temper."

"Indeed. Although she doesn't know I'm here on her behalf, she has expressed a desire to make your acquaintance."

"Has she?" Rowe felt Osbourne's shrewd gaze. "Do I detect more than a passing interest in the young lady on your part?"

"I only wish the best for her."

The elderly gentleman smiled. "Shields would have liked to see his sister married to a wealthy earl, I wager."

Rowe felt his color rise. Although it was true he was nearly beggared, he would prefer Mr. Osbourne remain unaware of that fact.

"I expect many wealthy and worthy gentlemen would welcome the opportunity to woo Miss Shields. She's beautiful, very talented with the harp, and exceedingly intelligent."

Osbourne stroked his beard. "Your description of the lass intrigues me." He frowned. "I had a daughter once, you know." He gestured toward a portrait of a pretty child, hung in a prominent spot over the fireplace. "She died of consumption before I could watch her grow up, and I always felt cheated."

"I'm so terribly sorry."

"Thank you."

Once more, Rowe felt Osbourne's eyes upon him...as if he were being weighed and measured. Had he unwittingly trespassed on the man's privacy or offended him in some way? *If so, my efforts to help Megan have been for naught.*

He cleared his throat. "Well...thank you for seeing me. With your permission, sir, I'll let Miss Shields know you were grieved to hear about her brother's death. That will mean a great deal to her, I'm sure."

Just as Rowe reached for his hat, Osbourne surprised him.

"You're nothing at all like your father."

"Pardon me?"

"Cecil Jensen Alderforth, the Sixth Earl of Rowe, was a fool and a gambler—two conditions that ought not be said in the same breath."

The hackles on Rowe's neck rose. If Osbourne had known his father, he must also know the entire family fortune had been lost. If so, why had he pretended otherwise by making a remark about Miss Shields marrying a wealthy earl? The man must be toying with him for some unknown reason.

"I didn't realize you were acquainted with my father, sir." His tone was deliberately chilly.

"I meant no offense. Perhaps I should have said I knew who you were right away, but I thought you'd be quite different. I confess, you've surprised me—which isn't easy at my age."

"I'm not understanding you."

"I thought you were here to ask for my help. Until now, I was unsure if I should give it."

Taken aback, Rowe peered at Osbourne. "Regarding what, exactly?"

"In recovering your estate."

Chapter Fifteen

Osbourne

Rowe was puzzled. "You have me at a loss, sir. As you must be well aware, my father squandered his fortune at the gaming tables. There's nothing to recover and no help you could offer."

"I beg to differ. Your father certainly never told you that he was cheated out of his fortune by a scurvy knave who ought to be behind bars. Are you acquainted with Sir Willard Vandenberg?"

"Sir Willard purchased our family estate—Symean House—when we were forced to sell it."

"With funds he stole from your father—and likely underpaid you for it to boot."

Rowe's jaw dropped. "What? Forgive me, but I have difficulty believing you, sir. My father never breathed a word to me about any of this, and during his lingering illness, he had ample opportunity."

"He didn't know." Osbourne gave Rowe a sympathetic glance. "Some men are consumed by vice. Your father was such a man. Unfortunately, Vandenberg knew of his predilection and took advantage of him by cheating at cards abominably."

"How do you come by your information?"

"I was there. I suspected Vandenberg had cheated at the time, but it was later confirmed to me by his former mistress."

"This is quite shocking. The man has even attempted to court my sister upon many occasions, but she wanted nothing to do with him."

"Vandenberg desired everything that was your father's. He couldn't manage to secure a barony, but he did buy himself the title of baronet by greasing the proper palms. Aren't you going to ask how we're to recover your fortune?"

"I'm quite curious, actually."

"Are you any good at cards?"

"Quite good, but I turned my back on gaming early on when I realized where it could lead."

"Unlike you, Vandenberg can't resist a high-stakes card game. We should provide one for him, when he's next in London."

"I understand he's here, to court Mrs. Aynsworth."

"Good! That will make it easier."

"What have you in mind?"

"We're going to wrest his ill-gotten gains away from him in the same manner he stole from your father. We'll cheat." He paused. "The only challenge will be in finding another fellow to work with us who could pose as a gambler—preferably a drunken foreigner whose enormous wealth would provide an irresistible temptation."

A slow smile spread across Rowe's face. "I know just the man."

••••

Arm in arm, Theo and Clarissa took a slow stroll in the garden. His new fiancée kept stealing solicitous looks at him, as if she feared he would lose consciousness. He found the attention to be endearing and heartwarming at the same time.

"You needn't think I'm about to keel over." He chuckled. "I'm quite on the mend."

"Nevertheless, I don't want you to become overtired."

"If I say I feel faint, will you kiss me?"

She slid her arms around his waist and planted a long, lingering kiss on his lips. He closed his eyes and relished the intoxicating sensations flowing through his veins.

"Mmm," he murmured. "Now I really do feel dizzy."

"Good." Clarissa pressed herself closer. "You may lean against me all you wish."

He nuzzled her neck. "Lucky thing your brother isn't here to raise any objections."

"I don't think he'd dare."

He pulled back slightly. "Speaking of Rowe, why did he depart for London so precipitously?"

"Come, let's sit in the gazebo and I'll explain everything."

Clarissa took him by the hand. As they stepped into the vine-covered structure and sat on one of the benches, she told him of her brother's effort to locate Mr. Osbourne on Megan's behalf.

"Apparently Miss Shields confided her wish to become acquainted with Mr. Osbourne. Jensen set off to make her wish come true...and find employment as well."

"He really is besotted with the lady, isn't he?"

"I've never seen him care for anyone more."

Theo shook his head. "Rowe and Miss Shields went at each other like a pair of Siamese fighting fish at first, but happily they found common ground. I wish he'd accept my help to marry her."

"If you were in his shoes, would you accept his help to marry me?"

"An unfair question if I ever heard one."

"Not at all. Pride can be difficult to overcome. You fought Brandon when he tried to reinstate your inheritance. If you were still penniless, would you have proposed to me?"

His eyebrows drew together. "If you put it that way, I suppose you're right...but I'd rather not think about it."

Theo moved in for another kiss, but then Seagate appeared with a silver salver in hand.

"Forgive the interruption, sir, but a message has arrived for you from Lord Rowe, marked urgent and confidential."

"What on earth?" Clarissa exclaimed. "I hope nothing is amiss!"

Alarmed, Theo took the message from the salver and opened it with the letter opener the butler proffered. "Thank you, Seagate."

As the butler turned away, Theo extracted the stationery from within the envelope and read the contents.

Clarissa clutched his arm. "Is Jensen in some sort of difficulty?"

"Wait a moment." Theo continued to scan the letter. "He's located Mr. Osbourne." His eyes widened as he read the next part. "Ha!"

"What is it?"

"I can't be more explicit just now, but your brother needs my assistance." He folded the letter, slipped it into his pocket, and stood. "I must reply to this right away, and advise my valet to pack my trunk. I'm taking the afternoon train to London."

Clarissa shot to her feet, her arms akimbo. "You must tell me what's going on!"

"Forgive me, but I can't betray your brother's confidence. Be assured, however, you'll know everything before long." He smiled and kissed her cheek. "For now, let's just say I'm to invest in a theatrical production."

••••

While Theo ate a quick lunch with Megan, Clarissa, and the rest of the family, servants loaded his packed trunk into the carriage. Even before the end of the meal, he left in order to catch the one o'clock train.

"I must dash, but please don't get up." Theo deposited a kiss onto Clarissa's cheek. "I'll send word when my business with Rowe is concluded."

He strode from the room, seemingly taking Clarissa's happy mood along with him. Although she knew he was helping her brother in some significant way, she wished she didn't have to give him up quite so soon after their engagement. Megan seemed to know how she was feeling because she gave her an encouraging smile.

"Perhaps this afternoon would be a good time to begin planning your wedding?"

"What a wonderful idea, Miss Shields," Larken said. "Perhaps the three of us can put our heads together after lunch?"

Clarissa was grateful for the suggestion. "I'd enjoy that very much."

Brandon chuckled. "You don't have to wait until then on my account. Myles and I are going riding in a few minutes, and I must change into riding clothes."

He folded his napkin next to his plate and hastened off.

Larken glanced at Clarissa. "I hope you've no objection to having the wedding breakfast at Graceling Hall. I long to have a splendid wedding celebration here, with beautiful hothouse flowers and all the trimmings. Oh, and the biggest cake imaginable!"

Her enthusiasm was infectious, and Clarissa felt her lips curve into a smile.

"Perhaps Miss Shields will agree to play the harp at the breakfast," Larken continued. "The guests would certainly enjoy a romantic ballad or two."

"Oh yes, Miss Shields, your music would make the day perfect," Clarissa said. "In fact, I'll be counting on you to help me with everything, if you're willing."

Larken nodded. "Indeed, my delicate condition will prevent me from doing quite as much as I might like. You'll help us, won't you, Miss Shields?"

Megan gave the both of them a level glance. "You aren't really needing my help, are you? I'm perfectly aware you're saying as much to keep me at Graceling Hall."

Clarissa's smile faded and Larken frowned.

"Nevertheless, I'd love to be a part of your wedding plans." Megan's eyes glistened. "Truth be told, the longer I stay here, the less I want to leave."

Larken brightened. "Put all thoughts of leaving aside, then, at least until the New Year."

"If I stay, you must allow me to be useful," Megan said.

"I've a task for you," Clarissa said. "Jensen doesn't want me to go to the cottage alone, but I have piano lessons to give the next few mornings. If you wouldn't mind accompanying me, that would be very helpful."

"I'd be glad to go with you, to be sure," Megan said.

Larken broached the topic of menus, but Clarissa was terribly pleased with herself and only half attended to the conversation. Megan had agreed to stay for the time being, and she looked forward to telling Rowe when she saw him next.

••••

Osbourne sat in the great room of his gentleman's club, seemingly engrossed in the morning newspaper.

"Osbourne!" came a familiar voice. "I haven't seen you here in a while."

The silver-haired man glanced up, feigning surprise. "If it isn't Sir Willard Vandenberg! How have you been?"

The baronet settled himself on a nearby chair. "Tolerably well, thank you."

"What brings you to town just now?"

"In pursuit of a lady, of course." Vandenberg chuckled. "And you?"

"Cards." Osbourne winked.

Vandenberg raised one eyebrow. "Must be a very interesting game to bring you out of retirement."

Osbourne waved his fingers, dismissively. "Oh, you know how it is..." He trailed off with a shrug.

A guffaw followed. "Come now, Osbourne. Up in Newcastle I hardly ever hear anything of interest. What's going on?"

"It's hardly worth the notice of a baronet."

Vandenberg's lips pressed together in a thin line. "I insist you tell me what's afoot and let me decide for myself."

"All right, but you won't want anything to do with it once you know who's involved. You remember Cecil Jensen Alderforth, the Sixth Earl of Rowe, don't you? You fleeced him rather thoroughly at one point."

Another guffaw. "He's not involved! Stupid chap's been six feet under for years."

"No, it's his son."

"Rowe? I didn't realize he'd taken up gaming."

"The idiotic lad is apparently desperate to regain a semblance of wealth so he can court some poor colleen."

"Ha! I caught a brief glimpse of an Irish girl at the King ball several days ago."

"That must be the one he's after."

"She's rather luscious, admittedly, but Rowe's a fool if he wants to marry her. He ought to bed the lass and be done with it."

Osbourne gritted his teeth in anger, but passed it off as a smile. "Indeed. The word is, Rowe has cultivated the company of some vulgar Yankee who made an ungodly amount of money in railroads and lumber in the west. He's rich as Croesus, and Rowe plans to best him at cards." He laughed. "I plan to best them both, of course."

"I think you've been had, old boy." Vandenburg's skepticism reeked from his pores like stale wine. "Rowe hasn't got any money to play deep."

"I've been assured his friends have advanced him a large sum, but I'll make sure the bank has verified his stake before the first hand is dealt."

"Probably the King brothers. Rowe and those two lads were always thick as thieves."

"Oh well, I knew you wouldn't be interested. Besides which, the Yank's game of choice is poker."

As Osbourne glanced at Vandenberg, he watched the man's pupils dilate with excitement.

"Wait just a moment! Poker, did you say? I happened to pick up the game when I was last in Bath."

"Did you now? I've studied poker myself. In truth, I'm rather good at it."

"I might like to sit in a hand or two."

"Would you really? The game's being held in a little private gambling hell near Chelsea, two nights hence." Osbourne produced his calling card and scribbled an address on it. "You'll have to bring this with you for admittance. The proprietress's name is Miss Josie."

"Jolly good."

When Vandenberg reached for the card, Osbourne held it in place with a fingertip. "Are you sure you want to come? Truly, this game won't be for the faint-hearted."

"No fair trying to discourage me now."

With a sigh, Osbourne slid the card over. "All right. Things will get started at ten o'clock sharp. If you're late, I can't guarantee you a spot at the table."

"And, er, what brand of cards am I to expect?"

"De La Rue, naturally."

Vandenberg pumped his hand. "Thank you, Osbourne."

"It should be a memorable evening. I can feel the excitement already."

••••

Although Brandon had offered Clarissa and Megan the use of a regular carriage, Rowe's sister insisted on taking her gig. They set off down the driveway the following morning, with Clarissa at the reins.

"I do believe you're as independent as I am, driving your own self and all," Megan said. "I thought most great ladies never lifted a finger to do anything."

"Perhaps some don't, but if I never lifted a finger to do anything, nothing would ever get done! After Jensen and I sold Symean House, we learned to shift for ourselves, more or less. We managed to retain a cook, a housekeeper, and a part-time gardener, but I look after my own clothes and arrange my own hair."

"I confess I've enjoyed having a lady's maid very much. Do you feel the lack?"

"After I'm married, I'd love to have a lady's maid again, but I think I'll always be a trifle more self-reliant than is strictly fashionable."

"That's why we get along so well, I'm thinking."

The two ladies shared a laugh. Megan enjoyed the relatively short drive through the neighborhood. Leaves were falling in earnest, and the formerly balmy weather had given way to a slight crisp, refreshing breeze.

"Winter's creeping a wee bit closer every day, I reckon."

"I hope we get a great deal of snow this year."

"I'd like that. Belfast never gets more than few days of snow."

As they passed the church and graveyard, Megan felt a tug on her heartstrings. Clarissa followed her gaze. "It's still very difficult for you, isn't it?"

"That it is. What's worse is remembering how angry I was, thinking my brother had abandoned me." She averted her eyes and took a deep, cleansing breath. "I hope Paddy forgives me."

"I'm sure he does. You were only thirteen when you lost contact with him, after all. I think your feelings were perfectly normal."

Megan glanced at Clarissa. "Are you afraid Mr. Quinlan is still lurking about?"

"Not at all. He'd have better sense than to hang around here, where he's more likely to be apprehended. The police questioned his driver—a man named Fergus—but he didn't seem to have a clue where his master had gone."

"I met Fergus. I'd take him at his word."

"Well, Fergus told the constable he'd taken his master home from the ball early. Graham's clothes were in disarray and he had bruises on his face, but he explained to Fergus that he'd had too much to drink and had taken a tumble down the patio stairs."

"What a cool liar!"

"Indeed. By the time the constable came to arrest Graham, a horse was missing from the stables and he'd gone without a word to any of his staff."

"I'm so glad you didn't marry him!"

Clarissa shuddered. "So am I. A man capable of murder surely would have had no compunction about hurting his wife."

Before long, they'd reached the cottage, which was a picturesque, two-story Tudor structure framed by majestic oaks and short trimmed hedges. In the back, Megan spied a pretty rose garden, surrounded by taller privacy hedges. A smile of pleasure spread across her lips.

"What a charming home!"

"It's where the former caretaker for Symean House used to live. Jensen partitioned the cottage, garden, and two acres of land for us, and sold the rest of the estate to Sir Willard. You can see our former home if you pass beyond that hedge in the back."

"It's a palace compared to what I'm used to."

After Clarissa drove the gig into the small barn, Megan helped her furnish the horse with a bucket of water and one of oats. Clarissa brushed off her hands afterwards and fished a ring of keys from a pocket. "Shall we go inside the house?"

The interior of the cozy cottage featured a great deal of wood, with oak floors and carved oak paneling. Many of the rooms had plasterwork ceilings decorated with floral and leaf medallions, and the multi-paned windows let in a great deal of light. While Clarissa met with her pupil in the parlor, where the piano was located, Megan went exploring. She sat in the library for a short while, admiring the number of volumes and breadth of subjects on the bookshelves. Rowe was certainly well-read, but judging from his conversation, she'd already known as much. Thereafter, she wandered through the kitchen and out the back, where the garden spread out in all its splendor. Although she had no doubt it would be more spectacular in spring, many of the rose bushes were still in bloom.

Halting piano chords were flowing from the cottage, and Megan marveled at Clarissa's patience with her somewhat unskilled pupil. She strolled through the garden and ducked through an opening in the privacy hedge, hoping to catch a glimpse of Symean House. A short walk later, the magnificent structure became visible—a neoclassical edifice of breathtaking beauty. Until now, she'd not quite realized the extent of terrible loss Clarissa and Rowe had suffered. Gazing at their former residence, Megan suddenly felt tiny and insignificant. If His Lordship still owned that estate, would he have ever given her a second glance?

With a sigh, she returned to the caretaker's garden and spent a few minutes perched on a bench, watching bees visit various blossoms. As she sat, her thoughts turned toward London. Rowe could not have been successful in finding employment if he needed Theo's help. Should he manage to secure some sort of position, however, would she reconsider his proposal? Could she ever make an earl truly content? Her heart said yes, a thousand times over, but her mind continued to have doubts. Lady Rowe, formerly known as Megan Shields? The notion sounded dreadfully far-fetched.

Movement at the break in the hedge caught her eye, making her jump. Was someone lurking about, watching her? A sudden chilly breeze made her shiver. As she stood, she swallowed her fear and decided to confront the voyeur. Before she'd taken more than a few steps, however, Clarissa appeared at the kitchen doorway and waved. Megan hesitated. The man on the other side of the hedge was undoubtedly a servant from Symean House who'd wondered why she was on the property without permission. In fact, there'd been a stand of apple trees not too far away, and he probably suspected her of scrumping! No sense in inviting censure for trespassing if she could avoid it, so Megan hastened toward the cottage without looking back.

Suzanne G. Rogers

Chapter Sixteen
Gambling Hell

Vandenberg presented himself at the address written on Osbourne's calling card, at a quarter to ten o'clock in the evening. The gruff doorman peered at the card in the illumination cast from the nearby gas streetlight before admitting him to the premises, which appeared to be a converted townhouse.

The smoke-filled gaming room, also known in the vernacular as a gambling hell, was filled with wealthy men and women in search of dice and vice. Liquor flowed freely from the bar, and several heavily rouged ladies circulated amongst the gentlemen, trying to drum up business of one sort or another.

As Vandenberg glanced around the room, he saw no one he knew. The glazed expressions of the well-heeled clientele as they went about the business of winning money, however, was very familiar to him. The hazard table seemed to be particularly lively, but even though it was surrounded by dandies and sumptuously clad ladies, it held no allure for him. Cards were his game, and he would stick to what worked. Nevertheless, the sound of rattling dice and cheers from the patrons always stirred his blood and quickened his pulse.

The proprietress, clad in a low-cut gown, greeted the baronet. "Welcome, sir. I'm Miss Josie." The pretty woman's smile was dazzling, but Vandenberg was so distracted by the scent of money, he barely noticed. "What can I get you to drink?"

"Brandy." The top of Osbourne's head, barely visible in the back, caught his eye. "Aha, I see my friend is already here. Be so kind as to have the brandy brought to my table."

"As you wish."

As Vandenberg moved toward Osbourne, an ebullient, florid-faced gentleman nearly bumped into him because he was so busy counting the cash in his hand.

"Oh, sorry, old boy." The man chortled with glee as he folded the stack of twenty-pound notes into his billfold. "I just won a bloody fortune at cribbage!"

"You have my congratulations."

"Thank you, sir!"

The man ambled toward the bar, and Vandenberg couldn't help but smile. By hook or by crook, he himself had strolled through many a gambling hell, just as satisfied. Continuing on his way, the thrill of anticipation lifted the hair at the back of his neck. The poker games he'd participated in during his sojourn to Bath had only whetted his appetite; he looked forward to winning some serious money tonight.

The poker table in the corner was separated from prying eyes by several potted plants and a wisp of a screen. Osbourne and two other gentlemen had already taken their seats at the table, but Rowe and the rich American had not yet arrived. A representative of the establishment's bank stood nearby with a tray of chips and a cash box.

Osbourne stood as Vandenberg drew near, and extended a hand. "Glad to see you're on time, Sir Willard."

"Good evening, Osbourne."

"Allow me to introduce our fellow players to you," Osbourne continued. "Mr. Edmund Jones, and Mr. William Bartleby."

Vandenberg nodded to the two earnest gentlemen, whom he sized up as pigeons. He only hoped they'd purchased a high enough stake to make taking their money worth his while. As Vandenberg was exchanging handshakes with the duo, Osbourne glanced toward the door.

"Lord Rowe has just arrived, along with the Yank."

Vandenberg looked over his shoulder. He recognized Lord Rowe, of course, but not the man by his side. Younger than Vandenberg had imagined, the American robber baron was clad in black evening wear, with a silk brocade waistcoat in a loud cherry red. His bushy mutton chop whiskers extended from his upper lip to his earlobes like draping curtains, and he wore a gleaming ebony stovepipe top hat. As Miss Josie hastened to greet him and Rowe, the fellow doffed the hat and gave her a broad grin and cheeky wink. When she turned to walk away, the American pinched her behind. Although the pretty woman giggled in response, Vandenberg rolled his eyes. He really didn't expect a Yank to have refined manners, but he dearly hoped the evening wouldn't grate on his nerves.

When Rowe spotted Osbourne's raised hand, he murmured to the American and then the two of them made their way over. As Rowe approached, he peered at Vandenberg in surprise.

"Sir Willard! I didn't expect to see you here."

"I ran into Osbourne at our club the other day, and he mentioned poker. I've just learned the game and I was hoping to stretch my skills a bit."

"Ah. Good." Rowe turned to the American. "Allow me to introduce Mr. Dallas Robinson of Texas."

The man extended his hand. "Call me Dallas."

The Yank reeked of whisky, and Vandenberg could barely keep his countenance at his common, coarse twanging accent. By the time Rowe had finished introducing Dallas to Osbourne and the two other poker players, Miss Josie had brought drinks on a tray. As she handed the American a glass of amber liquid, he gave her his hat and another wink.

"Sweetheart, bring over the bottle."

"Certainly."

Miss Josie, no fool, backed away from him this time. Dallas chuckled and tossed a fat wallet on the table, where it landed with a thunk.

"Well, amigos, let's get 'er started."

Vandenberg exchanged a surreptitious glance of amusement with Osbourne. He wished he'd made a side bet on how soon he managed to fleece the vulgar boor.

••••

Two hours later, Vandenberg was still working on his first snifter of brandy, but the bottle of whisky next to Dallas was half empty. Osbourne had similarly nursed his glass of port and looked alert. Rowe's glass of whisky had been refilled once. Although Jones and Bartleby had eschewed alcohol altogether, their ashtrays had been emptied by the staff several times during the course of play. Everyone's stash of playing chips had been noticeably depleted, except for Vandenberg. After he won the next hand, he quickly added up his winnings in his head. He was up over two thousand pounds—a goodly amount to be sure—but he knew he could do better. Dallas had begun to slur his words, and Rowe had become far too tentative in the game. Even Osbourne's mood had turned dour.

"I think we should up the stakes, gentlemen," Vandenberg said. "What do you say?"

Dallas's eyes widened, but then he chuckled. "That's mighty reckless of you, partner, but then reckless is my middle name."

Osbourne whistled softly and shook his head slightly. Rowe swallowed hard and as he took a sip of his whisky, his hand trembled.

Bartleby groaned and sat back. "I'm afraid it's just not been my night." He beckoned to the banker. "Cash me out, would you? I've had enough."

Jones, however, was sanguine about Vandenberg's proposal. He leaned back and gave him an appraising glance. "What sort of minimum do you propose?"

The baronet pushed his chips toward the center. "Two thousand pounds."

Dallas snorted. "You Englishmen are too cautious. I say five."

A slow smile spread across Vandenberg's lips. "Done." He noticed Rowe flinch. "Too rich for you, Your Lordship?"

"No. I...um...will you excuse me just one moment?" Looking green around the edges, the earl stood and headed off toward the gentlemen's room.

Osbourne pursed his lips. "I suppose I'm in—for now. Jones?"

With a slow shake of his head, the man frowned. "No, I'm with Bartleby. Luck has eluded me tonight." He gathered his chips and stood. "Thank you for the game, gentlemen. Perhaps we'll meet again on some other, more fortunate occasion."

As Jones departed, Vandenberg glanced around the table. "And then there were four. When Rowe returns, we'll resume."

Dallas guffawed. "That reminds me of a l'il story."

He proceeded to tell an off-color joke about an unmarried cowboy and the farmer's four daughters. Before he could reach the punchline, however, Vandenberg lost patience.

"Sir, you are no gentleman!"

Disappointment registered on Dallas's face. "Why...that's exactly right! I reckon you must have heard that joke already."

Moments later, Rowe sat down at the table, his spine ramrod stiff.

"We lost Jones," Osbourne said.

"I see." Rowe drained his whiskey. "Shall we continue?"

••••

It was nearing two a.m., and the atmosphere at the poker table was intense. Vandenberg's luck had clearly waned, but he wasn't worried. When the pot was large enough, he was ready to pounce with the winning hand tucked up in his shirtsleeve. Dallas had finally stopped drinking, and he was in the black considerably. Osbourne and Rowe had both seesawed back and forth, but at present looked as if they'd broken even.

"Let's take a short break, gentlemen." Vandenberg feigned discouragement as he called the banker over, but secretly he could scarcely contain his glee. "Will you accept my IOU for twenty-five thousand pounds?"

The man frowned. "That's vastly over our limit, sir."

"I'm good for it, most assuredly." Vandenberg nodded at Rowe. "Lord Rowe can vouch for me."

The earl cocked his head. "I'll vouch for you only if Symean Hall is your pledge."

Osbourne made a sound of protest. "I advise you to think carefully, Sir Willard. If you lose, you'll be ruined."

Dallas laughed. "And if he wins, *we'll* be ruined!"

"Perhaps *you* won't, sir," Rowe murmured.

"True, but it would leave a dent in my bottom line."

Vandenberg pretended to consider the matter, although he knew he would not lose. "All right. I pledge my estate against the twenty-five thousand pounds."

He signed a note to that effect, received his chips, and play resumed. With each successive hand, the tension rose. Finally, the moment came when it was time to strike. Vandenberg pushed all his chips into the center of the table, and his fellow players gaped.

Osbourne gave him a bleak glance, shook his head, and tossed his cards down. "Alas, I must fold."

A heady sense of power rushed through Vandenberg's veins. He lived to see that look of defeat on an opponent's face, the acknowledgment of his superiority and indomitability. In that moment, no king could have felt more alive. The only thing better would be to win against the final two, bringing the vulgar Yank and the upstart earl down to their knees.

As Dallas and Rowe considered their hands, Vandenberg gestured to one of the waiters. "Another brandy, if you please."

"Right away, sir."

The moment when all eyes naturally fixed themselves on the waiter was the lapse Vandenberg needed to switch out his cards for the winning hand. He fanned the new cards face down on the table, and slid the old ones into a pocket. Afterward, he folded his arms across his chest and waited. Finally, Dallas and Rowe pushed their chips into the center to call.

With a broad grin, Vandenberg laid out his cards, four aces and a jack. "Four of a kind."

Dallas let out a sharp noise and flinched—as if he'd been shot in the chest. "You got me, partner." He showed his hand. "Straight...nine high."

Vandenberg fixed his gaze on Rowe, who was deathly pale and breathing in a shallow fashion. "Best get it over with, Lord Rowe."

Rowe's brown eyes darted to Vandenberg's face. "Quite so." He laid down his hand. "Straight flush."

••••

Dallas and Osbourne gasped, but Vandenberg said nothing. As Rowe watched, the baronet's face suffused with color and his eyes narrowed. Finally he managed to find his tongue.

"That's impossible. You cheated!"

Without moving a muscle, Rowe locked his gaze onto Vandenberg. "Osbourne, will you summon a constable? It seems we have a dispute to settle, and I daresay Sir Willard has far more to lose from a search of his pockets than I do."

Vandenberg bristled. "How *dare* you!"

Osbourne stood, hastened over to Miss Josie, and whispered in her ear. Shortly thereafter, the two moved out of Rowe's range of vision. Dallas removed a small pistol from his coat and laid it on the table.

"I suggest you keep your hands where we can see them, Sir Willard."

The man blanched. "This is ridiculous! It's Rowe who cheated, not I!"

Rowe's temper flared. "You'd know all about cheating, wouldn't you—just like you cheated my father out of his wealth? You stole his money, used it to purchase Symean House and a baronetcy, and had the audacity to pursue my sister in the bargain. You ought to be in jail!"

Dallas gave Vandenberg a crooked grin. "In my neck of the woods, card sharps usually end up with lead poisoning."

Osbourne returned with Miss Josie, accompanied by a uniformed constable. The policeman kept his hand on his nightstick as he glanced around the table.

"I'm Officer Sloat. What seems to be the trouble?"

"We've had an allegation of cheating from Sir Willard," Rowe said. "I'm certainly willing to be searched to prove my innocence. I think if you check the right pocket of his coat, you'll find the five spare cards he discarded in favor of the hand he brought with him."

Vandenberg shot to his feet. "I did no such thing!"

By now, the other patrons realized a dispute was ongoing, and many clustered around to watch. All conversation and activity came to a halt, and the establishment became deadly quiet.

"If you're innocent, Sir Willard, you won't mind a search, will you?" Sloat asked.

"This is absurd! It's an outrage!" As Vandenberg shouted, spittle formed at the sides of his mouth. "I'm a baronet, and I won't be treated like a common criminal!"

Rowe stood. "If you withdraw your allegation against me, I think we can dispense with any further investigation. If not, you'll be revealed to be a cheat and a scoundrel in front of all these people. In addition to the wealth and property you've lost tonight, you'll also sacrifice your reputation and risk being sent to prison for a lengthy period of time. Which is it to be?"

Vandenberg's fists clenched at his side, and he seemed to coil like a snake. In the next moment, he hissed air through his teeth. "All this is beneath me, Lord Rowe. Under protest, I withdraw my allegation."

"Good." Rowe picked up several chips and handed them to the banker. "Cash these in and give the proceeds to Sir Willard. I wouldn't want to leave him penniless in the same heartless manner he treated my father. Oh, and I'll be closing on Symean House directly, Sir Willard. You have until the end of the month to move out any of your personal belongings."

Miss Josie cleared her throat. "There's a complimentary hansom waiting outside, sir, to take you home."

Vandenberg snatched the cash proffered to him by the banker and pushed his way through the crowd. A few moments later, he slammed out the front door. It seemed as if every patron in the gambling hell was holding his or her breath. Finally, the clip clop of horse's hooves could be heard as the cab left, and the doorman came inside.

"Sir Willard has gone."

A roaring cheer went up. Osbourne and Dallas slapped Rowe on the back, and the constable shook his hand. As Dallas peeled off his whiskers, revealing himself as Theo, Jones and Bartleby bolted from a back room to join the merriment.

Josie beamed. "I haven't had that much fun in ages!"

Theo stood and raised his hands for quiet. "Thank you, everyone! Tonight has been a tremendous success, and I'm sure we'd all like to get to bed."

The constable waved his nightstick. "What do we do with our props, Apollo?"

"They'll have to go back to the theater warehouse first thing tomorrow, but I have someone coming to pick them up in the morning. Change into your street clothes in one of the bedrooms, and then stack your costumes and props on the hazard tables on your way out. Mr. Grimsby will see that you get paid at the door." Theo grinned. "Really great work, everyone!"

A cacophony of noise and movement ensued, but Rowe's knees finally gave way and he sank into a chair. He clutched Vandenberg's note in his hand—the one which meant Symean House would soon be his again—and he was overcome with emotion. He glanced at Osbourne and Theo, who were grinning at him.

"Thank you both...for everything."

"I didn't do much, really." Osbourne jerked his head toward Theo. "It was King here who brought an entire company of stage actors to bear. It's not everyone who has access to a theater company and a warehouse full of props."

Rowe gazed at his friend, shaking his head in amazement. "Your performance as Dallas Robinson was truly impressive."

Osbourne nodded. "Indeed, I was convinced! How did you manage the accent?"

"It was easy, actually. My brother and I shared a private compartment with a Texan gentleman once, and we chatted all the way from London to Newcastle. It amused Brandon no end that I could reproduce the fellow's manner of speech thereafter."

Rowe brandished Vandenberg's IOU. "I'll deliver this to my attorney tomorrow so he can foreclose on the property forthwith." He chuckled. "And won't Clarissa be surprised to learn she has a dowry again!"

Osbourne gave him a sidelong glance. "I expect Miss Shields will look forward to a proposal from a wealthy earl in the very near future?"

Rowe affected an Irish brogue. "Och aye, that she will!"

Chapter Seventeen
Jack Be Nimble

As Megan entered the dining room for lunch with Clarissa and Larken, she noticed Brandon's seat was unoccupied. "Isn't Mr. King dining with us?"

"Not today," Larken replied. "He took Myles on an outing to Newcastle. The little fellow has been somewhat sad since Estella left, and Brandon means to spoil him a bit."

"It must be difficult, not having any children his own age to play with," Clarissa said.

"Indeed, and the new baby won't help matters. They'll be a full seven years apart in age."

When the servant brought in the soup course, Larken closed her eyes and turned pale. Megan and Clarissa exchanged a glance of alarm.

"Are you unwell?" Clarissa asked.

The fair-haired beauty opened her eyes and stood. "My stomach is a trifle unsteady today. I believe I'll go lie down." She hastened from the room with her napkin pressed against her lips.

Clarissa grimaced. "Should we summon a physician, do you suppose?"

Megan shook her head. "Her condition's perfectly normal, to be sure. It's like that for many women when they're with child, but usually it passes after three months."

Megan began to eat the fragrant soup set in front of her, but Rowe's sister took only two sips of hers before putting her spoon down. Megan cocked her head.

"You've no liking for squash soup, milady?"

"My throat is a little sore, to be truthful, and my nose feels stuffy."

"Och, there's been a chill in the air the last few days, right enough. Many of the staff have come down with a cold."

"I didn't realize the weather would turn cool quite so quickly, and I didn't think to bring any of my heavier dresses or shawls."

"Surely you could borrow a wrap from Mrs. King?"

"In her current condition, I don't want to disturb her."

The butler brought in a letter for Clarissa just then, from her brother. She opened it immediately and perused the contents.

"Jensen and Theo are returning later today!"

Megan's heart skipped a beat. "I'm so glad."

Clarissa pouted. "Yes, but I expect my nose will be red by the time they arrive and I'll not be fit to be seen! Every time I get a cold, I look as if my face has been dipped in hot water."

"Why don't you crawl back into bed and try to sleep? Perhaps you can stave off your cold with a nap and be presentable for Mr. King's return."

"Do you think so?"

"It certainly can't hurt. And in the meantime, I'll go to the cottage and pack a few winter gowns and shawls."

"Would you do that for me?"

"I insisted on making myself useful, didn't I? If you want to make a list of items you need, I'll be happy to bring them, too."

"But it's chilly, and you haven't a proper shawl to wear. Besides which, Rowe would be furious with me, letting you go alone."

"It was *you* he didn't want going to the cottage alone, not me. I'll borrow a scarf from Bess and I'll be fine. I imagine I'm more used to the cold than you are."

"Oh, Miss Shields, you're wonderful."

Megan laughed. "Och aye, it's my Irish showin'."

••••

When Megan checked on Larken after lunch, she discovered the woman resting quietly in her room with a basin within reach. Clarissa had also taken to her bed with a merry fire blazing in the grate. Megan was grateful to have an errand to run, otherwise she would have been without plans for the entire afternoon. She informed the cook she wouldn't be back for tea, and continued on to the stables to ask the stablehands to prepare Clarissa's gig. Then, with Bess's long woolen scarf wrapped over her head and neck, she set off for the cottage.

Along the way, she passed a local farmer, who raised his hat in greeting. "Afternoon, milady!"

Megan was startled, until she realized the man must have taken her for Rowe's sister. Since her features were largely obscured by a scarf, she was driving Clarissa's gig, and was clad in one of Her Ladyship's gowns, Megan supposed the mistake was a natural one. She merely nodded as her friend might have done, and drove on. The sky was overcast and dreary, but her thoughts were cheerful nevertheless. Rowe had been gone from Newcastle for nearly ten days, and she missed him dreadfully. What news he might have to impart was unclear, but she looked forward to seeing him and Theo again—hopefully before dinner.

She'd accompanied Clarissa to the cottage several times in the preceding week and knew the way well. The horse kept a good pace, and it took less than a half hour to reach her destination. After leaving the horse in the small barn as usual, she took the cottage keys and let herself into the home. As she entered, she hung Bess's scarf on a hook near the door, and made her way upstairs. The house was deathly quiet without Clarissa to keep her company, but Megan shrugged off a sudden prickle of apprehension. Until recently, solitude had been a frequent companion, and she was not afraid of the condition.

After retrieving a large tapestry bag from an armoire, Megan began to fill it with items from Clarissa's list. As she glanced out the window, she caught sight of Symean House in the distance. Although it was a lovely tableau, she wondered if Clarissa found it painful to be reminded daily of the family home she'd lost. In the next moment, Megan discarded the notion. Clarissa was generally so optimistic, she probably took comfort from the view.

A faint scent of burning leaves reached Megan's nostrils as she worked, but she didn't take too much notice. Fall was generally the season farmers raked up leaves, set them on fire, and used the residual ash to spread on fields and gardens to improve the soil for springtime planting. The chilly afternoon was perfect weather to enjoy a large bonfire and perhaps even roast potatoes in the embers. She had fond memories of participating in such activities when she was a young child.

Midway through packing the tapestry bag, Megan began to fear she wouldn't be able to carry it to the gig without straining her back. A second bag, or perhaps a small trunk, would halve the load, but a cursory search of Clarissa's room turned up nothing useful. Megan decided one of the other bedrooms would no doubt yield a suitable piece of luggage, so she checked across the hall. As soon as she opened the door, she realized immediately from the masculine furnishings the room must belong to Rowe. Although she knew she ought to respect the man's privacy, she nevertheless tiptoed over to the closet and spent a few stolen moments taking in the scent of his clothes.

It was then she realized the odor of burning leaves was becoming increasingly noxious. Whichever neighbor was responsible for the bonfire should be scolded for putting it downwind of the cottage. She hastened to the window to see if she could spot the offending fire...and her mouth went dry. Puffs of white smoke were billowing so close to the glass it could only be coming from the lawn below.

Megan picked up her skirts and ran downstairs, where smoke had seeped through the cracks in the doors and windows, and hung in the air like fog. When she wrenched the front door open, flames nearly set her skirt on fire. Someone had piled wood and kindling against the door and set it ablaze. With no way to pass through the inferno without burning to death, she slammed the door shut, turned around, and headed toward the back of the cottage.

Her heart pounded in her ears as she sped down the hall and into the kitchen. When she grasped the door handle, however, the heated metal burned her fingers. She cried out in pain, but tried to quell her rising panic. Smoke was roiling through the crack in the bottom of the door, and soon she'd be unable to breathe. She grabbed several dishtowels from a shelf and stopped up the leak as best she could. Coughing, she backed out of the kitchen and fled from room to room, searching for a window she could use to escape—to no avail. Flames seemed to be everywhere, as if the house were surrounded by a ring of fire, and she was trapped inside. When she reached the parlor, she spied a horribly familiar man standing on the lawn, laughing at his handiwork. Graham Quinlan had killed her brother, and it looked as if he was going to kill her, too.

Megan screamed.

•••

Rowe could scarcely believe his good fortune. With Osbourne and Theo's help, he'd won back Symean Hall, his family home. Although he hadn't managed to recoup the entirety of his father's massive wealth, he could count on the income from the tenant farmers associated with the estate to support himself. Furthermore, the rent from the caretaker's cottage would also provide a small, steady sum. A great deal of the cash he'd wrested from Sir Willard had gone to pay the expenses incurred in setting up the gambling hell subterfuge, such as compensating the actors who'd assisted with the ruse. Even so, Rowe felt flush for the first time in a long while, and filled with hope for the future—especially where Miss Shields was concerned.

Although he would have liked to bring Osbourne back to Newcastle immediately, the man stayed behind to tend to some matters of business. After Rowe extracted Osbourne's promise to visit Graceling Hall as soon as possible, he and Theo began their journey home. Rowe was light-hearted and jovial along the way. A ready smile sprang to his lips at the slightest provocation, and every ordinary happenstance seemed to increase his merriment. They'd caught the earliest train that morning, in the hope of reaching Graceling Hall in the late afternoon. Although Theo had brought a book along to read, Rowe was content to gaze out the train window and daydream. How sweet life was, at last! No longer would Clarissa be forced to give piano lessons to disinterested girls. Never again must he and his sister traipse across the countryside, tutoring the children of the gentry in the ways of the ballroom. If Clarissa wanted a trousseau for her upcoming marriage, she would have the finest one imaginable. In fact, she and Miss Shields could shop for their trousseaus together.

The train made good time and reached Newcastle a few minutes ahead of schedule. A cab was available to ferry the travelers to Graceling Hall, and as the hansom turned up the drive, Rowe was humming under his breath. Not even Theo's amused chuckling could dampen his spirits. As the carriage came to a stop, Seagate emerged from the house along with a footman, who opened the cab door.

When Rowe emerged, he noticed Quinlan's driver sitting on the front steps, a forlorn expression on his face. A lone horse was tied to a wrought iron tether nearby.

"Fergus? Why are you here?"

The man stood. "Nobody was at home to see me, so I waited." He gave Seagate an accusatory glare, but the butler was unmoved. "I thought ye should know about Mr. Quinlan. He's gone mad, he has."

"Do you know where he is?" Theo asked.

Fergus shook his head. "I can't tell ye where he's gone off to this moment, but I've caught glimpses o' him lurkin' in the neighborhood the last week, with his hair all wild and his clothes a mess. Today, he came back to the house for a change o' clothes. The staff was all in a tizzy, to be sure, so I offered to drive him to the constable to turn himself in. He weren't havin' none o' that, and said he wouldn't rest till he'd taken his revenge."

Rowe was bewildered. "Against whom?"

Fergus winced. "He said if he couldn't have Lady Clarissa, no one could."

Theo gasped. "How perfectly evil!"

"Fortunately, he can't hurt her," Rowe said. "She's been staying at Graceling Hall."

"I knew as much, but I said nothin' to tip him off. I've nothing but admiration for Lady Clarissa, ye see, and don't want her to get hurt."

Theo frowned. "I'll send someone to fetch the constable. He should know Quinlan's in the area and making threats."

"Lady Clarissa's here, isn't she, Seagate?" Rowe asked.

"Her Ladyship has gone to bed with a cold."

Rowe heaved a sigh of relief. "I'm sorry she's ill but thank heavens she's not at the cottage."

The butler's eyebrows drew together. "Forgive me, Your Lordship, but Miss Shields went to your cottage this afternoon to fetch some things for Her Ladyship. She's not yet returned."

Fergus gave an exclamation in Gaelic and pointed. "It looks like a fire over there, so it does!"

Rowe's head snapped toward the horizon, where a plume of smoke was rising. *Megan!* In the next breath, he untied Fergus's horse, leaped into the saddle, and dug his heels into the creature's flanks.

"I'll be along directly!" Theo shouted.

Rowe nodded, and as he practically flew down the driveway, a cold bead of sweat rolled down his temple. *If Quinlan has done anything to hurt her, I'll kill him with my bare hands.*

••••

The heat and smoke were so intense, Megan's eyes were streaming with tears. She grabbed Bess's scarf from the hook near the front door and tied it over her nose and mouth so she could breath. *Think! There must be a way out of this house!* She could tie bedsheets together upstairs and use them to climb out a window...but to where? The grass and bushes below were on fire. Wait...there was an oak tree right outside

Rowe's window. She used to be good at climbing trees, not so very long ago. If she jumped onto a branch, at least she'd be out of immediate danger. Her spine stiffened, along with her resolve. Anything was better than burning to death, and she wasn't going to die without a fight.

Megan darted up the stairs, burst into Rowe's room, and ran to the trio of tall casement windows. Although the opening was narrow, she could certainly squeeze through. After flinging the middle window open wide, she dragged the nearby chair over and used it to climb up. Lifted by the heated air, white burning ash was floating upward outside, like snow falling in the wrong direction. Nevertheless, she tried not to think about anything but the gnarled branch about three feet away. At about ten inches in diameter, it was far thinner than she would have liked, but she had little choice. The wooden beams in the Tudor cottage were crackling and groaning, and it couldn't be too much longer before the building was entirely engulfed in flames.

After murmuring a quick, silent prayer, Megan took a deep breath, and leaped out into space. Her foot skidded on the thick bark, but she managed to grab a perpendicular branch to steady herself. Her breath hissed through her teeth as the skin on her blistered fingers broke, but she couldn't afford to loosen her grip. Her weight had caused the branch to dip and sway, almost twenty feet in the air. Should the branch snap, she'd plunge to the hard ground and most assuredly break her neck. Two yards away, however, was the tree trunk. If she could make her way there, she'd be further away from the fire and her weight wouldn't stress the branch as much. Unfortunately, the soles of her shoes were too smooth for her feet to find purchase. Trembling with fear, Megan held onto the slender vertical branch with her uninjured hand and carefully reached down to remove first one slipper, and then the other. The shoes dropped to the grass. Then, with her bare feet, she edged forward.

"What a nimble minx!"

Startled, Megan was forced to seize the slender branch again or risk losing her balance. She glanced down to discover Quinlan standing almost directly beneath her, gazing up with a strange mixture of admiration and annoyance.

"I didn't realize a lady such as yourself could be so hoydenish."

A lady? Megan remembered the scarf wrapped around her nose and mouth; clearly Quinlan had mistaken her for Clarissa.

"No matter. There are more ways to kill a dog than hanging, as the proverb goes."

He left, disappearing from view around the side of the cottage. Megan wasted no time in traversing the distance between her and the tree trunk, stepping over a raised knot in the wood as she did so. When she'd reached a place of relative safety, she sat down on the branch and wondered what mischief Quinlan had in store for her next. Flames had burned their way from the ground floor of the cottage to the roof by that point and were blackening the wooden shingles. Burning embers were raining down onto the lawn, creating smoldering spots wherever they landed. The heat from the fire was radiating outward so strongly that Megan had begun to sweat in earnest. Rivulets of moisture ran down her forehead and into her eyes, which felt red and swollen. It was becoming increasingly more difficult to breath, and she began to worry she would lose consciousness.

When Quinlan reappeared with a long burning timber, Megan finally burst into tears. The murderous lunatic was determined to burn her alive, one way or another.

••••

As his horse galloped at top speed, Rowe flattened himself against the creature's neck. The cottage was almost fully engulfed by the time he arrived, but it was the strange sight in the side yard that caught his eye. Quinlan was brandishing a flaming stick of wood as he approached the oak tree nearest the house. Rowe urged his mount to jump over the short hedgerow separating the property from the thoroughfare. After the horse landed, however, the heat and ash made the animal rear in fright. Rowe dismounted, sped toward Quinlan, and tackled him just as he raised the firebrand toward one of the oak's lower-hanging branches. Quinlan lost his grip on the stick, which sailed into the grass and seemed to sputter out.

The two men grappled with one another, even as small, burning bits of wood settled onto their clothes and hair. Quinlan howled when one of the embers singed the skin under his eye, but Rowe was too enraged to care.

"Where is she? What have you done?" The earl punctuated his sentences with savage punches to the man's jaw.

Inexplicably, Quinlan dissolved into a paroxysm of laughter. Rowe's momentary confusion gave way to fury, and he drew his fist back once more. Before he could land another blow, however, he heard a blessedly sweet voice calling him from above.

"I'm here, Lord Rowe!"

As he glanced upward, his gaze locked onto Megan. Quinlan seized the moment, planted his boot into Rowe's midsection, and shoved him backward…into a burning patch of grass. The earl rolled over and over to avoid catching on fire, scrambled to his feet, and shed his smoldering jacket. With a mighty crashing noise, the cottage caved in on itself in the center, sending a new shower of burning debris airborne. Quinlan was nowhere to be seen, but Rowe had a new concern. Although the man had failed to ignite the oak, descending glowing embers had done his work for him. The tree's leaves, brown and dry due to the season, were catching fire. They burned merrily, like hundreds of candles, without regard for the young woman at their mercy.

"I'm going to get you down, Miss Shields!" he shouted. "Stay calm!"

Despite his words, Rowe was anything but calm. He ran toward the barn to fetch a coiled length of rope. As he sped back toward the oak with the coil over his shoulder, he was almost crushed by a falling piece of cottage wall. Fortunately, he saw it tipping toward him and managed to dart out of the way. Although the horse was skittish, Rowe grabbed his reins and practically dragged the beast underneath the tree. He hurled the end of the coiled rope over the branch overhead and gestured for Megan to take it.

"Tie the end around your waist!"

Because the noise of the fire was deafening, he had to pantomime what he needed her to do. Fortunately, she understood him, looped the rope around herself, and tied a knot. Rowe tied the other end of the rope onto the horse's pommel and led him far enough away until the line was taut. Would the colleen trust him enough to drop down on the other side?

••••

As soon as Rowe tossed the rope to Megan, she guessed at his plan. The only way to effect a rescue would be to lower her to the ground, using the branch as a hoist. If the branch or the rope broke, her death would be all but assured. Although her heart sank at the prospect of dangling in mid-air, she couldn't afford to dwell on the danger or waste time dithering about it. Rowe had already almost been burned to death because of her, and was still in mortal peril.

Megan tied the rope with a fisherman's knot her father had taught her long ago, and prepared to slide off the branch. When Rowe gave her the signal, she dropped first to her stomach, letting her legs dangle. She held onto the branch, hoping to ease off slowly, but the searing pain on her blistered palm made her let go sooner than she'd anticipated. As she dangled in the air, swinging to and fro, the thin rope bit into the skin of her waist. Rowe backed the horse toward the oak, and Megan descended toward the ground...lower and lower. Finally her bare feet were on the grass, and her raw fingers scrabbled to undo the knot she'd tied. The other end of the rope went slack as Rowe detached it from the horse's pommel, and he rushed toward her. A sickening cracking sound overhead made her freeze in fear, but the earl grabbed her by the arm and yanked her to safety. They ran to the edge of the lawn, and glanced back to see a large, burning tree branch had fallen where Megan had stood moments before. Fortunately, Rowe's horse had escaped injury by jumping over the hedge and into the lane beyond.

She pulled the scarf from her face and used it to brush embers from Rowe's hair and shoulders. Small sections of his white shirt had been burned through, and the skin underneath revealed a myriad of pink burns. Seemingly oblivious to the pain he must be feeling, Rowe grabbed Megan by her upper arms and peered into her face.

"Are you all right?"

Her throat was raw from smoke, so she just nodded. Without a word, Rowe wrapped his muscular arms around her and cradled her trembling body against his.

"If anything had happened to you, I would have lost my mind," he murmured.

Rowe reached down to take her blistered hand, but she shrieked in pain. When he saw the broken, oozing burns on her palm and fingers, she could see him fighting back tears.

"I'm so sorry you're hurt. I should have been here sooner."

After swallowing several times, Megan managed to speak. "'Tis nothin' but a scratch."

His laugh was tender. "Yes, in the same way my cottage is just a little scorched." He glanced down. "Since your shoes are missing, you must allow me to transport you to safety."

In the next moment, Rowe picked her up in his strong muscular arms as if she were a new bride. He carried her along the outskirts of the property, avoiding the worst of the smoke and ash, on his way to the barn. Fortunately, the small structure was far enough away from the burning cottage to still be intact. As Rowe was settling Megan into the gig, a commotion in the lane drew her attention. Theo had arrived with help. Men swarmed from a long line of carriages, gigs, and wagons with buckets in hand and formed a bucket brigade from the well to the cottage.

When Theo saw Megan and Rowe, he came running.

"Thank heavens you're both safe! What happened?"

"Quinlan tried to kill me by setting fire to the cottage." Megan's voice sounded like a croak. "He thought I was Clarissa."

Theo went pale.

"I'm taking Miss Shields to back to Graceling Hall," Rowe said. "She's going to need medical attention."

Theo's gaze swept over the condition of Rowe's garments. "So are you."

Chapter Eighteen
Forevermore

Megan knew her friends wanted her to relate the events of the afternoon, but she was in no mood to speak with anyone—least of all Clarissa. She couldn't bear to tell the woman her house had been destroyed, and that she'd indirectly been the cause. Although the physician was summoned immediately upon Megan's return to Graceling Hall, she insisted on a bath straightaway.

"Let the doctor tend to Lord Rowe first when he comes, otherwise he'll have to tend to me in the altogether. I smell like the inside of a fireplace and I can bear it no longer."

She managed most of her ablutions with her uninjured hand, but she had to ask Bess to wash her hair for her. Even so, she couldn't seem to get the smell of smoke out of her nostrils.

The maid didn't ask any questions, but as Megan relaxed a trifle, she felt obliged to tell her a little about what had happened.

Bess gasped. "It's a miracle you survived! I never would have had the courage to jump out the window the way you did."

"I expect you would have done the same thing. It's amazin' what a body will do to live, if given a chance."

As the maid combed her tresses out at the vanity afterward, Megan noticed her hair appeared to be singed in a few places. In addition, the whites of her eyes were red, her chest and throat felt sore, and she was seized with fits of coughing, despite the endless glasses of water Bess pressed on her. Furthermore, bruises ringed her body where the rope had chafed. Her dress, ruined by smoke and ash, had been discarded in a heap on the floor, along with the woolen scarf the maid had loaned her.

Megan gave her a sorrowful glance. "I've ruined your scarf, I'm afraid, but I promise to knit you a new one after my hand heals."

"After everything you've been through, you're worried about my scarf? Bless your heart, Miss Shields."

"Truth be told, I'm worried about more than the scarf." Moisture pooled in Megan's eyes. "Poor Lord Rowe and Lady Clarissa have had their house burned down and it's my doing."

Bess stared. "What?"

"If I hadn't gone to the cottage, Mr. Quinlan wouldn't have mistaken me for Lady Clarissa, and he wouldn't have set the house on fire." Tears slipped down her cheeks. "I hope they can forgive me."

"I've never heard of such silliness! You had no way to know what Mr. Quinlan was planning."

"But they already had so few possessions to their name already, and now everything is gone—including Her Ladyship's beautiful piano! I'm not sure how she can ever stand to look at me again."

"Miss Shields, I imagine His Lordship and Lady Clarissa are so relieved you're alive, they aren't thinking about material things."

When the doctor came, he tended Megan's throbbing hand with salve and bandages. As he worked, she asked about Rowe.

"He sustained a few burns and inhaled too much smoke, but with rest and fresh air, he'll be right as ninepence."

Although the news was good, Megan dissolved into tears nevertheless. Her emotions weren't usually so uncontrollable, but her brush with death and guilt about the fire had taken its toll on her nerves.

The doctor patted her shoulder. "You're overwrought, my dear, and it's little wonder."

Sobbing, she shook her head. "Ye don't understand! I've ruined everythin' and I won't ever feel better again!"

Clearly disconcerted by Megan's outburst, the man exchanged a puzzled glance with Bess. "Er...she should keep those bandages dry."

The maid nodded. "Yes, sir."

Shortly after the physician left the room, Clarissa rushed in without knocking and hastened to Megan's side.

"Oh, Miss Shields, I just heard what happened, and I'm so horribly sorry! I should never have sent you to the cottage by yourself, but I wasn't thinking clearly." Her gaze fell to Megan's bandaged hand and her eyes filled with tears. "Your poor hand! Can you ever forgive me for putting you in danger?"

Megan was astonished. "I should be beggin' your forgiveness, milady! Mr. Quinlan set your cottage afire because I was in it. Because of me, your piano and clothes and everything are gone!"

"My clothes were years out of date, and I hated that piano. It had a tinny sound I could never abide. I'm just so glad you're all right!"

She threw her arms around Megan and the two women burst into sobs. Finally, Clarissa pulled back. "Theo has returned to Graceling Hall, with the constable. If you're feeling up to it, he's waiting in the drawing room to speak with you. "

Megan dried her tears. "How is your cold?"

Clarissa laughed. "After I took a nap, I felt much better. And when I checked on Larken, I discovered she'd gone down to the kitchen and was eating enough food to feed an army!"

"Truly?" A smile finally stole its way onto Megan's lips. "I'll come down after Bess does something with my wet hair."

••••

The skin on Rowe's back and shoulders was smarting from a smattering of small burns. After a quick bath, some salve, and a change of clothes, his pressing need to see Miss Shields outweighed any lingering discomfort. As Clarissa hurried to the colleen's room to coax her downstairs, he went to the drawing room to wait. Even Myles insisted on lingering with everyone else waiting for her to appear.

When Clarissa escorted Megan into the room, Myles immediately rushed over to fling his arms around her waist. A spasm of pain crossed Megan's face, but she covered it with a smile.

"I'm glad you didn't burn up, Miss Shields."

Her voice was husky. "You shouldn't have worried a bit, lad. Lord Rowe came to my rescue."

Megan sought out Rowe's gaze as she spoke, and he hastened over to take her arm. Despite voluble assertions she was perfectly well, he led her to the sofa and sat by her side.

"Run along to the nursery, Myles," Larken said. "Miss Shields must speak to the constable."

"All right." Before he left, however, the young boy pressed a kiss onto Megan's cheek.

Her eyebrows rose. "Why, you really *are* a charmer, to be sure. I thank you very much!"

"You're welcome. And nobody dared me to do that, either. I just wanted to!"

As Myles darted from the room, his face pink with embarrassment, everyone was smiling.

Theo cleared his throat. "I think I can speak for everyone here when we say how relieved we are to see you safe and sound, Miss Shields." He gestured toward the uniformed policeman, standing nearby. "This is Mr. Horn. He's here to listen to your story."

As Megan began to speak, she reached out her uninjured hand toward Rowe. He grasped it, willing his own strength and comfort to flow into her. She related the afternoon's horrifying events in a brave and calm manner that filled him with pride, but when she reached the part about jumping from the cottage onto the branch, he gasped, "So that's how you ended up in the tree?"

She gave him a sidelong glance. "Perhaps you were thinking I flew?"

"Actually, until this very moment I didn't think about it at all. I was just so concerned about getting you to safety at the time, it never occurred to me to wonder how you'd managed to wind up twenty feet in the air."

"You did save me and risked your life to do it. I can't ever thank you enough."

He squeezed her hand, and she resumed her tale…ending with Quinlan's failed attempt to set fire to the tree, his subsequent fight with Rowe, and her ultimate rescue.

"If His Lordship hadn't arrived when he did, I wouldn't be here right now." Megan took a deep breath. "Mr. Quinlan escaped, I'm afraid. I dearly wish he hadn't."

The constable, who'd been listening quietly with rapt attention, finally spoke. "He didn't escape, actually." All eyes swiveled toward him. "A man's body was found under a wall near the back of the house. Mr. Theo King identified him as Quinlan."

Theo nodded. "I think he must have been fleeing toward the garden when that part of the cottage fell. I don't think he knew what hit him."

A long pause ensued as everyone digested the news.

"I feel sorry for the poor, tortured man," Megan said at last. "I hope his soul can find rest now."

"You're a better person than I am, Miss Shields," Rowe said. "All I feel is relief."

"As do I," Theo said. "I hate to speak ill of the dead, but I'm glad we don't have to worry about any more tragedies perpetrated by Quinlan."

The constable stood. "Well, I'm off to notify the man's next of kin. It'll be sad tidings for someone tonight."

Theo glanced at Megan. "Thank heavens, there are no sad tidings for our family this time."

"Hear, hear." Rowe nodded in agreement.

Brandon rang for the butler to show the policeman out. Afterward, Larken glanced around the drawing room, an expectant expression on her face. "I hope everyone has an appetite for dinner?"

Megan's stomach promptly growled so loudly, she burst into laughter along with everyone else.

"Och, aye, I'm more likely than not to drop dead of hunger right now if I don't get something to eat," she quipped.

Seagate appeared, as if on cue. "Dinner is served."

As the King family filed through the double doors on their way to the dining room, Rowe held Megan back. Theo glanced over his shoulder as he escorted Clarissa from the room. "Is everything all right?"

Rowe nodded and gave him a surreptitious wink. "We'll be with you in a moment."

The dawning light of comprehension appeared in Theo's eyes, and he reached for the doors to pull them shut. "Take your time."

When Rowe and Megan were alone, he cupped her face in his hands and captured her lips with his. His tender kisses did not go unanswered, and an explosion of passion left them both breathless.

"Yer a right charmer, I must say," she murmured.

Rowe affected his best Irish brogue. "That I am, Miss Shields, where you're concerned. And nobody dared me to do it, either. I've been wantin' to kiss ye for a long time, so I have."

"Have you indeed, sir?" She closed her eyes and leaned toward him for another kiss. "By all means, carry on."

They exchanged several more kisses.

"You're going to marry me," he murmured.

"Am I now?" Her words were soft, like a breath of spring.

"You are."

Megan suddenly seemed to snap out of the romantic spell he'd woven. "Are you daft? If you were too poor to marry me before, you're far too poor now!"

"I'm poor no longer. In fact, I've regained Symean House and a tidy sum besides."

She stared at him with narrowed eyes. "How?"

"A card game."

"What!"

He grinned. "The man who swindled my father out of his estate by cheating him at cards was Sir Willard. I bested him at poker while I was in London, and won a great deal of it back. We can marry as soon as you like!"

To his puzzlement, his good news seemed to leave her as cold as a marble tombstone.

"I've no intention of marrying a man who indulges in games of chance, Your Lordship. We'll not be marrying at all."

Megan flung open the doors and strode from the drawing room, even as he sputtered in protest. "Wait! You don't understand!"

"My father was a gambler, and he led my mother a merry chase. I won't be led the same way."

"I'm not a gambler, Miss Shields. I swear it."

She turned to give him an appraising glance. "What you just told me says differently."

"Give me a chance to explain, will you? After all, I saved your life!"

Her eyes widened. "And you'd use that against me?"

"I'll do anything it takes to convince you to marry me."

She turned her face away, but he thought he could see a hint of a smile.

"All right, Lord Rowe. Because you saved my life and because I burned your house down, I'll listen to you speak your piece. Right now, however, you're to take me into dinner before I change my mind!"

He placed her left hand in the crook of his elbow. "As you wish."

••••

After her brief romantic interlude with Rowe, Megan could almost forget the pain of her burns. Nevertheless, she'd been perfectly serious in her rebuff of his proposal. She'd always held gambling in the utmost contempt, since her father had frequently spent his meager pay losing at dice. Her keen disappointment in Rowe's revelation was juxtaposed with her utter admiration of him, and it was unclear which opinion would prevail. Any explanation was unlikely to win her over, but she owed him the opportunity to make his case. Secretly, she yearned for him to succeed.

Over hot soup, Rowe broached the subject of his London sojourn, detailing the creation of the fabricated gambling hell and the inveiglement of Sir Willard by a mutual friend named Osbourne.

Megan gave him a sharp glance. "Osbourne?"

Clarissa cast a guilty look in her direction. "Please forgive me for not telling you, Miss Shields, but Jensen swore me to secrecy. He went to London to find Mr. Osbourne on your behalf."

Megan was mystified. "Why?"

"He thought the both of you would profit from a mutual acquaintance."

Stunned, Megan's gaze slid over to Rowe. His every action had been for her, without a thought for himself. How could such a noble gentleman be involved in gambling?

"I went to see Mr. Osbourne on Miss Shields's behalf. To my surprise, I learned he'd been present when Sir Willard cheated my father out of Symean Hall," Rowe said.

Brandon gaped. "What a bounder! If I'd known as much, I never would have allowed Sir Willard into the house!"

Clarissa gasped. "Sir Willard is really a cheat?"

Rowe nodded. "An extraordinarily successful one, too."

"Until now." Theo chuckled.

"Osbourne knew Sir Willard would not be able to resist a high-stakes game of poker, and so he helped set the trap. Theo was to play the part of a rich American robber baron, and he also brought his former acting troupe to the mix." Rowe grinned. "He was absolutely brilliant."

Larken beamed. "Did Josie play a part?"

"Oh, yes, she was the gambling hell proprietress!" Theo laughed. "We all had a capital time—except for Sir Willard. When he finally played the hand he'd tucked into his sleeve, Rowe finished him off. I doubt if the man will have the stomach for gaming in the future."

"Especially not after he lost Symean House to me," Rowe added.

Clarissa shook her head in disbelief. "You're not joking, are you? Please tell me you're not!"

"I'm perfectly serious. As soon as our attorney closes on Sir Willard's note, the house is ours once more...and a bit of cash besides."

Excited conversation ensued, interrupted only by the arrival of rack of lamb with mint sauce.

"So the game of poker wasn't really a game at all," Megan said. "Not truly."

Rowe gave her a tender smile. "That's it, exactly. It was all scripted, from beginning to end. I hope you won't hold it against me."

"And what did you make of Mr. Osbourne?" she asked.

"I can see why your brother liked him so. He's a clever chap, with a highly developed moral code."

"I found him quite amiable," Theo said.

"I'm happy to report he's coming to Graceling Hall for a visit very soon, Miss Shields, and looking forward to meeting you at long last," Rowe said.

Although he and Theo went on to discuss the gambling ruse in greater detail, Megan's attentions were divided. She listened to the conversation but said nothing more until after the dessert of raspberry-filled sandwich cake arrived. After the plates were set on the table, Clarissa gave her a worried glance.

"You've been exceedingly quiet, Miss Shields. I hope you're not feeling any additional ill effects from your ordeal?"

"To be truthful, my thoughts have been elsewhere. It seems I've decided on a change of plans that affects all of you at this table."

Clarissa's eyes grew round, and Larken's brow furrowed. Although Rowe's visage didn't betray his emotions, his face lost color.

"Oh, please don't say you're leaving Graceling Hall!" Clarissa exclaimed.

Larken frowned. "I thought it was all settled!"

"I must, I'm afraid. It's unavoidable." Megan bit the inside of her cheek to avoid laughing.

"Can you tell us why?" Theo asked.

"Because Lord Rowe and I are to marry and live at Symean House." She smiled at him. "If he'll have me."

A broad grin spread across his face. "Oh, I'll have you, Miss Shields. Now and forevermore."

Suzanne G. Rogers

Chapter Nineteen

Just Desserts and Cake

Sylvia preened in the latest Parisian fashion as she arrived at The Adelphi Theatre with her daughter and brand-new husband. While the man bought a matinée program for Estella in the lobby, one of Sylvia's friends beckoned her over.

"Hello, Mrs. Aynsworth. I adore your gown!"

"Thank you. Actually, it's Lady Vandenberg now."

"No! When did that happen?"

Sylvia giggled. "Sir Willard and I eloped. We were married less than two weeks ago."

"Why, you sly fox! You never said a word to me, so you can't have known him long."

"It was a whirlwind courtship, as they say." She lowered her voice. "His haste will likely appear unseemly, but I'd no wish to wait, to be truthful." She giggled. "I'm the wife of a baronet now."

"So you are! I wouldn't have stood on ceremony, either."

Sylvia retrieved a rectangular card out of her reticule and gave it to her friend. "Here's my calling card, with my new name."

The woman's eyebrows rose. "You're at the same address as before?"

"Yes, Willie is selling his London townhouse. In the meantime, he's moved in with Estella and me."

"I'll call on you tomorrow afternoon, and we'll plan a ladies' tea in honor of the new bride!"

"Won't that be lovely! I'll see you then."

When Sylvia returned to her husband's side, Estella's nose was buried in her newly purchased program for *The Mademoiselle and the Mysterious Mystery*. Vandenberg had purchased a program for Sylvia as well and rented her a pair of opera glasses.

"How thoughtful of you, Willie! Thank you."

He acknowledged her thanks with a nod and gestured toward the lobby doors. "Shall we take our seats?"

Estella wiggled with happiness. "I can't wait!"

"I can't either," Sylvia said. "I haven't been to a matinée in ever so long."

Vandenberg escorted them into a box which afforded an excellent view of the proscenium. Estella sat between him and her mother.

"Lord Apollo used to perform here, Mama."

Estella's curious statement roused her curiosity. "Who is Lord Apollo, dearest?"

"Mr. Theo King, of course."

"Oh? Yes, I believe he did mention having been an actor once, but I never managed to get the particulars."

Vandenberg overheard. "Theo King was an *actor*, was he? I shouldn't think he would admit it."

The little girl glanced at him, clearly puzzled. "Why not?"

"Acting isn't a respectable profession. In fact, having an actor in the family casts quite a shadow on the Kings." He paused and his eyes flicked toward Sylvia. "Er...it's a good thing I've sold Symean House. I've no wish to be neighbors to dreadful people like that."

A flash of annoyance made Sylvia frown. She'd known her husband was selling his London townhouse, but he never mentioned anything about his Newcastle estate. Since the theater lights dimmed just then, she had no opportunity to inquire about it. As the overture commenced, her daughter gave a little bounce in her crimson velvet-covered seat.

"I wish Myles were here!"

"Myles?" Vandenberg murmured.

"Estella made friends with Brandon King's ward during our visit," Sylvia whispered over her daughter's head.

He frowned. "You're not to have anything to do with him, Estella."

The girl's curls danced as she tossed her head. "You're not my papa and you can't tell me what to do!"

Vandenberg swelled up with indignation, looking like a cat whose fur had been set on end. "What did you say?"

"Apologize to Willie, Estella," Sylvia said.

The curls danced once more. "Hmph!"

Vandenberg frowned. "Never mind. I'm sure your daughter will feel sorry when she gets no dessert at dinner tonight."

Estella leaned forward, ignoring her stepfather as hard as a six-year-old could possibly do. Sylvia sighed; the child had been spoiled dreadfully and would have to be brought to task. She'd speak with Estella's nanny about it just as soon as possible. On stage, the curtains rolled away, revealing a drawing room set. The performance commenced when a very pretty ingenue—an actress named Elysium Fields, according to the program—ran on stage and hid something in between a pair of seat cushions.

Vandenberg gasped, "Miss Josie!"

He reached across Estella to snatch the opera glasses out of Sylvia's hands. The behavior was terribly rude, and he didn't even have the grace to acknowledge the scowl she shot in his direction. He peered through the opera glasses, gasping a second time when a constable appeared on stage and began to argue with the ingenue.

"Officer Sloat?" he muttered. "No, it can't be!"

People seated nearby began to hush Sylvia's husband, and her enjoyment of the matinée was blunted. As the play unfolded, her husband continued to make peculiar gasping noises every time a new character appeared. Sylvia folded her arms across her chest and stared at the stage in humiliation. Perhaps her whirlwind courtship had been too short for her to recognize the baronet's foibles. It had been the same way with her first husband, actually, who'd humiliated her by passing away very publicly in the arms of his Parisian paramour. Indeed, older men seemed to possess more eccentricities than younger ones—but then they also had more money. Well, she was married now, so it was too late for regrets. In the future, however, maybe she'd take her daughter to the theater alone!

Toward the end of the first act, Sylvia glanced over at Vandenberg. He'd lowered the opera glasses to his lap and was staring at the stage, fixedly. Although it was rather boorish of him to keep the glasses to himself, at least he'd stopped making odd sounds and disturbing the other patrons.

When intermission arrived, the gaslights were turned up and illumination filled the theater. Patrons stood and began to file out toward the lobby to partake of refreshments. Estella tugged on her sleeve. "Mama, I'm thirsty."

"Yes, so am I."

Sylvia became exasperated when Vandenberg sat unmoving and silent as a tombstone. She wondered briefly if he'd fallen asleep, but then she noticed his eyes were wide open.

"Dearest, do you suppose Estella and I could have a drink?"

He made no reply, so she reached across to jostle his shoulder. Vandenberg slumped to one side, quite obviously dead, and Estella shrieked in horror. Sylvia groaned. What horrible luck! She was a young widow twice over, and tongues would surely wag. Why, she might never manage to marry again!

••••

Two months later...

Guests were assembled in the chapel as the organist began to play. Although the chapel was decorated for a traditional wedding, little angels had been added to the floral arrangements to indicate the Christmas season. Theo stood in front of the altar, waiting for his bride-to-be. Larken and Brandon sat in the front pew, watching proudly as Myles came down the aisle first, as ring bearer. When Clarissa appeared in the doorway on her brother's arm, a smile of joy lit Theo's face. Clad in a wedding gown of white silk and tulle, she was ethereal. Pleated netting covered her shoulders, and a pearl necklace graced her throat. Netting also cascaded from the crown of delicate white flowers in her hair, blending with the trailing hem of her gown in a symphony of movement. Rowe escorted her down the aisle, where he relinquished her to Theo with a nod.

Instead of taking a seat in the front pew, however, the earl turned and waited for his own bride. In the doorway, Megan appeared with Mr. Osbourne as her escort. She was dressed in a snowy white satin wedding gown trimmed with ermine at the collar, shoulder seams, and at the wrists. Dainty pleats finished the hem and long train, and embroidered netting cascaded from the lace-covered bridal headband in her hair. As the colleen walked toward him, Rowe seemed to stand taller. When Megan and

Osbourne reached the altar, the older gentleman gave her a gentle kiss on the cheek before stepping back to take his place in the pew.

The vicar stepped forward and began the ceremony. Myles pulled on his collar occasionally and shifted his weight from foot to foot throughout. He performed creditably, however, when it was time for him to present the rings on a satin pillow. Afterward, when the grooms were allowed to kiss their brides, the young lad turned toward Larken and Brandon and exclaimed, "It's time for cake!"

The End

Lord Apollo & the Colleen

My Fair Guardian

When Bethany is saddled with an unwanted, unrefined, and decidedly common guardian, she must polish him up before he's fit for good society. As for Willoughby Winter, all that stands between him and his inheritance is to marry Bethany off. Can he succeed in his efforts before his past becomes known or will she manage to distract him from his goal—by hook or by crook?

Here's a sneak peek:

Excerpt from
My Fair Guardian

Bethany paced as she waited with Mr. Ingalls in her study. The solicitor polished his spectacles with a handkerchief and gave her a pained glance.

"You'll not make the situation any more palatable by punishing the carpet in that fashion, Miss Christensen. Your life doesn't necessarily have to change overmuch."

"I beg to differ. I've met—"

"Excuse me, Miss Christensen?" Richmond stood in the doorway. "Mr. Winter has arrived."

Will walked into the room with his cloth cap crushed in one hand. His curly brown hair was so damp with perspiration it looked almost black. Furthermore, his work shirt was nearly transparent with moisture, his boots were dusty, and the smell emanating from his body sent Bethany rushing over to unlatch the window. After she threw it open wide, she turned to address him—more formally this time, considering his change of status.

"Thank you for coming, Mr. Winter. Is it raining?"

He gave her a puzzled glance. "No, but it's hot and I was sweating like a pig."

Bethany glanced at the butler. "Richmond, please bring Mr. Winter a glass of water."

"Very good, miss." The butler bowed and disappeared down the hallway.

Will drew his sleeve across his face. "Thank you, Miss Christensen. Some water would set me up right nicely." He glanced down at himself. "Can't sit, I'm afraid. I've been shoveling dirt all day."

Bethany remained standing by the window, yearning for a breeze. "This is Mr. Ingalls. He was Mr. Leopold's solicitor and he now advises me."

The elderly man stood. "It's a pleasure to meet you, sir." He nodded instead of attempting to shake Will's dirty hand.

"Likewise."

Mr. Ingalls cleared his throat. "I have good news to impart to you, sir."

Will's eyebrows rose. "Oh?"

Bethany frowned. "The rolled-up paper you discovered in Mr. Leopold's desk turned out to be a codicil."

"A coddy-what?" Will shook his head. "I don't understand."

"A codicil is a document that modifies the terms of a pre-existing will," the solicitor said. "As it so happens, the terms are in your favor."

Before Mr. Ingalls could continue, Richmond arrived with the glass of water. Will gulped the water down and belched as he returned the glass to the butler's tray.

"Oh, 'scuse me."

Bethany's eyes flickered toward the ceiling. "That will be all, Richmond."

The butler left, seemingly biting back a smile.

Will gave the solicitor a quizzical glance. "So, my cousin decided to give me a few quid or some such thing? I'm touched."

"Mr. Leopold was not your cousin, Mr. Winter." Bethany took a deep breath. "He was your father."

Several seconds passed before Will burst into laughter. When neither Bethany nor Mr. Ingalls joined in, however, his merriment faded.

"Wait...you're serious?"

Bethany gestured toward the old journal, which was open on the desk blotter. "Mr. Leopold wrote about his romance twenty-four years ago with a Mrs. Clementine Aldersgate. She was a lady married to a sea captain who was gone for months at a time. When the woman died giving birth to Mr. Leopold's child, he fostered the boy with his cousin, Agnes Leopold Winter and her husband, Edgar."

Will continued to shake his head. "Even if that's true, I don't understand why Frederick wouldn't want to raise me himself."

"Mr. Leopold had your welfare uppermost in mind," Bethany said. "According to his journal, he paid the midwife to tell the captain that the baby was stillborn. Mr. Leopold feared that if Captain Aldersgate discovered you had lived, the man would have tried to kill you." Bethany held up a newspaper obituary, which had been tucked into the journal. "The captain died a few days before the date of the codicil. I expect Mr. Leopold thought it was finally safe to change his will in your favor."

"A change that only came to light because of your serendipitous discovery, Mr. Winter." The solicitor gestured with the codicil. "According to the terms of this document, Frederick Leopold wished for you to be appointed as the new guardian to Miss Bethany Christensen and Miss Jane Christensen until such time as the elder sister marries or attains the age of twenty-five years. For your service, you are to be given a salary and the run of Lansings Lodge."

Will was gripping his cap so firmly, Bethany wondered if he meant to wring out some of the perspiration soaked therein.

"What happens to me when the lady marries or turns twenty-five?" His expression was wary.

"At that point, you cease your guardianship, and you inherit half the estate. Until then, however, the title of Lansings Lodge will be held in a trust."

Will crossed his arms. "So, all I have to do is to get Miss Christensen paired off as quick as I can?"

Bethany burst out with, "How dare you, sir!"

A Personal Request

I love to write, but I can't do it without you. If you enjoyed *Lord Apollo & the Colleen*, would you consider leaving a review? Not only would I like to hear your thoughts, but also your review is very helpful to other readers. Thank you in advance!

Suzanne G. Rogers

About the Author

Originally from Southern California, Suzanne G. Rogers currently resides in beautiful Savannah, Georgia on an island populated by exotic birds, deer, turtles, otters, and gators. Tab is her beverage of choice, but a cranberry vodka martini doesn't go amiss.

For notification of freebies, sales, and new releases, sign up here: https://tinyurl.com/y4nya7pb

Visit her historical romance blog:
http://suzannegrogers.com

Visit her fantasy blog:
https://childofyden.wordpress.com

Find her on Facebook at:
https://www.facebook.com/SuzanneGRogers

Follow her on Gab:
https://gab.com/Suzanne_G_Rogers

Suzanne G. Rogers

Historical Romance

Graceling Hall Series
Larken (Book One)*
Lord Apollo & the Colleen (Book Two)

The Beaucroft Girls Series
Ruse & Romance (Book One)*
Rake & Romance (Book Two)*

The Mannequin Series
The Mannequin (Book One)*
Grace Unmasked (Book Two)
The Star-Crossed Seamstress (Book Three)
A Chance of Rayne (Book Four)

Standalone Titles
A Gift for Fiona
Spinster*
Lady Fallows' Secrets
My Fair Guardian
Jessamine's Folly*
Duke of a Gilded Age
The Ice Captain's Daughter*
An American in Paris of the West
Rumer Has It

*Audiobook available

Fantasy

The Yden Series
The Last Great Wizard of Yden (Book One)
Dragon Clan of Yden (Book Two)
Secrets of Yden (Book Three)
Kira (Prequel to the Yden Trilogy)

Standalone Titles
Dani & the Immortals
The Dragon Rider's Daughter*
Clash of Wills
Tournament of Chance: Dragon Rebel
Magical Misperception
Whimsical Tendencies*
Something Wicked in L.A.
Royal Promenade

*Audiobook Available

Made in the USA
Coppell, TX
20 June 2023